FOG COAST RUNAWAY

Linda B. Myers

To Sarah —
Enjoy the Journey!
Linda B. Myers

ABOUT THIS BOOK

Fog Coast Runaway is a work of historical fiction, set among actual locations and events of the 1800s. Characters, names, and happenings are from the author's imagination. Any resemblance to actual persons - living or dead - is entirely coincidental.

Published by Mycomm One

Cover design by www.introstudio.me
Interior design by Heidi Hansen

ISBN: 978-0-9986747-7-3

For updates and chatter:
www.LindaBMyers.com
Facebook.com/lindabmyers.author
myerslindab@gmail.com

DEDICATION

To my sister, Donna L. Whichello

Chapter One

April 1893

Adelia Wright had a case of the morbs. Her dog was dead, her Pa fuddled with booze, her brother a muttonhead. And now this. Adelia was bleeding.

"What a blasted time," she swore to nobody now that Shep wasn't there to hear her. What on earth was happening to her body? She had no one to ask...certainly not Pa who wouldn't listen or brother Wiley who would only taunt. She needed a mother's help with this mystery. The blood soaking her bloomers just couldn't be a good thing.

The closest female neighbor was old Cora Dixon who held school classes in her home. It was a mile trek through the damp forest to the west, toward the ocean.

Adelia couldn't go without a gift. She snatched up a bouquet of adder's tongue, trillium, and fawn lilies from the orchard meadow behind the cabin. Then she traipsed on her way, switching the flowers back and forth in agitation as she went.

Cora Dixon came to her door hunched forward on a sturdy branch that doubled as a cane. Her mouth tightened as she peered down at Adelia on her stoop. "Gracious, is that blood on your frock?"

Adelia shoved the bouquet to the old woman. "These are for you. Am I dying?"

"Don't be batty, child." A crimson blush moved up the loose skin on Cora's neck to land on her wrinkled cheeks. "But you cannot walk around in public like this." She took the flowers and ushered Adelia inside.

"Your father still has that heathen, don't he? Can she not explain what is upon you?"

If she could, I wouldn't be here, Adelia thought but said, "Lilac does not speak English, ma'am. Why am I bleeding from under my belly?"

Mrs. Dixon put the flowers in the soapstone sink, then fluttered her hands like a hatchling attempting to fly. "People do not talk about these things," she whispered even though they were alone. "But your menses have begun. I will teach you how to get your rags up, and then no more will be said about it."

The old woman showed the young girl how to make a belt from muslin strips with safety pins and how to create pads by folding soft rags. "Use flannel or cotton or whatever absorbent rags you can find. Wash them at night and keep them for the next time."

When all was secure, Cora Dixon shooed Adelia out the door with a final warning. "This will happen once a month until you have babies. You are a woman now."

"Have babies? I am a woman?" Adelia thought maybe Lilac would have been easier to understand after all.

"Menses come monthly until you marry. Then you keep having babies and breastfeeding them. If you are lucky, you may not suffer the curse again for years."

Isn't that the beatingest thing? Adelia did not feel much like a woman, nor did she have a firm grip on the process of babies, but she was most thankful her innards were normal. Still, bleeding seemed like an undeserved punishment for growing up. She wondered what boys went through, not that she'd ask Wiley about it.

A mother might explain it to her in more detail. But she'd never known her mother. As Pa told it, he'd come home from the lighthouse one day to find baby Adelia in her cradle, shrieking in outrage, hunger, and sodden clothing. Her mother had vanished. "Not worth looking for the whore," he often added when talking about her perfidy.

That was twelve years back. Wiley said it was Adelia's fault. He was four years older and claimed to remember their mother. And to miss her. He'd never liked his little sister, calling her a pestilence when Pa wasn't around to hear.

As she neared the cabin, Wiley yelled from the vegetable patch. "Where you been? You ain't even dug out the weeds."

"Appears you must manage it yourself. I have to help Lilac with the meal." Causing Wiley extra work was the only good thing about the week so far.

* * *

"You know where that ol' bitch of a dog come from don't you, girl?" Her father George Wright asked. They were at the table. Through the cabin's open door, early spring sun rays cut across the dirt floor and plank table in strong bands of shadow and radiance.

Adelia couldn't keep her eyes from glancing at the rug near the fireplace. Shep's rug, now empty. She fought back tears, unwilling for Wiley to see how she ached.

You tell me she was a bum often enough, Adelia wanted to snap at her father. But she settled for, "Yes, sir." George spoke right over her as he reached into the pot for another elk short rib. He poured the last of the liquor into his glass. "From that last shipwreck before the light was lit. That's where. When the dark and the fog lifted, they found her howling amid a dozen dead men on the beach."

"Yes, sir." Adelia couldn't remember her father

ever talking about much of anything but the lighthouse when he was home from his three-month stints on it. She'd given up trying to interest him in her life.

"Bitch was the only living thing survived. Musta swum a mile to shore. Been the settlement bum ever since, surviving on handouts."

She'd heard her father's story before, how Shep's crew might have survived if Tillamook Rock Lighthouse, off the north Oregon Coast, had been completed three weeks earlier. But its lamp wasn't quite ready, so the ship had no warning light to keep it off the rocks.

Wiley pinched her thigh under the table and twisted until she cringed. "Know what she did, Pa? Fed that dog our meat when you were gone."

"We're not to waste food. Hear me, girl? You mind Wiley when I'm not here."

Adelia knew her father wouldn't remember giving her that order. He forgot a lot, getting liquored up pretty quick and staying mostly boozy for the two weeks before he went back to the lighthouse. There he had three months to dry out before his next leave.

"Seems strange to me, her just dying on the stoop like that," Adelia said, staring an evil eye at her brother. "Seems something must have happened to her."

Wiley sneered. "I suppose somebody could of strangled her. Old as she was, she wouldn't put up much of a fight. I woulda put her out of her misery with the Springfield long ago, Pa, if you'd let me use it."

"Ain't gonna tell you again, boy. That gun stays right where I put it."

This time, Adelia sneered at Wiley.

George Wright pushed back from the table, signaling the end of the meal. But he still had his drink. "Was a terrible gale the night the *Lupatia* went down. Lighthouse crew heard sailors scream even through the raging storm. Sails slapped and rigging creaked. Commander was crying, 'Hard aport.'"

Her father was off and running. The tale might have scared her more if Adelia hadn't heard it so many times before.

"They saw running lights, then all went dark. By morning light, they picked out the remains of the *Lupatia* in the surf. Twelve of the sixteen corpses were strewn along the beach. The rest are out there still."

Adelia picked up plates and left the table quietly to join the Indian woman cleaning dishes. They called her Lilac since they couldn't pronounce her name. She didn't speak English, and they couldn't handle the Clatsop language. Adelia liked this one, but her father replaced his women fairly often. Chinese or Clatsop women. Adelia put an enamel pan of water on the wood stove to heat and listened to her father drone.

"A lighthouse a mile out to sea, helluva thing. First foozler who tried to survey it fell into the sea. His body was never found. Helluva thing. Makes a man crazy, living out there on a God forsaken rock that wants you dead."

You ever listen to yourself? Adelia figured it was the lighthouse that made him daft. He'd been an assistant keeper for years on the light they nicknamed Terrible Tilly. That had to knock a man off his chump.

In the dark that night, Adelia listened to the moaning and grunting of the Indian woman and her father. It was the only language they shared, as the bed frame squeaked along with them. They were directly over her in the cabin loft. Her bed was on the dirt floor, as was Wiley's, with a ragged curtain drawn between the two.

Lilac gasped.

"What you suppose he's up to now?" Adelia whispered to her brother.

"Shut yer tater trap, or I might come show you."

Adelia had seen animals mate so she had a rough idea of what was going on. It was hard to picture what humans did, though. She had no interest in taking part, especially with an all-fired ratbag like her brother. She rolled on her side to face the wall. In the morning she would go to the creek and wash the rags Cora Dixon had given her. Hang them to dry on a vine maple where her brother or father would never see them. She didn't think she could survive that kind of humiliation.

She wished Shep was at the foot of her bed, but

that wise old dog, her only source of affection, was gone. She'd carried the shepherd's body from the stoop into the woods to bury, deep enough for forest creatures to leave it alone. What she felt was new to her. It wasn't sadness. That was a part of life around here.

This was intense grief. It hurt worse than a burn at the stove when fat exploded or when Wiley punched her in the arm. This agony was on the inside, slicing through her where she couldn't rub it or administer one of Lilac's salves.

Adelia used to be able to talk to Wiley, when they were little enough. Before he became such a bully-boy. Had he killed her dog? If she could ever prove it, she'd use Pa's Springfield on him. Maybe not to fix his flint for good, but at least to scare the bejesus out of him. She had to find where her father hid the ammunition first. She'd never admit it, but she was afraid of her brother now, every time her father went back out to the light.

Loss of her dog, mistrust of Wiley, and this bloody curse, all in one week. Life is a sneaky opponent that blindsides you whenever it chooses. Adelia was damn sure of that.

* * *

Two days later, George Wright left for his next three-month shift on Tillamook Rock Lighthouse.

Wiley headed off to drink with friends or check his traps or whatever he did to get through the day. Adelia did not care as long as he was gone from her sight. She knew she was not really safe at home anymore. And she couldn't see things getting any better. Maybe she could make some money then leave. Sew or clean for other settlers maybe. She decided to work on a plan.

But time was not on her side. The next day, she was cleaning the coop, singing to soothe the chickens:

Oh I went down South for to see my Sal
Play polly wolly doodle all the day
My Sally is a spunky gal..

Her brother broke in with a liquor-slurred verse of his own. *"Oh my Sis she is a maiden fair, play polly wolly doodle all the day."*

A bolt shot through Adelia as she looked into his eyes, crazed with rotgut and lust. Wiley blocked the entrance. At sixteen, he was big, randy, and cruel. His shirt was filthy, his old boots smelled of manure from the field, and his pants of human sweat.

He smiled at Adelia, breathing out fumes of alcohol. "I'll show you what happens to maidens fair."

Her only weapon was the broom. She swung it at him, scratching his face. On her next swing, he grabbed the stiff straw, pulled the stick from her hands, and tossed it aside. Adelia tried to dodge past him, and nearly succeeded, but he caught one wrist, then the other, forcing her down. She yelled. The chickens squawked and flew in panic.

Wiley ripped through her thin bloomers and tried to shove himself inside. Alcohol impeded his finesse, and her struggle landed a knee in his groin hard enough for him to cry out. For a moment all was still, except downy feathers from the panicky birds flurrying like snow.

Then he started at it again, but the cocking sound of a chambered bullet stopped him. Wiley turned toward it, as did Adelia. There was the Indian woman, Springfield rifle in hand.

"You go," she hissed. Adelia realized Lilac had learned all the English she needed.

Wiley stood bent over, his hand in his groin where Adelia had kicked him. Blood trickled from the broom scratches on his face. He growled, "You will be sorry. You both will be sorry."

"You go."

He limped away. Adelia rose from the hard packed dirt. Her head was pounding and she couldn't catch her breath, but she realized she wasn't really hurt on the outside. Sore, scraped, and bruised but not really hurt. Bruises and scrapes were common as dirt.

Lilac looked at her and said, "You go." This time her voice was gentler.

Lilac was right. Adelia had to leave. They both did.

Wiley would return. That knowledge curled like smoke around grief for her dead dog and fear of the unknown.

Adelia went to the cabin, put on her only other pair of bloomers, and packed an ancient valise with what little she had. She saw her brother's boots, the new ones he'd purchased with such pride. She tied the laces together then slung them over her shoulder. He would miss them, and she was delighted by that. Finally, she removed all the money from the old lard tin on the shelf. She gave half of it to Lilac.

Then Adelia left her home. She planned on never coming back.

Chapter Two

April 1893

Adelia rushed along a deer path through the Douglas fir and cedars. Blackberry brambles and maple vine reached out to trip her, but she ripped through them. Grief, anger, and fear fueled her flight. Although she'd never been fearful of the wilderness before, Adelia was spooked by every forest noise now. The idea that Wiley was trailing her, well, her heart raced even though she knew it was bunkum.

"Stop running and start thinking," she lectured aloud, willing herself to slow down and listen to her own reason. A mossy log that crossed a creek proved inviting, and she sat, dangling her feet just above the water. Tadpoles half-grown into frogs darted about in the quiet water below her. She took a couple deep breaths and listened to a pileated woodpecker hammer at a hole. Bees worked the Oregon lilies and lupine along the bank. A hive of wildflower honey would not be far away.

The sounds and scents drained her fear, soothing her enough to consider her situation realistically. Wiley was not thundering along behind her. He probably didn't know she was gone yet.

"And in truth, he is unlikely to come looking," she pronounced. A shard of grief for Shep sliced through her. Tadpoles and birds were no replacements at conversation.

Wiley should never want her back, on the off chance her father would believe her about what happened. "If he thinks at all, he's thinking good riddance." Of course, he might come after the money she had taken. She sighed at the puzzle. Then she moved to the next item on her mental checklist.

She needed a safe place for the night, somewhere her brother wouldn't find her if he did hunt for her. It took a while with her brow furled in deep thought. She picked a blackberry bramble from the end of her long ash blonde braid. At last, the perfect place flashed into her memory. "Let's go," she said, lifting her valise and heading onward. She wondered how long it would take her to stop talking to a dead dog.

It was another two miles or so to the old dairy barn. Its backside shoved up against a sharp rising hill so the door faced south, away from most winds. Adelia had seen it before when she passed this way. Wild rose bushes not far from the barn provided her cover to await the farmer who would no doubt soon appear to do the evening milking.

When he arrived, he seemed a hardy fellow, cheeks and nose red above a massive dark beard of wildly curling hair. Adelia snuck to the outside wall of the barn and peered through an accommodating chink. The farmer burst into *The Old Settler*, singing to his trio of Holsteins as he began to milk.

No longer the slave of ambition,
I laugh at the world and its shams,
As I think of my pleasant condition,
Surrounded by acres of clams.

Except he modified the last line to *Surrounded by acres of teats.* Then he guffawed to his trio. Squeezing a teat of the cow before him, he shot a stream of milk to a ratter cat perched on her back haunches, awaiting her treat. Adelia clasped a hand across her mouth to smother a giggle, and the cows covered for her. They mooed for the farmer to hurry and unload their swollen udders.

As he left the barn, he called, "Good evening, Milky, Clara, and Clover. I thank you each for all."

Adelia watched while he moved the heavily laden pail into his cold store, deep in the side of the same hill that supported the barn. She did not know how cheese or butter was made, but she knew the milk would soon be one or the other. The thought made her hungry. Hungrier.

When she felt sure the farmer would not return that evening, she snuck into the barn. She knew these particular cows, having petted one in their pasture on an earlier day. Two rolled their eyes and moved away, but the mostly white bossy came close for a scratch around the horns then behind the ears. "Good girl, Milky," Adelia said, thinking that was a fine name for her. The cow gave her a raspy lick on the arm with a sandpaper tongue, causing her a second rare giggle. The others settled and accepted Adelia's presence. At least they didn't bawl for the farmer's attention.

She found a space between the barn wall and a pile of scratchy rope. She tamped down a small mat of clean dry straw, removed a horse blanket from a peg, and spread it over the nest. Using her valise as a pillow, she pulled her knees to her chest and covered herself with her cape. Her hidey hole was just large enough for a child, and when the ratter cat came to curl up there, too, Adelia was warm enough to feel drowsy.

Everything ached, spirit and body. When she thought of her brother, the ache spread in the way of a disease, building in malignancy. She was forsaken by parents and sibling, alike. She was a nobody, worse, a nothing. But that line of thinking would get her nowhere, and she whispered as much to the cat. Besides, the farmer had given her an idea. She now knew exactly what she would do the next day. A one-day plan was enough to help her sleep, that and the restorative power of a purring cat.

* * *

The growl in her belly awakened Adelia. It disturbed the cat, too, who stretched then disappeared on its early rounds. It was still dark, but Adelia knew she must leave before the farmer returned for the morning milking. She picked up her few things and replaced the horse blanket. In the process, her motion alerted the cows, who'd forgotten she was there. The two skittish ones mooed. First low, then loud. No amount of shushing appeased them, so Adelia ran from the barn, smack into the farmer. He held a lantern high, but dropped an empty milk pail and grabbed her wrist.

"See here, see here," he blustered in a startled voice, repeating it again as she squirmed. He struggled not to drop the oil lantern so close to the barn. Her wrist was very small and his hand very large. It was as if he couldn't quite tighten down so she slipped free.

Adelia ran with the speed of a young deer, her legs leaping through a field of new corn. It was dark, but she knew there would be woods soon, in any direction. Behind her she heard another "See here!" and plaintive mooing, then all was quiet except the chitchat of the earliest birds.

When she reached the safety of the trees, Adelia darted under a cedar, its lowest boughs dipping to the ground. She sucked down great gulps of air, thinking she was catching her breath. But the gulps didn't stop, nor did her eyes stop watering. Beneath the massive tree, the child mourned for the love she'd never had, for the few comforts she'd lost, and for the many fears she'd found.

But crying was a waste of time. It was a simple fact, and a childish thing she could no longer afford. She wiped her eyes on a dress sleeve. Adelia's stomach forced her out of her cedar den, its noisy protest for food becoming more important than safety.

She wondered what the farmer would think when he found the nearly new pair of boots she had left for him in the barn, the ones that belonged to Wiley. The thought brought a bit of cheer to her morning.

She was very close to the ocean, with small hill farms all around this stand of cedar and fir. As the sky began to lighten toward the east, she found a vegetable garden. It was too early in the year for most plants to mature, but she saw the shoulders of carrots that had overwintered. She grabbed four before courage failed her, and she ran.

It was her second theft, following the removal of cash from the lard can on the high shelf back home. She thought about how it felt, being a criminal, how she should be suffering deep shame. Certainly the reverend had taught her it was a sin when he preached at the church service held in settlers' homes, on days when there was no school. But when carrots tasted this good, thieving was its own reward. She wished she'd tried for some of the cheese she imagined in the farmer's cold store.

Adelia stayed close to the bank of Elk Creek following it toward the beach. It was wide here so it flowed lazily toward the ocean. She stopped now and then to skip a stone across the water or to braid fawn lilies into her hair, but she did not dawdle long. She wished Shep was with her. Distress bit her again. She simply must try not to think about the dog.

The stream led her to the south end of the new Elk Creek Road. The so-called road punched through the forest following an ancient Indian path. It was the only route over Tillamook Head, a bluff over a thousand feet high, dangerous where the ground was unstable at the coast. The road zigzagged up and over, eventually ending on the other side of the headland at Seaside, Oregon. Adelia's father followed this route on days he met the tender boat that took him to or from the lighthouse.

Elk Creek Road was a pair of barely passable ruts through a hundred jolting, nasty curves, and yet it was so much better than the preceding foot trail that a toll was demanded of anyone riding on it. If Adelia had a horse, it would cost her a quarter. If she had a wagon, she'd pay seventy-five cents for the bone-jarring commute. *If wishes were horses, beggars would ride.*

She could ask a teamster if she could hitch a ride; that is what her father did. And there was an ox team heading out, hauling a load of butchered pork to the meat market in Seaside. But she was too worried that the driver might know either George or Wiley. Besides, she was far too reticent to approach a strange man: her luck hadn't been all that great with the ones she knew.

The sun was just rising. She quietly slipped out of the woods, around the toll gate and onto the road to walk the eight miles to Seaside. If she heard a wagon coming, she would disappear into the trees until the conveyance passed her by.

The first two miles twisted sharply uphill. Adelia began to sweat although it was still cool. In sunny spots along the road she found salmonberry shrubs with early fruit just ripening to orange, and she gobbled as she walked on. She picked an enormous skunk cabbage leaf to use as a berry bowl, keeping an eye out for bears.

When she heard a wagon coming, she crouched behind a massive stand of ferns that dripped with morning dew. Her teeth began to chatter. Her head felt light. The berries weren't filling the empty pit in her stomach fast enough. Adelia needed to eat.

As the wagon approached, she heard singing. She

wondered if everyone sang songs when they didn't know someone was listening. Unlike the farmer singing to his cows, this woman's voice was high and appealing. Adelia was not afraid of women.

Sweet violets, sweeter than the roses,
Covered all over from head to toe,
Covered all over with sweet violets.

Adelia had never begged before. She supposed if she could learn to steal, she could learn to plead. She stepped out into the road, startling the chunky little mare that pulled a buckboard. The horse snorted, the woman driver yelped, and Adelia spoke. "Morning, ma'am."

"Goodness, child. You gave us a start."

"Yes, ma'am. Sorry, ma'am." Adelia did her best to smile since people seemed to like that sort of thing. Cora Dixon had once said she had dimples whatever that meant. She held up the wide leaf with its load of berries. "Wondered if you might have some other food to trade for these salmonberries. They're nearly ripe."

The woman looked down at her from the high bench seat. "You hungry?"

It was hard to admit. Adelia blushed but forced herself to say, "Yes, ma'am. I am hungry."

"No shame in that." The woman turned on her seat and dug into a basket beside her. "Keep the berries.

And here is corn bread. Stale, I'm afraid, but fillin' when you need it."

"It is perfect." Adelia's stomach urged her on as she reached for the large yellow square.

"Now jump in the back of the wagon if you want a ride to Seaside."

Adelia set her food prizes into the flatbed and clambered up.

"My name is Ida Rose. Yours?"

"Adelia," she said when she had gulped down a dry chunk.

"Well, Miss Adelia, don't get crumbs on those blankets. They're for Seaside tourists to handle."

Adelia looked at the folded woolens with their bold native wildlife patterns. She recognized the look, but felt confused by Ida Rose's very fair skin. "You a Clatsop?"

"Nope, but one taught me how to make 'em. I be a used up white woman. Too old and ornery to worry about being on the road alone."

"They are so pretty," Adelia said, wanting to touch one of the blankets but afraid the berry juice on her hands would stick. "Have to be addle-pated not to want one. Seems to me you could sell all you make if some Clatsop and Chinook ladies helped out. I've seen those Seaside tourist before. They buy a lot." It had been so long since Adelia talked with someone who seemed interested. Someone who seemed kind.

"Well ain't you just a Joan Jacob Astor," the woman said with a chuckle. "A couple of them work with me carding the wool, spinning it, knitting it. Then I sell door to door in Seaside or on the street to visitors. Even an ugly white woman like me gets more than Indians moneywise, so I front for them. Nobody needs to know who makes what."

"Takes grit for that, Ida Rose, ma'am."

"Hornswaggling tourists, you mean? Not at all, girl. They go happy, Indians go happy, I go happy. Nobody gets hurt. Giddap, hoss."

The horse plodded, and Adelia ate. The stale bread tasted like heaven.

The sounds around them were of a world going about its morning: the cry of an eagle, wind in the trees, a roar of breakers on the beach far below, the protests of the wagon lurching over ruts. At the top of Tillamook Head, Ida Rose stopped her mare once more. She grabbed up a book, climbed down from her seat, and walked to the cliff. There she stood.

Adelia followed along, coming to a halt beside her, the twelve-year-old not much shorter than this tiny adult. She stared where the woman was staring.

"Know what Mr. William Clark said about this spot? He and Sacagawea and them must have stood right about here." She rifled through pages of the dog-eared book. "Let me see...here. He wrote this view is one of 'the grandest and most pleasing prospects which my eyes ever surveyed...the Seas rageing with emence wave and brakeing with great force from the rocks....'"

Adelia saw just that, along with Tillamook Rock Lighthouse far at sea.

"Ain't that somethin'? And Mr. William Clark went across the country. He seen a thing or two. And now here we are. You and me."

By the time they crested Tillamook Head and the wagon picked up speed down the other side, they both were singing *Sweet Violets*. When they arrived in Seaside, Adelia jumped down, waved a good-bye to Ida Rose, and walked to the beach where she sat in the sand, still humming the song.

She warmed in the mid-morning sun, the sand hot under her butt and legs. She needed rest from her journey. On this side of the Head, she could still pick out the lighthouse and the vastness of the sea beyond. Her father told her there was land over there somewhere, a place called China from whence trader ships came filled with arcane booty. They aimed at the mouth of the Columbia, just to the north of Seaside.

George Wright claimed Terrible Tilly kept them from smashing against the coastal rocks that gave this place the nickname Graveyard of the Pacific. "Two thousand ships went down before the light went up," he'd said to her. She tried to think of her father as a hero.

She rested in the sun while the tide ebbed, enjoying the arguments of seabirds amidst the happier sounds of people on the beach. In time, she stood and scavenged a sturdy stick of driftwood with a hook shape on one end. And as Lilac had taught her, she began to dig for razor clams.

As she worked, she gave a thought to the farmer. He had reminded her of this skill. She saluted him by singing his song, with the proper lyric in its proper place.

No longer the slave of ambition,
I laugh at the world and its shams,
As I think of my pleasant condition,
Surrounded by acres of clams.

Chapter Three

April 1893

Seaside, Oregon epitomized fabulous wealth to a girl in a shabby cotton frock. Her father's Chinese woman had taught Adelia to sew. Lilac dyed this dress green from lichens, but Adelia had no idea who made it to begin with. She let out the seams through the years as she grew. It was too short now, revealing the tops of her lace-up work boots, but there was no more material left to make it longer. She had one better dress in her valise, but it was also too short. Both dresses were getting tight across the chest, and thinking about that made her blush. Her bonnet was frayed around the brim, but it still protected her from the sun as she dug for clams. She hid in plain sight among the other diggers on the slight chance her brother was on her trail.

Adelia's plan was to ride from Seaside to Astoria,

but the stagecoach didn't leave until tomorrow afternoon. She'd have to bed down somewhere overnight. No way could she hide in a fancy hotel or a smart shop among the stylish ladies. She'd find another barn or shed outside town.

As she gathered clams, she watched the tourists from the elegant Seaside House resort, the one that had given the town its name. It was like a palace from a picture book to Adelia, built on the isolated beach more than a decade earlier by a railroad tycoon. She thought the tourist men looked pretty much like the men she knew, except they favored large manicured mustaches over long untrimmed beards. Their coats fit tighter, their hats had narrower brims, and they smelled better, less like sweat and more like spice.

But the women! They were exotic shorebirds from a world apart. Even on the beach, every bit of skin was hidden from the sun and from view. Their colorful hats were enormous affairs with veils, lace, and flowers piled high. Their dresses billowed out in the back like their bottoms were abnormally large. And those sleeves were as puffy as the tinned marshmallows she'd seen in the penny candy store.

These upper class people toured in fine carriages, strolled through the shops, had afternoon tea on the seaside verandah, bought whatever caught their eye. Adelia was astounded, since even her next meal was in question. Her father had told her the rich came from as far as San Francisco and Portland, by ship or train or stage just to vacation here where the ocean breeze cooled the summer.

Adelia wondered if people with money always scared people with none. They scared her plenty so she avoided them when she could. But that didn't stop her from being amused at them. Her own dress might be shabby but it allowed her freedom in the sun, with no boned underwear to lace or bind. She only owned bloomers and a thin petticoat.

She took her clams, held in her skirt, to a wagon at the top of the beach. The ground was hard enough for wheels and hooves not to sink in the sand. It belonged to Clarence Adams and his wife, Bess. Together they loaded it with clams then sold them to guest houses and hotels. Adelia made two pennies apiece for each large razor clam in an unbroken shell.

"Looks like another twenty four cents," Bess Adams said as she rummaged a purse from between her massive breasts. She handed coins to Adelia then replaced the purse. The woman allowed herself the freedom of rolling up her sleeves as far as her elbows. It was a look too scandalous for town, but must be okay here on the beach, at least for a woman of ample proportions and advancing years. As Adelia turned back to dig for more, Mrs. Adams called, "Here. Take this bucket. You can carry more at a time that way."

"Thank you, Mrs. Adams," Adelia answered, too

shy to say more but glad of any assistance.

As the sun climbed to noon and Adelia kept digging, she became aware she had an audience. A small boy watched her every move. He was four, or maybe five, in a costume that looked more girly than anything the boys she knew would wear.

"What is that you have on?" she asked.

The boy didn't answer, pretending disinterest. He drew a circle in the sand with a stick.

"Are you dressed in your mama's under things?" Adelia teased.

"This is my bathing suit," he said with a huff as a shock of coppery hair fluffed in the breeze. "I can get wet if I want."

"Oh yes? Spin around. Let me see." The top was a navy blouse with white buttons and puffy sleeves. The short bottoms were loose pantaloons that matched the top. The boy spun again and again until he fell in the sand.

"Might be good for swimming but not so good for flying."

"Flying? I cannot fly." He stood dizzily.

"See what I mean?"

He giggled. Adelia did, too. Being silly made you feel less sad.

"What are you doing?" he asked.

"Digging razor clams."

"What is that?"

"Come closer. Watch."

She eyed the wet sand, cocking her head in concentration. "See! There!" She pointed.

"What?"

A dimple in the fluid sand appeared to spit out a bit of water and air.

"That's where he is. Now we dig. Fast." She jabbed the hooked end of her cedar branch deep into the sand with all the force she could muster. "Mr. Clam is trying to dig faster. But I am going to catch up." With the hook deep in the sand, she dropped to a knee then pulled backward on the branch. It broke the surface tension of the sand, and she gave it a wiggle to dislodge even more. Then she dug with both hands like a dog, scooping out sand as fast as she could. She stopped, peered into the hole, reached in deep.

"You must be quick. It can dig fast. Maybe all the way to China." In triumph, she hauled up a pale tubular body, extending from a shell which was at least six inches long. "It is really sharp along there. Why it is called a razor." She dropped the bivalve into her bucket.

The boy frowned, staring at it and its captive neighbors. "What you do with them?"

"People eat them, silly. Fried in butter. Cut up in chowder."

"Eeeuuu," the child said.

"Not good to kill what you do not intend to eat."

She dug up another and another with the little boy beside her, both of them soaked in sand that sucked at their feet. "Like quicksand," she said. "We need to be careful. A little kid like you might disappear below the surface and be eaten by a whale."

She saw his look of concern and relented. "You want to try to catch a clam?"

"Could I?"

She shepherded him through the process from finding the dimple to raising the clam in the air like a trophy.

He vibrated with joy. "Mama!" he shrieked. "Mama, look!" A lady watching them from a table on the hotel's verandah, rose and picked her way through the sand.

"Ernest, what are you up to?" she called out.

The closer the lady got, the more nervous Adelia got. Should she run? But that would call attention to herself. She tried to smooth her wet skirt and kick sand from her feet. Then she jammed her hands in her pockets, crossed one foot over the other, and waited for the boy's mother to arrive.

The lady was the most beautiful thing she had ever seen in her life, other than maybe a fawn. Or the sunset over the ocean. Now sun high in the sky turned the woman's red hair into fire and added a shiny glint to her light blue eyes. Even her dress seemed lighter and airier than the other women wore.

"Mama, look! A razor clam. Careful not to cut yourself."

"I would need to touch it to cut myself, Ernest, and I intend to do no such thing." She clutched the towels she was carrying tighter to her breast. "Who is your new friend?"

The boy considered this weighty issue. "I do not know. I found her on the beach."

Adelia felt she had been collected, like a seashell or fishbone.

"I like her." Ernest completed his assessment.

"Ernest does not take a shine to just anyone. He is often shy." The woman's smile was as radiant as her hair. Her voice was music. She smelled of flowers. Adelia had read about goddesses in school. She never thought to meet one in Seaside, Oregon.

"Me, too. I am shy. Ma'am." Adelia, tongue-tied, fought to get out this many words in a row.

"What is your name?"

"Adelia. Ma'am."

"And I am Florence Munro. Is your mother here, Adelia?" The woman looked around.

"No, ma'am."

"Father? Friends?"

"No, ma'am."

"You are alone?"

"Yes, ma'am."

Mrs. Munro's eyes narrowed for a second, looking

Adelia up and down. The girl flinched in humiliation at her ragged gown.

"It is my oldest dress," she said as though she had many. "I work in it."

"I can see it has been designed very cleverly. Were those pockets at one time cuffs? How fun."

"I cut the cuffs off when the sleeves got too short for my arms, then I sewed them to the skirt. You know, to hold stuff." Adelia stashed treasures there, a colorful pebble or a knot of wood shaped like a heart. Of course, she could only hide such riches when she didn't have her hands jammed into the pockets as she did when nervous. Like now.

"I can see the stitches are tiny and fine. Well done, Adelia."

Adelia felt a quiver of pride. Or was this woman making fun of her? But no, those eyes weren't lying and neither was that smile.

The lady gave a towel to Adelia and a second to Ernest. As she briskly rubbed the boy, she said, "Dry yourselves, children. Both of you. Now then. It is time for lunch. We are eating there on the verandah. You come join us, Adelia."

"Oh, no. Ma'am." The idea was inconceivable. She was not properly dressed, educated, or experienced to enter such a foreign land. She was unworthy.

"I insist."

Adelia was without further resistance. When *no*

didn't work, she was out of words. With a large intake of breathy resolve, she followed mother and son up the beach to the magnificent hotel, set down her pail at the steps of the verandah, and marched onward to meet her doom.

"Since I already have a table, we need not go through the front and bother with the maitre d'."

If the lady meant that to reassure, it worried Adelia all the more. *What is a maytardee*?

As she seated herself in a white wicker chair on the narrow verandah, Mrs. Munro chattered. "It is too warm outside for most of the guests at the noon day meal. But I love the sun. And you children will dry fast out here. Now sit. Ernest, you here next to me. Adelia across so we can talk."

The little boy clambered up with a helping hand from his new beach friend. Then Adelia sat, stiff with mortification, well aware of the stir she was causing at the next table.

Mrs. Munro noticed, too. She spoke to the neighboring couple. "A fine day for walking the beach. The perfect place for children. Such a lovely shore for us all to leave our worries behind, do you not agree? And are you not enjoying the string quartet? I do so love classical music." The couple managed tight smiles before returning to their chicken salads.

"Nosy Nellies," Mrs. Munro leaned forward and whispered to the children. Adelia fell in love with her right then and there.

Adelia could read the menu but had no idea what to do with it. And the prices! Clam chowder and tea, a dime each. Porterhouse steak, twenty cents. Elk for fifteen. Cranberry pie, a whole nickel. Mrs. Munro solved the problem when the waiter appeared. "We will each have a bowl of the chowder, a bit of the salmon with fried potatoes. And, I think, two sarsaparillas plus one tea. With strawberries in cream for dessert." She leaned toward Adelia and murmured, "It is all my treat to thank you for helping my boy have fun this morning."

As the waiter left, the maitre d' appeared. Adelia had no way of knowing who this big man was, standing too close to the table in a jacket far blacker and less yielding than any she'd seen before. "Good day, Mrs. Munro," he said with a taut bow of his upper body. "I see you have an extra child today." To Adelia's way of thinking, he might as well have said an extra worm.

"Why, yes. Ernest has made a friend."

Adelia looked up into the stern countenance of disapproving manhood. She felt like a worm.

"I see," he said. "I thought the child was possibly bothering you. We could feed her in the kitchen, if you wish."

Adelia was not the only one to hear the disapproval. "No, no. She is fine right here with me. I am sure Mr. Munro would agree. He arrives again this evening for the weekend. And of course, I shall be here all summer if we so choose."

"Ah, yes. Such a pleasure. Then enjoy your meal." The man turned sharply to strut away to another table. As he left, a waft of nutmeg and cinnamon hit Adelia's nose.

"Smells like a spice cabinet," Mrs. Munro said, this time not in a whisper and with a wrinkle to her nose. "Far too much hair tonic, I believe." Then she grinned, and Adelia joined in.

Adelia was ravenous. When the food was served, she couldn't believe the generous portion was all for her. She forgot about embarrassment or nerves and dug into the hot dishes. She'd never had a sarsaparilla, and Ernest delighted in teaching her how to use a straw.

"No, not out, silly. You suck in!"

For the first time in her life, Adelia was truly happy. She looked out at Tillamook Rock Lighthouse. What would her father think if he could see her now? And her brother would never find her here, not in this grand hotel where he'd fear to tread. Even if he did, this angel she'd just met would surely protect her.

By meal's end, life appeared to have possibilities she'd never known before, at least until Mrs. Munro asked her if she could come stay with Ernest each afternoon. "It would give him pleasure and allow me a little free time. I would pay you, of course."

"Oh please, Adel...Adel...Addy!" Ernest said, grappling with pronunciation. And so a nickname was born.

A prick of reality burst Adelia's bubble. Such joy just couldn't last. "I cannot. I have no place to stay, you see. I am to catch the stage to Astoria."

"Is someone meeting you there?"

"Well...well...no." Adelia may have experienced thieving and begging, but lying to this woman was out of the question.

"Then I believe we could make arrangements here. I know a hotel like this, so far from other towns with competent workers, must need to hire from time to time. I will speak to the management about it."

Adelia cringed. If that *maytardee* had anything to do with it, her new career was over before it began.

Chapter Four

April 1893

George Wright had cared for modern Fresnel lenses before, like the one on Terrible Tilly. The thin lights, designed in France, had great visibility. Diamonds in the sky, he'd heard them called.

The light was all well and good, but George despised the thunderous noise of the double-barreled foghorn. He stuffed cotton deep into his ear canals, then wore a deerstalker with the flaps down, even tried a Foot Ball Head Harness. Nothing worked although it gave the other assistant keepers a good laugh at his expense.

Now he no longer bothered. He was resigned. Insomnia and pounding headaches were a part of his existence. Life on Terrible Tilly was easier to bear if you concentrated on one day at a time.

This morning, the horns were quiet since the

weather was clear. He cleaned them to a mirror-like shine and removed the seaweed, rocks, and fish pitched into their throats by massive waves during the last storm.

Now it was time for lunch. One of the other men had allowed crumbs to scatter across the kitchen counter. "Scallywag," George snapped. He determined not to speak to the man for a week, a severe punishment on that hellish rock, marooned as they were.

George never knew what was going on at home, not unless one of his children sent a letter. It would come across on a supply boat whenever the weather was clear. His son Wiley, like George himself, was not much of a hand with a pen. Adelia used to send little drawings and notes about Shep or a skill she'd learned from Lilac. But that stopped, maybe because he never had anything to say, so he didn't write back.

Besides, his daughter made him think about his wife. So he did his best not to think about his daughter.

* * *

Adelia was decidedly not thinking about her father either. Nor was she party to whatever conversation passed between Mrs. Munro and the hotel manager following lunch on the verandah. Instead, she took Ernest with her to deliver her pail of clams to Mrs. Adams. Then she raced him down to the shore where they constructed a sandcastle that looked like Seaside House, if only to them. It stayed sturdy until a wave inundated it, and it collapsed.

"Could that happen to the real hotel?" Ernest asked, wrinkling his fair forehead under the floppy sun hat that Mrs. Munro insisted he wear.

"Nothing to worry about. The hotel promised your Pa no floods for the length of your stay," Adelia assured him.

"Well, that is good news," said Mrs. Munro, coming up behind them. "Another concern off my list."

Adelia gasped "Gee willikers!" as Florence Munro plopped down on a towel beside her. The woman had on a bathing suit! Her calves were naked except for straps crisscrossing up from little slippers. Wide pantaloons covered her knees and the high middy blouse neckline hid her collar bones, but the wide white sleeves were so short they revealed her upper arms. Adelia had never seen these parts on any female body except her own. She was relieved her arms and legs looked enough like Mrs. Munro's to know she was normal.

"You look...you look..."

"Yes, I know. *Scandalous*. I shall be the talk of the beach." Her blue eyes flashed with delight under the frivolous white cap that covered few of her red curls.

Sure enough, other women on the beach, enrobed

head to toe, were staring. They gathered in whispery groups. Mrs. Munro crossed her naked arms. "This is the latest look on the east coast. And I am nothing if not fashion forward here in the west."

"They are gathering like hens for a good clucking party," Adelia said. "They may come peck at you."

"I have no doubt." Mrs. Munro grabbed up Ernest and made a beak of her hand. She clucked and pecked at his tummy while he squirmed and giggled. She stopped long enough to address Adelia again. "Now, then. Important news. You have a place to stay and a place to work in the mornings, so you can care for Ernest in the afternoons. It has all been arranged. The compensation is commensurate with the position. In other words, hardly a living wage."

Adelia was taken aback. "I have a place to stay and work? I do?"

"You do. Go to the rear of the hotel, to the servants' entrance. The hotel manager will have the maitre d' meet you there. Run along, and I will stay with Ernest. We shall see you again tomorrow afternoon."

Adelia was overjoyed, thrilled that finding friends and an occupation had come so easily. And at such a hoity-toity place. Wouldn't her father be proud! Wouldn't Wiley be jealous! Hadn't she worried for nothing at all! Wasn't life just the darnedest thing!

The lecture from the *maytardee* soon sobered her. He appeared to be furious. He said Mrs. Munro had gone above his position to his supervisor, and that he had to hire Adelia, but he did not have to like it...or her. "It is scullery work for you. You will not be allowed to touch the fine china, not a snot-nosed urchin who acquired her employment by pulling the wool over the eyes of an esteemed but naive hotel guest." He added she was to report in the morning at 5 a.m. to Katja, the head scullery maid who would instruct her, since he was not in the habit of dealing with the lower staff himself.

Adelia, with a chastened exterior while joy fluttered in her heart, was escorted by a bellboy to the staff hall. The short wing behind Seaside House had a covered entrance to the back kitchen stairs, so workers stayed dry as they scurried back and forth, invisible to the sensitive eyes of the well-to-do.

"What's yer name, then?" asked the bellboy who looked no older than she did. "I'm Billy. Folks call me Billy Bell. 'Cause of my job and all."

"I am Adelia."

"Think I'll call you Dele."

"Dele is not my name. It is Adelia. That is what I answer to." *Cheeky boy.*

"Yes, madam," he said with a snort. "And here is your suite." With an exaggerated bow, he whistled his way back down the hall.

The room she was assigned housed three other girls. They arrived off and on through the evening, each older than she. That was reason enough for them to ignore her. They were also housemaids while she was a scullery maid, the lowest of household staff. Her presence among them appeared to be an offense. She'd said hello and been rebuffed. All in all, that was okay with her. Adelia didn't know much about talking to other girls anyway. She'd never had friends her age.

The bed was narrow as a cot with a straw-filled mattress. She had a small stand with one tiny drawer plus four pegs on the wall. It was far more room than she needed for the few items in her valise. Adelia stuffed her underwear in the drawer and hung her other dress on a peg with her cape next to it.

She place a small wooden figurine of Terrible Tilly on her nightstand. It was one of the few things her father had ever given her. Only once had he brought Adelia and Wiley to Seaside for fun. They'd eaten too much ice cream and popcorn while staring at rich vacationers and so many things to buy. He'd presented Adelia with a Seaside souvenir, this little carved replica with the legend, *May Your Light Always Shine.*

She sat on the edge of the bed, brushed a strand of hair off her forehead, and tucked it behind an ear. She was hungry again but too shy to ask anyone where or what she could eat. Instead, Adelia reclined on her side, curled into a ball and read again, *May Your Light Always Shine.*

Maybe her light was shining at last. Maybe the bad

times were behind her. But Adelia was no gigglemug. She knew this safe place could be temporary. Mrs. Munro might well be the flibbertigibbet the *maytardee* said she was. Her favor could be capricious, and she might soon move on to the next idea that crossed her mind. Adelia resolved to work so hard she would prove her own worth and not be dependent on the largesse of another. In time, she drifted off and slept through the night, one very tired little girl.

* * *

The next morning she resolutely faced her first shift as a hotel employee, reporting to Katja Heikkinen. The short, stocky woman was a Finn, gnarled as a tree burl. A name like Mrs. Troll seemed apt to Adelia, but her mirth died when the gnome waggled a finger in her face, saying, "You work here like Finnhorse, hard. Pay attention. Pull your load." She placed a large apron on the child, twirling her to wrap the straps around and around, tying them in the back.

Katja showed Adelia to an alcove off the main kitchen, a work area large enough for four enormous ceramic sinks, each with one tap for cold water. Two were in use by men, one peeling potatoes and the other filleting salmon. A woman washed china in a large wooden bowl set inside a third sink. The fourth sink was where Adelia was stationed on a wooden box, sleeves pushed back, to scrub cauldrons, sauce pans and muffin tins.

"Now you wash," Katja said.

And wash she did. For hours.

So far, Katja was the only kitchen worker that Adelia had taken a good look at, fearing she'd be caught in the act of wasting time. As she began to scrub another food-encrusted pot, she thought about the two hotel employees she'd dealt with so far.

The *maytardee* was an Englishman named Mr. Stapleton which probably accounted for the highfalutin way he talked. His last words to her had been that she bloody well better watch her step. She wondered what bloody meant. Would he actually wound her? Adelia scrubbed a little harder. Regarding Katja, Adelia never knew a white woman whose English was so hard to decipher. Until meeting the Englishman and the Finn, she'd thought all white people spoke the same language.

Her hands burned. She thought it was from the hot water for the dozens of pans she had begun to scour. The china in the next sink over was washed with a gentler soap for delicate dishware. Its aroma of lemon was obvious to Adelia, but she didn't recognize the floral scents. The soap she used on pots and kettles was far harsher for hard scrubbing.

"Don't rub yer eyes. Could blind yerself," Katja said, looking over her shoulder at the child's progress.

The woman washing the china said, "That soap has traces of lye. It isn't hot water burning your hands but caustic chemicals. I will give you a salve when we break for a meal."

The morning went on forever. Adelia was strong for a girl so young, having worked hard doing chores at home. But her hands hurt, she was tired of standing on a box, and she was wearing out. She knew about workhouses because her teacher had read aloud from *Oliver Twist*. She never thought she'd be employed in one herself.

At least the alcove was sunny, with a large window to give them plenty of light for their toil. Someone had even placed a violet plant on the sill. Not so *Oliver Twist* after all, Adelia thought.

When her pots were not only spotless but dry, Adelia carried them to a pantry to the right of the scullery alcove. It gave her time to stretch her back and dry her suffering hands. It also gave her an astounding view of stacks and stacks of plates and bowls, glittering crystal glasses and goblets, a treasury of silverware. She hadn't the slightest idea what most of it was for, but these riches made her gasp. How many plates and utensils did rich people need in order to eat?

To the left of the scullery alcove, many pots and kettles of water boiled on a huge wood stove belching out heat that stifled everyone. The kettles were simply too heavy for Adelia to handle; her small wrists hardly moved them off a burner much less across a room. So Katja regularly poured more boiling water into the sink where Adelia worked. She often splattered the girl until Adelia learned to squirm far to the left or right when Katja approached with a steaming kettle in each hand. While dodging, she bumped into the woman working to her left.

"Pardon, ma'am," she muttered, taking a quick peek at the woman who had told her about the soap. Her brown hair was piled high on her head as though small birds had built a messy nest to make her look taller. She was short and curvaceous, with facial features as fine as the china she washed. A long slender nose, thin pink lips, eyebrows arched as though perpetually surprised.

"I'm not ma'am. I'm Harriet," she said then smiled as she a dried a dozen paper thin teacups she had just washed. She leaned close to add in a whisper, "Katja means well, but she's rough. We call her a cow in a china shop. Behind her back, of course."

"I am Adelia," the newcomer said, glad to know she could use her voice in the scullery at all. She watched as Harriet left, carrying a tray of cups and saucers toward the pantry.

"I am Ephraim," a young male voice called from the sink at the opposite end. "Pleased to meet you."

"Albin here, young miss," said the next as he pulled a whole skeleton away from the fish. Was that a peg leg he had? She wanted to stare but turned back to her sink.

Something in Adelia warmed. It had nothing to do with the stove or the heat in the sink. These strangers did indeed seem strange. They were all so...so kind.

Just when she thought she could not scrub one more pot, her three sink mates stopped working. "Take off your apron and come with us," said Harriet. "We eat in the larder." They marched in unison to a wooden table in a large room off the main kitchen. The walls were white and lined with cabinetry. What on earth was behind each door?

"One thing for sure, young miss. You won't have to wash your hands before you eat," Albin huffed with a cheerful snort. "They're clean as a whistle by now."

"Red as a beet, too," Ephraim added as he pushed a lock of hair back from his eyes.

"The Castile soap I use on the delicates is a lot milder," added Harriet. "I shred it into Ivory flakes then boil with essential oils into a smooth liquid. None of the lye you use on the pots."

They all took chairs where spoons and bowls were arranged on the table. Adelia's stomach did cartwheels of glee when Katja sailed in with a large tureen redolent of venison and gravy. An unknown girl followed with hot loaves of bread and a dish of butter. Katja said a grace that no one could understand. And they ate.

It was eleven in the morning. Adelia had worked since five. The food and rest were bliss. No one spoke until bowls started to empty. Then words began to replace mouthfuls of food. "We eat in shifts, first us then the cooks, then the serving staff, when them upstairs has settled down," said Albin. "We be between the breakfast and lunch rush now. So this is a good time to catch your breath."

Harriet removed a small vial from her apron pocket. "Rub some of this into your hands. Magnolia Balm. It will soothe the red."

"You get used to it in time," said Katja holding up her own hands whose palms and fingers looked tough as bear paws. "See?" Everyone laughed.

"I'm thinkin' our young miss is a bit more delicate than an ol' Finnish boot like you, Katja," said Albin just before belching.

"Or you, ya addled hoppin' Swede," Katja smacked the tabletop with a "Ha" at her own joke. Adelia wondered about Albin's peg leg but would never have asked. Had he been a pirate? A Viking maybe? She'd seen pictures of them wearing horns.

"Lost my foot when a Finnish gal size of Katja crushed it while dancin." Albin winked at Adelia.

"Who are you, Adelia?" Ephraim asked. "How did a littl'un like you get here?"

The boy didn't look that much older to her. She squared her shoulders and for the first time, stared him right in the eyes. "I am not so little. I came to town to find a job." She felt it wiser to keep anything more to herself.

"And found a benefactress from what I hear," said the unknown person who'd followed Katja to the table. This tall pale girl stared at Adelia. Her brows and lashes were so light they seemed nonexistent. It made her look ashen, even a bit ghostly.

"Mrs. Munro wants me to keep tabs on her boy Ernest in the afternoons. She helped me get a job here mornings so I could do that in the afternoons. But it's not charity. I will work hard. I can be a big help to you. You will see."

"Yes, I'm sure you will," said the ghostly girl in a tone that indicated her doubt.

"Now everyone. To work!" announced Katja. To Adelia, she said, "Except you. You go to the staff hall, clean yourself up, then go to the Munro room."

As Adelia headed toward the employee quarters, she looked at her hands. So far, the Magnolia Balm was a great disappointment. *They burn but they will heal,* she thought as she changed into her other dress.

Her few possessions had been pawed through. Nothing was gone, just moved. Adelia was glad she had taken her money with her while she worked, wrapped in an old handkerchief of her father's, and pinned to the underside of her petticoat. The idea that she was getting clever in the ways of thieves brought a smile to her lips.

Her blue dress suited her, but it was too small. Mrs. Munro would take a look at her and regret hiring her to stay with Ernest. New clothes were the first thing she needed to arrange for herself. The money she'd stolen from home would go fast, but maybe the rag and bone man would have an old cloth she could buy. A curtain or table cloth. Some used material, dyed a cheery color as Lilac had shown her, didn't look bad if it wasn't so old it frayed.

Strange how things happen, she thought as she walked nervously down the corridor that led to the guest rooms. She'd planned to catch the stage to Astoria today, to seek her fortune there. It was the big city, rich with promise. Instead she had new friends, a good job, and a full stomach only two days after leaving home. She liked that Harriet person. And what was the story behind Albin's peg leg?

Maybe Seaside was a safe haven after all.

* * *

Ernest opened the door to her knock and shrieked in delight, "Addieee!"

From a distance Adelia heard his mother. "Well, ask her in then. Be a gentleman. You know how."

"Please come in," he said with a bow, trying hard to curb his enthusiasm. "How nice to see you again."

"Thank you, Ernest." She could think of nothing more to say as her eyes took in the astounding room. It was hard enough to remember to close her mouth as she considered what money could buy.

The walls were papered and flocked with immense red roses, and the floor carpeted with a wildly patterned rug. Tapestry drapes in yet another pattern framed a window view of the Pacific Ocean. A tufted settee had intricate carved wooden leaves and flowers that arched high across its back. The little desk...

"Some people call this style Rococo," said Mrs. Munro, interrupting Adelia's train of thought. "I myself call it Dark Ages." A cloud of sweet scent had bustled into the parlor along with her. "Wait until you see the headboards in the bed chambers, even the one for little Ernest. Enough to give our darling boy nightmares."

"I...I am sure it is all very fine," Adelia managed. Mrs. Munro might make light, but it was definitely not the place of a scullery maid to laugh at such excess. Nonetheless, she did have to suppress a giggle at the gold piping which was absolutely everywhere it could be piped.

"Go ahead and laugh. I won't tell. Although I warn you that Mr. Munro likes it. He says it is modeled on the posh coaches of the railroad magnate who built Seaside House. He informs me that the patterns and colors work together in order to create a close, cozy room. I pretend to agree. However, even Joseph, that's Mr. Munro, admits it is a touch too dark when the sun is not pouring in."

Mrs. Munro held two dresses over her arms and turned attention to them. "I finally found them, these dresses altogether too tight for me after a month of this restaurant. They were hiding in the back of the closet. With your talent for sewing and mine for fashion, I think we can make the sweetest little frocks for you. Girl clothes are so much more fun than boy clothes, not that I'm complaining about you, Ernest, my love. It is hardly your fault men look so drab these days. *They* used to be the fashion show, and we women were the little brown wrens."

As she spoke she held one dress then the other up in front of Adelia whose mouth appeared frozen in a silent O as she eyed first the stripes and then the pattern of spring leaves. "Can you do needle magic on these, do you think? I know how they should look but not how to get them there. I'm quite useless, you know. A featherhead, Mr. Munro calls me. Here is a sewing kit I'm sure you can use." Like the room, the little case was a burst of colorful thread.

Tea was brought into the room on a cart by one of the girls who roomed with Adelia. Her eyes grew narrow when she saw the scullery maid *sitting* in the guest room. Adelia didn't try to hold back the tiniest of smirks.

For once, Adelia was too full to eat. She examined the seams of the dresses as Ernest and Mrs. Munro nibbled. The material felt so smooth, so fine to her roughened hands. She had never worked with fabric like this. Oh, the dresses she would make!

"Ernest will nap after lunch, then there are some picture books you can read to him. It is too gray for the beach today, I detect, but he loves games, and two can play Lookabout in here." Mrs. Munro stood before a mirror and arranged a hat before pinning it in place. "I will return in time for dinner. Since Mr. Munro is still in Portland, you may dine in here with us. I am afraid it is inappropriate to use the dining room, now that you are an official employee. Mr. Stapleton would be so indignant he would surely have a conniption fit."

"Yes, ma'am, he surely would."

"I am spending the afternoon at my friend's home. Then shopping. After dinner Ernest, you and I can all play Charades or Pass the Slipper." She crushed Ernest in a hug.

When Mrs. Munro swept from the room, part of the light went with her. Adelia saw the crestfallen look on the little boy's face. "We'll do just fine, Ernest. And your mother will be back for dinner."

"Sometimes," Ernest said then sighed. "Sometimes she is not."

* * *

Ernest and Adelia didn't hear Mrs. Munro return, probably because they were under the dining table. The little boy's clay marbles had burst free from his silk pouch and scattered across the floor, each rolling for cover. "I got them in town yesterday with Mama," he mourned. "Twenty four of them. All different colors. Now they are lost!"

"No they are not. But you have to work for a peewee to make it your own forever." Adelia created a game of finding them. They both got down on all fours. She made him squeeze his eyes shut then, sighting a speckled green ball, she directed him to it by tapping the closest hand. In the process she taught him left and right.

"Land sakes!" Mrs. Munro exclaimed. "I thought I would have dinner with my two favorite children, but they seemed to have disappeared. Where in thunderation could they be?"

"Mama!" cried Ernest in delight. He clambered out and grabbed her around the legs. "We're finding marbles. Only one to go."

"Far better than losing them, my love," she said. "Adelia, are you under that table, too?"

"Yes, ma'am." Adelia crawled out and stood, blushing.

"Really, my dear. When we finish your new frocks, you cannot crawl around on the floor."

"No, ma'am."

"Or maybe you can." Mrs. Munro dropped to all fours, her laugh like music as she stretched for a robin's egg blue escapee wedged behind a table leg. "Number twenty four, I believe," she said, holding her prize aloft.

After dinner, Adelia was sent on her way. She thought about Ernest's comment, that sometimes his mother returned when she said and sometimes she didn't.

From Adelia's experience, adults never told a child what was going on. Ernest didn't realize that. It was as though he thought he was the central element in his mother's life. Maybe Adelia should help him understand that couldn't be true. Children weren't that important.

Still and all, the boy might not be all wrong. His mother certainly acted like she liked him. She played games and hugged him. Maybe Mrs. Munro was the one out of step. Or maybe it was Adelia. She was still wrestling with it when she entered her room in the staff hall. Two other girls were already there.

"Here comes our royalty now," said the housemaid who had seen Adelia in the Munro suite. "Imagine a scullery maid in the parlor. Sitting there like a queen."

"The Munro woman ain't got the sense God gave a goose," said the other.

Adelia might not understand Mrs. Munro, but she understood these two. Any chance of friendship with their kind was out of the question. She would waste no effort trying because she was here to work, not to be liked. She put them in the same category as medicine. You might not like it, but you took it however bitter a pill to swallow.

Chapter Five

Spring 1893

Adelia learned quickly about her place within the food service operation of a posh hotel. The kitchen was a spotless warren of separate work stations in separate rooms, so one function would not infringe on another. Food plating and serving was far to the other end from the scullery. It was a metaphor for the staff hierarchy at Seaside House as well, with scullery workers at the bottom of the pecking order. Hotel staff that was visible to guests looked down on the kitchen staff; Harriet explained that the highest a scullery maid like Adelia could ever attain was assistant to the cook. Harriet hoped to achieve that lofty status herself, maybe even beyond.

And yet, Adelia had come to the notice of an honored guest. This break in the invisible wall gave her stature in the scullery but marked her as trouble to those who outranked her. To the lower, Adelia was their ragamuffin; to the higher, she was a guttersnipe.

Two of the housemaids punished her on her second day for rising above her station. When Adelia returned to her room that night, the striped dress given to her by Mrs. Munro had been ripped to pieces, its sad tatters strewn on her bed like fallen leaves.

"Oh goodness," said one of the girls. "What on earth have you done to that dress?"

"A shame you cannot keep better care of your things," said another. "You have little enough to keep track of."

Adelia tucked the travesty away and bided her time. She carefully folded the second dress and carried it with her to work the next day. It wouldn't leave her sight until she could ask Mrs. Munro if she could leave it in her suite until the alterations were complete.

In time, she became more confident talking with the people around her. Ephraim, Albin, Harriet, the Ghostly Girl, and Katja were her scullery team. For the first time ever, she belonged somewhere. She'd known the work would be hard, but she'd never anticipated her own curiosity about co-workers. Her brother would have called it nosiness.

Since Harriet worked right next to her, the petite bundle of efficiency became her source of information.

"Why do you have that old wooden bowl in your sink?" Adelia asked.

"Keeps the delicates from breaking," Harriet answered as she carefully set a stack of saucers into the steaming water.

"Why was I assigned to a room with the housecleaning staff?"

Harriet passed the question on to Katja. The old gnome gasped, dried her hands on a soft strip of feed sack, then stomped off muttering in a mash-up of English and Finnish.

Harriet translated for Adelia. "You'll soon learn the language of Katja if you work your ears as hard as your hands. She's saying Mr. Stapleton done that to make you as uncomfortable as possible...encourage you to leave." She added more saucers to the water in her sink. "That man surely has it in for you."

Adelia attacked a cast iron pot with a scrubber of tough boar bristles, clutched tight in her sore hand. "He doesn't know a trifle like that would never discourage me."

Harriet smiled at the girl wrestling the pot that outweighed her head. "No. I'm sure he hasn't reckoned on a bobcat in the scullery."

When Katja returned, Adelia had a new room assignment with Harriet and the Ghostly Girl. "Anything else?" the Finn said, hands on hips and looking for back talk.

"No, ma'am. Bobcats know when to keep still." Adelia peeked up at Harriet who pretended a deep concern with an invisible spot on the delicate spout of a china cream pitcher.

Adelia also used tea and meal breaks to gather intelligence or, as Ephraim accused with a wink, to pry. "You're a right little inquisitor, you are."

Even with his teasing, Adelia couldn't be stopped. "Why do you boil so much water?" she asked pointing at the stove in the scullery where blistering hot pots belched heat and steam all day.

"Remember what curiosity did to the cat," the Ghostly Girl replied.

"Tain't all for your tea, young miss," said Albin. "Gallons for them upstairs. Takes gallons to wash away the sins of the wealthy."

"Big mouth Swede. Do not poison brain of girl with rot." Katja said, "Twenty gallons per guest per day. For laundry and baths and cleaning of rooms."

"You girls start out scrubbing pots," said Albin. "Boys like Ephraim here start by chopping wood for that stove. Chop most of the day. Scrubbing spuds and rutabagas was a promotion, right lad?"

"How I got my muscles, all that chopping," said Ephraim, flexing a bicep in Adelia's direction. "I'm on to blacking out gent's boots next. Sky's the limit."

Adelia turned her attention away from the young man's arm to the scone crumbs still on her plate. She'd die of humiliation if Ephraim guessed she'd like to know what that muscle felt like.

"Long as we're lookin' at each other's limbs, I've seen you eyin' my peg of a leg, young miss. Left my real one back in Virginia afore I hightailed it to a safer sort of territory."

"You mean you ran away from the Rebs?" Adelia knew little of the war except that Southerners were a scurrilous lot. At least, that's what old men said when they gathered together and talked about the war.

"None of that, none of that. I was a fisherman fresh from Sweden, come over with a trade broker's gang. We was at the docks when the Yanks came with guns and invited us into the Union army. Did my time on the Potomac Flotilla patrolling the river to keep supply lines open for the boys fighting in Chesapeake Bay. Knew about rebels and bullets and all kinds of fish. But I knew damn all about snake bite. Head cook cut off my leg with a butcher knife to stop the poison."

"Then served Leg of Albin for dinner." Katja pounded the table in delight.

"Katja!" cried Harriet. "That's terrible."

"Made it out of Virginia as far and fast as I could on one leg. Pacific Ocean got me stopped, or I'd still be going. That's what, twenty some year ago? Nearer thirty? Anyhoo, fish out here ain't so different from fish back there. I'm still a master of the art." He pantomimed the splitting of a salmon head to tail with the slash of the knife.

The Ghostly Girl actually had a name. Felicity. It was such a misnomer it seemed a joke at her expense. Adelia wanted to know more about her, but she was as distant as Terrible Tilly. As unpleasant, too. Nonetheless, Adelia admired how hard she worked. Felicity oversaw the gallons of boiling water and cleaned the tops of those stoves that baked all day long. She kept soot from falling through the stove tops into the cakes and buns in the enormous ovens below. It was hard work only noticed when done wrong. Soot in a guest's food was an unthinkable infraction.

* * *

Unthinkable infractions took place on Terrible Tilly, as well. George Wright ought to know. He was cleaning the toilet once again. Next time he would laugh at the head keeper's lubberwort of a joke, longer and louder than the rest of the crew.

The toilet was little more than a hole in the side of the lighthouse. You sat your bare buttocks in the cranny provided and dropped your business into the ocean swells below. *All of life is a piss pot,* George thought as he scrubbed down the walls with carbolic and considered the letter from a neighbor lady that had come on the last tender boat.

Cora Dixon, interfering old biddy, wrote that his daughter had disappeared. He supposed he was expected to do something about it. First his wife and now his daughter. Did all women disappear the minute a man turned his back? Not worth a fart in a whirlwind, the whole lot of them.

What was to be done about it, anyway? Gone is gone. But why hadn't his son written about it? Wiley might be worth even less than his daughter, come to think of it.

* * *

As the warm weeks went by, Adelia flourished with her scullery friends. She learned things that had never been part of life in the cabin where she was born: family things such as how to share, how to tease, how to cover for each other when Mr. Stapleton blew through the scullery looking for anyone to blast away.

But it was with Mrs. Munro that Adelia's secret-self believed she actually belonged. Surely it was destiny they found each other. The reason Adelia's own family let her go must be to become a part of this one. She was needed here. In the process of justifying her situation, she developed an eye, an ear, and a taste for nicer things than she had ever known. Finer foods, silkier clothes, better diction, neater hair, and shoes like these that actually fit her feet. Her benefactress had purchased the low heeled pumps just for her. *Imagine being the first owner of a pair of shoes.*

Mrs. Munro threatened to go to hotel management

about the ruination of the dress by the housemaids. Adelia begged her not to, not wanting this lovely lady anywhere near those dreadful girls. What if she preferred them? Who knew what they might say? Adelia would handle it herself in due time. Thinking of the possibilities amused her.

Finally, Mrs. Munro let it go. "I've had things destroyed, too." she said in a wistful voice. "Things ruined by the actions of others."

Adelia was curious, but nothing else was said. A new concept broadened her horizon a little bit more: even the rich must have their problems.

Mrs. Munro took her to the dry goods counter of a local store and bought material to replace the destroyed dress. Soon Adelia had a smart two-piece cotton skirt and jacket the color of blueberries, with a blouse beneath pinstriped to match. She also altered the leafy print dress that had survived the maids. She showed her benefactress how darting for ample bosoms like Mrs. Munro's could be varied to create a smaller space for her own.

"How clever you are!" the woman exclaimed. "You could be the seamstress for the hotel."

Adelia nearly purred with delight at such a compliment. *A seamstress! Maybe even a dressmaker one day!*

In the afternoons, when Mrs. Munro was 'off to visit a friend' or 'taking in a concert,' Adelia put on her old work dress then took Ernest into the forest where they built forts from cedar boughs or performed high wire acts on mossy logs fallen over creeks. They visited the hotel's race horses in their stables and captured frogs to hold races of their own. Ernest collected bouquets of wildflowers for Mrs. Munro nearly every day.

"Tiger lilies are her special favorite," he said when Adelia suggested columbine this time.

"Tell her sniffing them will give her freckles," Adelia warned.

"Will they really?" Ernest asked, staring wide-eyed at the flowers' speckled yellow-orange faces.

"That's how I got mine." Adelia wiggled her nose and the freckles there danced.

On the beach, she sometimes let Ernest play with the little lighthouse her father had given her. And she taught him the silly lyrics to *Sweet Violets,* those that she'd learned from Ida Rose on their trek along Elk Creek Road to Seaside. Adelia had no way to know how much the woman had cleaned up the original. That evening, hands joined and dancing in a circle around the hotel room, the little boy and growing girl belted out a performance for his mother:

One day I forgot my suspenders and took my girl out to a dance
While dancing I heard someone calling,
Hey mister you're losing your –
Sweet violets, sweeter than the roses,

covered all over from head to toe,
covered all over with sweet violets.

Mrs. Munro exuded delight as the two children performed the bawdy dancehall song. "Applause! Applause for my two whooperups! I do so love the opera!" She hugged them both then pronounced the need of ice cream for the entire cast.

The weeks were a joy. But on the weekends, Adelia was not required by the Munro family. In fact, they shut her out. She found herself jealous of Mr. Munro.

Each Friday afternoon Adelia could feel Ernest and his mother shift focus to the imminent arrival of his father and her husband. They sobered, losing the dash of silly that Adelia so loved. Their attention turned away from her and onto him.

Joseph Munro rejoined his family on the weekend train from Portland to Seaside via Astoria. It brought so many men out to the coast, where their families escaped the inland heat for the summer, that it was dubbed the Daddy Train.

The hotel bustled from the arrival of the men until they departed on Sunday afternoons. Everyone in the scullery worked overlapping shifts. Adelia had little time to sulk about lost afternoons with Mrs. Munro. Yet her curiosity battled with her jealousy of the man who took Ernest and his mother away from her. What was he like? He must be very handsome to have married such a beauty, and when she once caught sight of them on the beach, she could see that he was.

Why can't I be part of that family? In Adelia's mind, Joseph Munro became selfish, a man who thought of nobody but himself. She couldn't wait for him to be gone so she could reclaim his wife and son. She eagerly wished for Mondays.

* * *

On Sunday late afternoons, the kitchen slowed its pace. The scullery crew alternated taking a few hours off. Sometimes Adelia and Harriet walked up the street made of clam shells into the town, splurging on a bag of penny candy and a bit of gossip.

"You know where Katja spends her time off, don't you?" Harriet was older than Adelia by many years and privy to worldlier wisdom.

"No. Where?"

"In Albin's room."

"And what does she do there?"

Harriet looked around, making sure nobody else was near whenever she had a particularly juicy nugget to impart. "A bit of belly bumping, I should think."

Adelia was shocked. "Belly bumping? You mean..."

"Yes, that's exactly what I mean. Good thing she's past the point of bearing Swede Finn babes."

"She does...she does...*that* of her own accord?"

Adelia envisioned the stench and terror of her brother's attack.

Harriet held her hand to her mouth, squelching a snicker. "It can be quite nice, you know." Adelia had never told anyone about Wiley's violence, but Harriet was no stranger to the way things were for womenfolk.

"But...they are so old."

"Snow on the roof, fire in the furnace." Harriet shrugged. "Besides, they have an agreement. They will marry when they no longer both work for the hotel."

Adelia required a period of silence to mull this over. After her treatment by Wiley, she'd vowed never to try that disgusting and painful act of her own accord. But if even old people liked it, there must be something to it. What a mystery.

She recalled an afternoon when she was walking on her own in the town. She had run into Billy Bell, the bellboy who called her Dele. He looked at her in a way that reminded her of her brother. A leer from him frightened her, yet a smile from Ephraim warmed her heart. Mating was most bizarre.

One Sunday when Harriet stayed behind, Adelia trekked up Elk Creek Road to the top of Tillamook Head. The climb up was a good deal harder than the ride down in Ida Rose's buckboard. Muddy patches, clods of manure, and rock-hard ruts made for difficult footing. At the top of the rise, she stopped and breathed deep. Sea air dried her perspiration as she stared north to the new state of Washington, then south down the Oregon coast. Was the Orient just over the Pacific horizon? If she squinted on a clear day would she see it? What was her father doing right this minute out on the lighthouse? Would he miss her at all when he knew she was gone?

The wind masked all but the shrill bickering of gulls and murres, at least until a voice very near her ear joined the raucous flock. "Quite a sight, is it not?"

Adelia spun around, and the cliff rubble gave way under a heel. As she lost her balance, arms windmilling, Ephraim reached out and grabbed her, his hands on her waist.

She was not sure whether the near fall or Ephraim's nearness startled her the most, making her heart leap like a cottontail. She did know she was disappointed when he let go of her and delivered a superior-sort of comment. "There now, Adelia. Why would you think it safe so close to the edge?"

Her fear turned to embarrassment. "Why did you sneak up on me?" She wiped non-existent dust from her dress to give her hands something to do.

"I thought you must surely have heard me." Ephraim smiled. It was a slight smile, just below the sparse blonde mustache battling to take hold on his Nordic face. His fair skin was ruddy from the wind, and traces of bygone acne marked his high-boned cheeks. Another observer might have found him an average looking lad, but to Adelia, the hint of humor always dancing in his eyes lured her like a trout to a wooly worm fly.

"Why were you following me?" she demanded.

"I was not following you!" Ephraim protested. "I was hiking. It is my day off as truly as it is yours. But what in the Sam Hill is a girl doing walking alone way up here?"

"I have always gone walking alone."

"But you have not always been the girl you are growing into. It is not safe to be on your own."

The girl I am growing into.

Adelia had passed her thirteenth birthday, unnoticed by one and all. No presents, no cake, no song. She was used to it. Celebrations had not been her father's way. Yet, now she discovered that Ephraim had noticed she was changing.

Adelia lifted an arm and pointed toward the sea. "I come to look out there."

"At the waves? Yes, it is beautiful. But I do not believe you made this climb just for the scenery." His eyes followed her finger. "Ah! You mean the lighthouse, do you not?"

"Yes. Terrible Tilly it is called. They built it a mile out to sea because there is so much fog up here, that it often would not have been seen by sailors."

Ephraim proved quick-witted. "You come to stare because you have someone on the light?"

"Yes. My father."

"You must miss him way out there."

"No. Not so much anymore. But he may be missing me. Or else he is not."

They clambered back down the hill together. Ephraim sometimes took her hand to help her around puddles or over limbs fallen onto the track. She told him about her father, her missing mother, her Chinese and Clatsop mother replacements. She did not mention the experience with her brother Wiley. How he had hurt her, how he had caused Shep's demise. Those secrets were hers alone to bear.

Adelia was ready to grow up. Only a dumb Dora would stay an urchin when adulthood beckoned so near. It was exciting to think about it, that she might actually get by on her own. But, oh, the conflicts between child and womanhood!

When she was building sandcastles in the sun with Ernest, when they were singing ludicrous songs, then her worries slipped away. She played as she never had before. She knew she should not be so mindless, that she should act mature and formulate a plan for her own survival. Yet, try as she might, her thoughts were impossible to control. She was never sure whether the sight of a fat man's fall or the sound of a songbird would lead her to laughter or tears. Her moods were as wanton as any young animal's, and all the patina of advancing age could not control them. Sometimes she felt as though a rushing river split her innards wide open, depositing new ideas then wiping them away as the old bedrock of fear and subordination returned.

Certainly, this boy, this Ephraim, older than her brother but not by much, did nothing to quell the turmoil in her. With him, she felt quite grown up. She found herself willing to talk to him, to tell him things she told no one else.

By the time they returned to the kitchen, Harriet and Katja were setting out bread and stew for supper. The Ghostly Girl looked up from arranging the cutlery and scowled at them. "Should have known you would show for supper."

"Now then," said Albin following grace as he tucked a cloth into his shirt collar. "What did you do while the rest of us were covering for you?"

"As I cover for you on your days off," Ephraim answered back. "Today, I climbed to the top of the headland, and I found -"

" - found me on the beach when he came back down. I was looking through magazines left behind by the guests." Adelia was not ready to share her time with Ephraim or the location of her father.

The Ghostly Girl cast a baleful look from one to the other. Whatever she was about to say - if she was about to say anything at all - was silenced by the entry of Billy Bell.

"I been sent for her. Dele there," the boy said to

Kajka as he pointed at Adelia. "She's wanted in the Munro suite. Now."

This had never happened before. Sunday nights Mrs. Munro always spent alone with Ernest after Mr. Munro departed for the Daddy Train.

Adelia ran to her room and quickly replaced Wiley's hand-me-down boots with the shoes purchased for her by Mrs. Munro. Then she pulled off the work frock and threw on one of her better dresses. She was still fastening the tiny buttons on the bodice as she knocked on the Munro door. And knocked again. Then again.

The door was finally opened a crack by Ernest. His eyes were red.

"Hello, Ernest. Are you well? Is your mother here?" Adelia touched his shoulder and peeked over his head into the darkened room.

He flung the door open and delivered a frantic hug. For a moment, she could not release herself from his grasp. Then she knelt to hold him at arm's length and stare into his terrified face. "What has happened? Where is your mother?" She felt her own fear rise like a tide.

"She is in her bedroom. She said to say she is not well. And that you should give me my bath tonight."

"Of course, Ernest. Of course I will. But first, I'll look in on your..."

"No, Addy! She said take me to the bathroom, and

let her rest."

Adelia could hardly restrain herself from bursting into the bed chamber. Instead, she followed orders. She walked Ernest down the hall to the room where the oak-rimmed tub waited on its decorative iron feet for the next bather. At only four years old, Ernest usually loved to play in it. But not tonight.

She poured hot water from the warming stove into the tub, added cold to temper it, then undressed the little boy. As she lifted him into the water, he winced and yelped. Adelia turned him and saw the angry red welt on his bottom that crossed from one buttock to another.

"Ernie! What happened?" she gasped.

"I am not allowed to say." The boy began to sob in stinging pain and sorrow. Adelia got to her knees beside the tub. She soothed him with an enormous sponge and hummed the tune of *All the Pretty Little Horses*.

When he finally quieted, she wrapped him in a pure linen towel warmed near the stove. Its loose huckaback weave dried him with the gentlest touch. He was groggy from his bath and from the power of his outburst, eyes puffy and sore.

She carried him back to the Munro suite and helped him into his softest flannel nightshirt. After placing him in his bed, Adelia began to read a favorite book to him. He fell thoroughly asleep after one of *The*

Merry Adventures of Robin Hood. Only then did Adelia creep off his bed and out of his room. She knocked lightly on Mrs. Munro's bedroom door.

"Come in," she heard Mrs. Munro whisper and then, in a stronger voice add, "Do not turn on a lamp."

With only the wash of light from the sitting room to enhance her way, Adelia moved toward the absurdly ornate four-poster bed. She could see the form of Mrs. Munro with a Mariner Star quilt pulled up to her chin. Her curls were a wild tangle across the pillow. It was too dim for Adelia to see her features, but the whole of her face looked pale as a moon.

Do fathers attack wives as well as children? Are women and children worth so little?

Adelia touched the beloved cheek. "It is me. What can I do?"

"Adelia, my dear." Mrs. Munro turned slightly toward her, the luxurious sheets whispering a satiny rustle. "Is Ernest well?"

"Yes. Bathed and warm. He is asleep, but Robin Hood is in a bit of a pickle."

Mrs. Munro gave a wan smile. She moved one arm from under the covers and took Adelia's hand. She moaned lightly as though the activity cost her dearly. "Good. You are a good girl, Adelia. Can you get some ice?"

"Of course." Adelia had no idea how to order ice to the hotel room, but she knew just where to find it. She flew through the corridor and down the backstairs to the kitchen. It was well after dinner, and the night crew had no interest in a scullery girl.

Adelia went to the oak ice box. The behemoth was at least eight feet long and a foot taller than her own height. It held large blocks of ice that were delivered to the hotel for the chilling of dairy products and cold drinks. Albin had told her the ice journeyed down from Alaska to Astoria in the hulls of ships, carried below the cold water line. From there, it arrived at the hotel by stage coach or train.

Opening one of the ice box's many heavy doors, Adelia found an ice pick atop one of the blocks and cracked off a large chuck. She wrapped it in a kitchen towel and soon discovered that the side of a meat clever excelled at breaking ice into chips the size of dice.

Harriet sometimes put ice in a towel on her head when it ached, especially during her menses. Adelia thought Mrs. Munro would do the same. Instead, her benefactress lowered the ice pack under the covers, placing it with a gasp at a point that Adelia could not see.

"I saw Ernest's welt. Have you one, too?"

There was no immediate response in words, just a groan as the woman appeared to adjust the pack in the area of her ribs. Then she turned her face toward Adelia. "Yes. We fell, you see. We rented horses to ride with Mr. Munro. A wasp stung Ernest's pony. It bucked him off and kicked mine in the process. My horse reared and threw me."

"His wound looks like a whip mark. It is narrow and deep."

"Ah. Well, he hit a tree branch hard when he landed. I rolled. May have damaged a rib or two."

It was the first lie that Adelia knew Mrs. Munro had told her, and it was a real thumper. A pony and horse cause such a calamity? Most improbable. She'd seen the gentle dobbins that the hotel reserved for guests.

Adelia stayed with Mrs. Munro until she, too, slept. After a final look in on Ernest, she returned to the room she shared with Harriet and the Ghostly Girl. They were already asleep, recharging for the next scullery day. Adelia slipped on her nightgown and tumbled onto her cot. She listened to the deep breathing of the two slumbering workers, then thought of the walk with Ephraim, especially when he took her hand where the track grew rough.

Knowing her scullery team surrounded her made her feel comfortable, even safe. But tonight, Adelia wondered just how safe anyone was if the man who should protect you was the one you must fear.

She was no longer sure a family was such a great loss.

Chapter Six

Summer 1893

On the lighthouse, George Wright composed a note to the neighbor lady who had written that his daughter had disappeared. He refrained from calling her a meddling nosebag. He asked her to tell his son to write if she happened to see the boy.

His letter left the island as all human things left the island, delivered by pulley and derrick to a rocking supply ship at the other end of the rope. There was always a canvas bag of outgoing mail just as there was always an incoming bag.

In time, an answer from his son arrived when another supply ship could get near enough to Terrible Tilly to employ the derrick. Wiley said that, yes, Adelia was gone, and so was the Indian. There was nobody to cook for him or wash his clothes. He had to sell the chickens to a neighbor because he couldn't handle all the chores alone. When he went to put the payment into the lard bucket, he saw the rest of the household money was gone. The little thief must have stolen it. Could his father send more?

George sighed at the burden he carried so unfairly. He was shut away from society here on this godforsaken light perched on a rock in the ocean, doing his best to support a family. But it was never enough. Had his wife not run off all those years ago, maybe Adelia would have had reason to stay. But no. Like mother, like child. He could see it must have been lonely for a youngster of the fickle sex, but he'd done what he could for her, providing shelter and food.

His son's letter contained no information on whether Wiley had tried to find his little sister. Since she was gone now for some weeks, George could see no reason to request time off to go home. Her trail would be as cold as Wiley's note. The best he could think to do was send a classified ad to *The Daily Morning Astorian*:

> *LOST- girl thirteen gone missing. Blonde, freckled, Protestant, good teeth. Quiet. Mannerly. Sews, cleans, cooks. If such applies for work or otherwise crosses your path, say her father seeks her. Your payment is my good blessings or state your terms. George Wright, Third Keeper, Tillamook Rock Light.*

There. His duty was done. Someone would answer or not. A time might come when he could use a daughter. But at this particular point in his life, he couldn't see why.

* * *

Recent events reminded Adelia of the bagatelle table in the lobby for guests' amusement. Her emotions ricocheted like the pin balls in the game although she found it anything but amusing.

Neither Mrs. Munro nor Ernest told her what really happened that Sunday. Her curiosity burned like the Tillamook Light. Walking the beach Monday afternoon with Ernest in hand, she coaxed him to talk. "Does your mama hit you?"

"No, silly."

"But the bruise..."

"The pony did it."

"Really, Ernest? Not your Daddy?"

"I cannot say, Addy. I cannot."

"That's okay then," she relented.

But two steps closer to the water, he whispered with a trembling lip, "Sometimes I make him mad. When I cry sometimes."

Adelia let the matter drop, saving the child from the angst of either lying to his friend or breaking a promise to his parent.

In the afternoon, when they played pickup sticks

with Mrs. Munro at the parlor table, Adelia could see the woman's pain in the stiffness of her movements. "What can I do to help?"

"Maybe loosen my corset strings," Mrs. Munro said as she lifted one ivory stick off another. "The fashion of the day is not good for a bruised torso."

"Why not take it off?"

Mrs. Munro set aside the stick and reached for a hand of each child.

"Dear ones, listen to me. It is imperative nobody know that we had an accident with the horses. We would not want Domino or Happy punished for misbehaving, now would we?"

"No, mama."

"No, ma'am."

"Then I shall wear my corset, and I shall heal. Ernest shall sit on a cushion, and he shall heal. Adelia shall curb her curiosity, and she shall say no more about it."

Things calmed on Tuesday. Mrs. Munro even felt up to going for a stroll with her friend. It was Wednesday before Adelia's world was rocked again.

Ephraim left the kitchen carting a bucket of scraps from the vegetables he had prepared. He took them to the pit out back where debris burned. It was at the end of her shift, so Adelia followed him out, meaning to ask a favor about the scraps.

And there he was, not far from the flames, his arms

around the Ghostly Girl. Their lips pressed tight, and his hand cupped her bottom.

They parted when Adelia yelped. "Oh! I thought...I thought..."

Ephraim looked sheepish, but Felicity was matter-of-fact. "You thought Ephraim loved you? You aren't much more than a child." She was not unkind so much as direct. "He said you got all googly-eyed which I can understand. But he is mine."

Ephraim tucked down his chin in a gesture of shyness. "You did not know that Felicity has my heart. And I could not tell you. No one must know lest one of us loses our job."

"But you took my hand..."

"To help 'round obstacles. Politeness, Adelia, a gesture of affection but no more. I like you. We all do."

Adelia stared a moment longer, mouth agape. Shame spread until her entire soul quaked on the verge of explosion. She turned and ran toward the servants quarters.

"Wait, Adelia!" Ephraim called.

"Let her go," the Ghostly Girl said. "She needs us out of her sight for a while."

Adelia tore off her work dress, kicked off her boots, and donned her leaf print dress and shoes. She tried to keep this overbearing humiliation to herself as she climbed the stairs to the guest wing, but the minute Mrs. Munro opened her door, the game was up. Adelia bawled like an offended calf.

"Adelia, my darling. Whatever has happened?"

Such genuine concern caused Adelia to sob all the more. Through great gulpings of air, she told her benefactress about the perfidy and betrayal by the lad she loved.

Holding Adelia as she sobbed, Mrs. Munro said, "There now, there now. I believe the boy is what is called your crush."

"I do not (*gasp, sniffle*) know what that means."

"It is a new use of an old word that I read in the *Godey's Lady's Book*. In all the world, the one person you are infatuated with is your crush. He makes your heart flutter, even if a reason is not obvious."

"Yes. He is my crush. *Was* my crush." Mrs. Munro dug out a handkerchief, and Adelia blew like a windstorm. "I'll...I'll wash this for you."

"Fine, fine. Now Adelia, as *Godey's* explains, crushes are short-lived. You may not even care by tomorrow. I do not think he meant to lie or hurt you. It sounds as though you have mistaken his manners for romance."

"I have no experience with boys who have manners." Maybe because her emotions were high, she finally told someone about her brother's attack, how he held her down in the filth, bruised her, tore at her clothing before he was forced to stop. "I know what he was about to do, and I could not stop it."

Mrs. Munro listened quietly, maybe even knowingly. "My darling girl. Ephraim may be an innocent, but your brother should be horsewhipped."

"I am not sure about the innocence. But on the horsewhipping, we agree."

"You have many friends here now, Adelia. As you get a little older, you will learn more about crushes and the breaking of hearts. Why, maybe there is somebody's heart *you* are breaking without even knowing it. You may be somebody else's crush."

Adelia doubted that. And she would never be able to face her scullery family again lest they laugh at her. But then she realized Felicity and Ephraim could not gossip about her without revealing their own entanglement. All three of them were bound to secrecy in the scullery. It wouldn't be so awful after all. She would not have to run away again.

But what a problematic poser the whole thing was. Bad men could hurt you. Good men could hurt you. Maybe it was better to stay away from them altogether.

* * *

When Friday afternoon came around, Adelia had to admit that the crush was dead as a clinker brick. In fact, when Ephraim smiled at her during the morning break, she realized how crooked his teeth were. And how pasty his skin. She actually began to think the

Ghostly Girl might want to do a little unpledging of her troth. Adelia was a far more subdued girl when she knocked on the Munro suite door that afternoon. The subject of Mr. Munro's impending arrival remained unmentioned.

It was a rainy day so they all stayed inside. Mrs. Munro was walking far less stiffly, and Ernest showed no more effects of his accident with the pony or whatever it had been. Adelia helped him draw the hotel, the beach, the lighthouse. Then she used flash cards to improve his addition.

While Ernest played with two toy horses and wagons, Adelia showed Mrs. Munro how to do a curving chain stitch to embroider the surface layer of fabric only. For all the woman's intelligence and accomplishment, she really was a dullard when it came to needle and thread.

"I am a dullard with needle and thread."

"Yes, you are. But it gives me something I can do for you."

Adelia was aware that Mrs. Munro was staring at her, as if trying to make a decision. Finally, her benefactress said, "There is something else you can do for me."

"Anything."

Mrs. Munro went to the escritoire and located a sheet of paper in the center drawer. Dipping the metal nib of a swan quill into a cut glass bottle of ink, she wrote for a moment, blotted the paper, and brought the note to Adelia.

"This is where my friend lives. The one I go out with in the afternoons. The address and directions are here. It is not far. Just two streets over."

"Do you need me to go there now?"

"No. But if another time comes when my husband is here...if you ever find me stricken...the next time I fall off my horse, I want you to take Ernest there for me."

"You mean to your friend?"

"Yes. And Adelia, if that happens, be sure, be very sure, you avoid Mr. Munro. Do not tell him where you are going. Do not stop to help me. Just get Ernest away, and my friend will know what to do."

Adelia understood exactly what was being asked of her. It terrified her. But there was nothing else to say other than, "I promise," and nothing else to do but nod. Then, because the lull in the conversation was getting very loud, Adelia continued the lesson. "Now see, Mrs. Munro, how the needle pulls the thread through this loop then doubles back..."

* * *

Weeks passed, and days began to shorten. Nights grew cooler on the Oregon Coast. Summer vacations for the Seaside House guests would soon come to an end. Mothers and children would return to their city homes for the school year, the holidays, the winter.

The Seaside House staff made plans, too, for the months when the tourist trade dwindled then virtually disappeared. The restaurant would all but close, feeding only a small staff and a handful of offseason guests. In the scullery, Katja and Albin would be employed through the winter as they were the two with the most seniority. The rest would be welcomed back in the spring but would go unpaid over the winter.

"Who among us can afford that?" Harriet said with a breathy sigh, over tea in the scullery.

"I will go to my uncle's farm," Ephraim said, buttering one of the biscuits left over from the guest breakfast hours. "He pays me what he can. Winter's when we rebuild fences and repair harnesses and such. He needs a new milk shed, too. And lambing season in the new year, of course."

"My mother sends me out to clean houses and gives me a stipend from that. Hardly worth the effort, though," said the Ghostly Girl. Adelia didn't believe her, not unless one of those houses she cleaned happened to belong to Ephraim's uncle. Somehow Felicity and Ephraim would stay as close to each other as magnets.

Adelia had actually caught Felicity in the act of humming one evening when she entered their room after an afternoon with Ernest. "What song is that?" she asked. And much to her surprise, the Ghostly Girl burst into the lyrics.

'Twas at a ball held in the west, on me he first did glance,
So gently he my fingers prest and asked me out to dance.
I blushed and whispered, no, no, no.
Then smiling dropped my fan,
For how could I refuse to dance,
he was such a nice young man!

Adelia giggled. "Now just replace the 'he' with 'Ephraim' in your mind."

Felicity gave her the ghost of a smile. "I am glad you came to our scullery, Adelia. Ephraim and I know you have kept our secret, and we both thank you for that. Trust is rare."

"When the time comes for a ceremony, remember I can sew. I would gladly help with your dress."

Refilling the cups of tea around the servant table, Harriet said she would be a cookee at the same logging operation she went to last fall.

"Cookee?" Adelia asked.

"Cookee. That's what they call assistants to the head cook. I know him well." The job was with the same crew but at a different location, one closer to Astoria. The bunkhouses and cookhouse were on skids so they could be hauled from one site to the next as the crew logged out an area. "They're always looking for cookees who can dish out any number of hearty squares a day. I leave next Thursday on the morning train to the Skipanon dock. Take a boat from there to the camp."

"How about you, Adelia?" Albin asked before slurping the cream he'd overpoured into his saucer.

She had no idea. It hadn't dawned on her that there'd be no work once the summer trade was gone. She blushed at her ignorance and at the aloneness of having nowhere to go. "Well...maybe Mrs. Munro will ask me home with them. To care for Ernest, you know."

A silence settled like snow. Even Katja held her tongue. At last it was Harriet who said what they all knew. "Guests can be unreliable no matter how kind they seem."

"But Mrs. Munro would never -"

"- I'm sure she would not want to disappoint you. But if that does not work out, Adelia, I mean if the Munros already have another girl back in their home so they cannot use you again until next summer...if that happens, you can come with me. To the cook camp, I mean. Nothing glamorous but flunkeys clean, wait tables, and such. You could do that. We'll earn our keep through the winter. And stay warm and fed in the process."

Chapter Seven

Late August 1893

It was mid afternoon, the last Friday of the month. Mrs. Munro was out with her friend. In the suite, Ernest and Adelia made a ring on the floor from a long strip of yellow zigzag trim. They both crouched, patooties up and faces down, doing their best to capture each other's marbles. Adelia was tickled by the boy's frown of concentration as he cradled the shooter in the crook of his index finger then flicked it with his thumb. She used to let him win. During the course of the summer, he'd become such a deadly aim that he no longer needed her help. His shooter killed her final marble by knocking it outside the ring.

"I win! I win!" he exclaimed with big-eyed joy and followed up with a chortle of pure pleasure.

"You're too good for me!" she said, sitting back on her knees as he began to replace his marbles in their little pouch.

That was when the door to the Munro suite burst open. "Florence! I'm here by the early train. A surprise!"

The jovial man nodded at the two children on the floor. From down there, he looked very tall and very dashing to Adelia. But Ernest tensed then inched closer to her. She put a hand on the boy's shoulder.

The man advanced into the main bedroom, then Ernest's room, yelling, "Florrie, where are you?" He circled back to the children.

"Who are you, sir?" Adelia asked, although she knew.

"That is Father," Ernest said. Adelia heard the angst in his little voice. To her ears, it sounded more like the arrival of a hangman than a father.

Yet, the man smiled broadly at them through a turned-up mustache. His eyes flashed with good cheer. This demeanor confused Adelia. She had no understanding that a person could take pleasure in causing pain. In this, Ernest was more knowledgeable than she.

"Yes, and come greet your father properly, laddy," he boomed. Ernie, still clutching his pouch of marbles, began to stand. But the man swooped him roughly in his arms, tossed him up in the air, then crushed him in a tight hug. "That's my big boy."

Adelia saw pain in her charge's face. Or fear. *Both?*

Mr. Munro grinned again at Adelia, but her instincts now signaled danger. "More to the point, girl," he demanded. "Who might you be?"

"I am Adelia Wright, sir."

"And a pretty little thing you are. But why are you here?"

"I take care of...I mean, I came to play marbles with Ernest."

"Fine. But where is my wife, Adelia?"

"She had business, sir. An errand to run. To the shop. For more of this adornment, you see." She picked up the zigzag trim. "To make a bigger circle now that your son is so good at the game. He wins over a mere girl every time. You have a proper young man here. Sir."

The attempt to smooth ruffled feathers failed. Mr. Munro rolled his eyes and scoffed, "Such fimble-famble." Adelia felt threat in the air. His smile remained, but it appeared taut, artificial. "So you are the little guttersnipe who takes care of my heir while my wife enjoys a bit of horizontal refreshment elsewhere."

"No, sir. Well, yes, but I..."

"Tell no lies or your nose will grow and ruin your pretty face."

He slid Ernest to the ground and lurched to grab Adelia's hair. He yanked on the braid that wrapped around her head, scattered the pins, and pulled her to her feet. "Tell me in whose bed I will find my wife fucking."

The pain made her yelp, and she grabbed at his hand. "I'm sure I do not know what you are talking about, sir."

The smile was gone as Mr. Munro slapped her across the face, scratching her cheek with his gold signet ring. "What did I say about lying?"

He pulled back a fist to hit her, but Ernest yelled, "Let her go!" and threw the pouch of marbles at him. It bounced off his father's chest, a useless weapon, but the marbles spilled and rolled across the floor. "Don't hurt Addy, please don't," the child cried.

"Quit that crying," the man snapped, rounding on the boy while releasing Adelia's hair. "Boys don't cry. I've told you that again and again."

He made a move toward Ernest, but Adelia grabbed his arm. When he swung back to her, he stepped on marbles that had scattered this way and that. His feet churned and he crashed to the floor, landing so hard he bounced like a felled tree. It would have been funny if the children weren't so terrified. They stared, jaws dropped. In that stunning moment, Mrs. Munro appeared in the doorway.

"Joseph!" she gasped.

"Whore," he growled, beginning to rise.

"Adelia, go! Go!" the woman hissed, pushing her husband off his feet again. "Keep quiet and go."

Adelia grabbed Ernest's hand and pulled him into the hall. Mrs. Munro slammed the door behind them. In a split second, Adelia heard a thud on the other side of the heavy wood.

"Mama!" Ernest called and pulled back. Adelia picked him up and scampered away. She wanted to shriek for help, but her benefactress had ordered her to silence. She shushed Ernest as she ran down the hall, her loose braid bouncing behind her.

Mid afternoon was the time many guests were resting in their suites before dinner. Adelia was desperate to disturb no one as she dashed to the servant quarters. When she reached her room, she collapsed onto her cot, setting Ernest beside her. Both were trembling. She wiped his runny nose with a scrap of cloth she'd been saving for a pillow cover.

Harriet whisked into the room along with the aroma of kitchen soap. It was the end of her work shift. She gasped when she saw Ernest. "Adelia! You cannot have that boy here. It's against the rules for any guest to be here."

"I know, I know, and please don't tell. I'll have him gone soon."

"But what is wrong? The child looks scared. *You* look scared."

"I will tell you all, but later. Now I must rush. There is danger."

Harriet argued no more. She opened the door and

peered into the servants hall. "Nobody coming yet. But I'll keep watch."

Adelia was filled with fear for Ernest and fury at his father, but she made note of what she owed her scullery co-worker.

"Where's mama?" Ernie asked then demanded, "Addy! Find her."

"She is right behind us, Ernie. It's like a game. Like hide and seek." As Adelia babbled she stuffed a few items into a valise.

"Are you coming back?" asked Harriet as she alternated between peeking into the hall and watching Adelia repair her hair with new pins.

"Yes. I'm just taking a few things. In case I don't get back 'til late." To the boy she said, "We're off to meet your mama, Ernest. We're on a merry adventure, like Robin Hood. You must take heart."

"Okay." He clambered off the bed, dejected, a child who feared the worse could still happen.

Adelia hugged Harriet and whispered in her ear, "Say nothing. I beg you. I will explain when I get back."

Harriet returned the hug. "The law protects cows better than children. Save the boy," she whispered to Adelia. Then to them both, "Now rattle your hocks, both of you."

As quickly as possible Adelia and Ernest snuck from the servants quarters, out to the Seaside's courtyard, and away toward the town. They soon slowed to a pace Ernest could handle. Guests often saw the two of them out and about together. Nothing must appear suspicious now.

The name and address of Hydrangea House were written on the paper that Mrs. Munro had given her. Adelia was sure she could get Ernest there safely. In fact, they both knew where it was. They'd played Pinkerton men and shadowed Mrs. Munro to the house more than once, although they hadn't told her that. They'd had a good snoop around the spacious wood-shingled vacation home, but they'd never caught a peek at its resident.

A picket fence surrounded the two-story house, and a climbing hydrangea looped through and around the fence then over the arched gateway. There were few floral clusters left this late in the summer, but the deep green leaves framed the pink rose bushes that hugged the fence line. All that Adelia had ever grown were vegetables to feed her father and brother. To her eyes, the blossoms were an extravagance, very butter upon bacon. A rich person must abide here in this fairyland home.

Adelia and Ernest climbed the stairs to the porch, big steps for the boy's short legs. His tight hold on her hand was beginning to ache, but she didn't let go. She knocked with the other hand. They waited, her anticipation rising. What would Mrs. Munro's man friend be like?

She wasn't a man at all. When the woman opened the door, Adelia gawked.

"Yes children? What is it?" The woman was tiny.

"Ah, um...here," Adelia managed, handing the woman her slip of paper. "Mrs. Munro said you would know what to do."

"Oh, dash it! Come in. Quickly, children."

As Adelia passed by, she was aware Mrs. Munro's friend smelled of her rose garden.

The woman peered out toward the road. "I see no one following." She shut the door and turned toward the children. "You must be Adelia. I am Mrs. Emma Watson."

"How did you know my name?"

"Florrie said there might be a time when a lovely girl named Adelia would appear with Ernest. And we planned just what to do if that should occur. Hello, young master," she added with a smile, but Ernest tucked himself firmly behind Adelia's knees. Adelia wished they were a steadier support for him. Curiosity about what would come next was all that held her anxiety in check.

Mrs. Watson led them to a small room at the back of the house. "It is very cozy in here, my favorite room." The floral upholsteries and wallpaper, each splashed with cabbage roses, vines, butterflies and peacocks, felt cloying to Adelia. Like the suite in the hotel, it was an overgrown tropical grove. But this room was small.

She would have preferred a place with a second exit or at least a large open window. From one of the prissy chairs, a mass of white fur raised a moon-sized face. "Meeeooow."

"This fat fellow is Zeus," Mrs. Watson said as she flitted about, lighting matching art deco parlor lamps. She was so tiny, she made normal women look bovine. "Here you are, safe now. There are some playing cards in the campaign chest, and books are just there. I have things to which I must attend. Arrangements to be made."

"Will you help Mrs. Munro?" Adelia asked. They stood nearly eye to eye.

"That is my aim, child. Wait here. Comfort the boy. That's what she needs you to do."

"Will you go for the man who is her special friend? Will he help, too?"

Mrs. Watson cocked her head like a songbird with a question. "Man? What man? There is no man."

"But I thought she had a...a..."

"Balderdash, child. Although her cuss of a blasted husband thinks the same thing. I must prepare now."

Adelia dropped onto the sofa. Ernest pushed next to her and put his head on her lap. He seemed to be calming a bit. Maybe the small room felt more cozy than confining to him. She'd never seen him suck his thumb before but decided to let him do it if it gave him comfort. Adelia ran her hand over his head, smoothing down his coppery hair, damp from fear and haste.

Zeus stared at them both as though aliens had intruded into his private space. He appeared especially fascinated by Ernest. In his experience, two-leggers were far bigger than this boy kitten.

Adelia swallowed hard. She had been wrong all along. Mrs. Munro had not taken a lover, at least if this friend of hers was right. Mr. Munro had misunderstood the situation, but so had she. Adelia felt an unpleasant flip in the pit of her stomach. It made her queasy as heat spread up her body. She had never felt like this before, but she knew it for what it was: shame.

Adelia vowed she would never doubt Mrs. Munro again.

All was quiet for a half hour, maybe more. Ernest drifted off, tuckered from his horrible afternoon. Adelia rubbed her cheek where she had been slapped. It felt tender in the spot scraped by Mr. Munro's ring.

She looked at the sweet face of the sleeping boy on her lap. Would he grow into a cruel adult, like her brother, like his father? She would protect him from brutality as best she could. Of course. But could she keep him from becoming brutal himself when violence was all around them?

The clopping and jangling and 'Whoa' sounds of a carriage out front startled Adelia. Zeus had managed to heave his great self onto the arm of the sofa, the better to stare at Ernest. Adelia quietly slipped the child's head off her lap and onto a silk pillow embroidered with hydrangeas. She had been told to stay put, but it was not a possibility once she heard the front door open and shut. Then the beloved voice said, "I am here. The children?"

Mrs. Watson said, "Yes. They are fine, my dear." She paid the driver of the horse-drawn taxi and shooed him away as soon as he brought in two large travel cases and a satchel.

Then Adelia ran to Mrs. Munro and hugged her tight. When she looked up she saw that Mrs. Munro had affixed a long scarf over her hat, trying to hide the wound. Her face was swollen on the left side, and the skin across her cheek had broken. Her eyes were red, and she was very pale. Adelia gasped. "He hit you again. Is he following? Does he know where you are?"

"I am safe. For now. Go back to Ernest. I will be with you as soon as Emma and I have time to talk."

"But I..."

"Adelia. Be with Ernest now." Adelia heard the iron in the tired voice, and against every desire to argue, she turned and walked back to the floral cave. Zeus had curled himself next to the sleeping child, giving and taking body warmth. Adelia paced the length and width of the little room again and again. She had no clock, but she could tell by long shadows through the window that the afternoon was growing late.

Think. What can I do? What will happen to us?

It seemed forever before the two women came into the room. Mrs. Munro confessed to Adelia, "Joseph is dead. I left his body in the suite. Authorities will soon be after me."

"Dead? You must have hit back. He deserved..."

"Emma and I have a plan. Please, Emma, tell Adelia." Then she awakened Ernest to cradle him in her arms.

While Mrs. Munro whispered mother-isms to her boy, Emma explained quietly to Adelia. "The hotel will raise the alarm for a woman and child traveling together. It is likely nobody yet knows they are gone. They probably won't tonight unless a maid comes in to straighten up this evening. Whether the authorities are contacted late tonight or early tomorrow, they will certainly be watching the train by the time it leaves in the morning. So Florrie and I will take the mail stagecoach this evening. It stops at Skipanon boat landing, just this side of Astoria. We will catch a ferry from there into the city. Nobody is seeking two women. We will be well."

"Can she not stay here?" Adelia felt the terror of abandonment breathing down her neck.

"No, nowhere in Seaside. When the thousands of summer guests depart, only seventy people live here.

She will be hounded down in a place this small. Astoria, too, for that matter. Searchers will not just give up."

"But what about..."

"Florrie has money she took from her hotel room. She will book passage on a steamer out of Astoria. When she is gone, I will return here. I'll be able to tell you then where she is headed."

"Can I..."

Mrs. Munro interrupted. "Adelia, you must stay with Ernest. I trust you. More important, *he* trusts you. You are like a big sister." Her benefactress handed her a thick envelope. "There is money. And a letter to you."

"But I cannot take him to my room in the hotel. They won't allow it!"

"You will stay here until I return," Emma Watson said. "I was soon to leave for Portland for the winter, so most rooms in the house are already shut down. No staff will come in. Keep quiet, remain inside, and you should be safe. I will be back in two days, three at the most."

Mrs. Munro's voice trembled. "After that, we will have to see. One day at a time. It is certain Ernest is safer with you than with me until I know the searchers have lost our trail. And then I will come for my darling boy."

"But how will I know where you are? How can I reach you?" Adelia was close to panic. She wanted to run with Mrs. Munro, but she couldn't. She had to stay for Ernest's sake. Fear was paralyzing her brain.

Think.

"Advertisements, Adelia. Until we each have an address for mail, we will employ personal ads in *The Morning Astorian*. I will use the name Sweet Violets so you know it is me. And what name would you like to use?"

Adelia tried to focus. One day at a time, one thought at a time, one heartbreak at a time. "Tilly. I will be Tilly. It is the right name when things are terrible."

"A fine name. Now we must rest until it is time to catch the stage. We have nearly two hours."

Think.

Adelia stood. "I have one errand I must attend while you're still here to watch over Ernest. I will not be long." Without waiting for approval, Adelia ran out the front door and scampered away. She couldn't tell them she was going back to the hotel, placing herself at risk once again. Mrs. Munro would never have allowed it. But there was a job that must be done.

* * *

Adelia got back to Hydrangea House before the women left to catch the stagecoach. Mrs. Munro's good-bye to Ernest had been almost unbearable to hear. "You must be bricky now, Ernest. Very brave.

Take care of Adelia until I come back to take care of you both."

"Don't go, don't go," he pleaded until Mrs. Munro, in tears herself, handed him to Adelia and rushed from the room, from the house, from Seaside.

When Adelia set him down, he crumpled into a heap and pounded the floor with his fists. It was Zeus who offered the most comfort. Ernest rolled over, sat up and held out his arms. The corpulent white cat snuggled close. Zeus purred loud enough for them all to hear.

Mrs. Munro left behind a satchel with clothes for Ernest. Adelia also found his tin horses and wagons in it. She gave him her lighthouse to play with. In time, the toys distracted the four-year-old. He created a game of crashing the wagons into the spindly carved legs of Mrs. Watson's furniture. Zeus made an obliging effort to cuff the toys this way and that.

With his attention diverted, Adelia opened the envelop from Mrs. Munro. There was more money than she had ever seen. She unfolded the letter.

Dearest Adelia:

Mr. Munro never believed I was spending time with women friends and not with a man. His jealousy flamed. I could no longer let him near Ernest. I feared he might kill us both.

Mrs. Watson cannot keep Ernest for me. She has a husband and grown children in Portland and will soon return there for the winter. Questions would be asked. You are my best hope.

Adelia, you are young, but more a woman now than a girl. You are the closest thing to a guardian that Ernest has until I safely return to you both. I beg you to keep him for me. Be very careful. Be wise. I doubt the authorities will look for you, but they will certainly look for us. You must be more cunning, more vigilant than they. I believe that you are.

I will not ask where you will go for fear I would not be able to stay away, which could bring harm upon my darling boy. I will not be truly alive again until the day we are reunited.

The money with this letter should be enough to see you both through a winter and more, but I will surely be back with you before spring.

Warmest regards, my dear one,
Florence Munro

Adelia stumbled over a word or two, but managed to work them all out. She blinked her eyes dry, stiffened her spine with resolve, and felt justified about the errand she had run. It had been the right thing to do, might even buy Mrs. Munro more time to disappear. She slipped the money and the letter into her valise.

As Ernest and Zeus became more deeply involved in their game, she went to the kitchen. She opened the back door and peeked out to a small yard. All seemed quiet. A scent of roses drifted in. Adelia shut the door again, fastening the hook-and-eye closure. On the kitchen counter she found a loaf of bread, cheese, a bowl with apples and half of a chocolate cake. In the ice box she located milk for Zeus. Then she put the food on a silver tray and carried it back to the flower cave. The three of them ate in silence. When the sun was finally down and moonlight began to appear through the window, Adelia said, "She is on the stagecoach by now, Ernest. Your mother is safe."

"I'm scared, Addy."

"I know you are. But I know just what to do. And Zeus is a particularly fine guard cat. We are safe."

Adelia found blankets in a bedroom, but they preferred to stay together in the flower cave. They bedded down on the sofa, Ernest at one end, Adelia at the other, and Zeus in the middle. There were no children's books, but Adelia found a heavy tome entitled *The Language of Flowers*. She began to read aloud. It was so dull, the boy drifted away in next to no time.

She put the book down and lay awake, listening to Zeus purr. She finally had time to think back on her errand, to consider whether there was anything she had forgotten or gotten wrong.

She had returned to the Munro hotel room. She had to. With Mr. Munro dead, Mrs. Munro would be hounded for murder. So the room must not look like she was the one who killed her husband. It must look like wife and child had been kidnapped by a hideous rogue or maybe two. At the very least, there had to be doubt. Either way, Mrs. Munro would be pursued but maybe as a victim, not a murderous wife. A woman stolen by men was surely not as bad as a woman who murdered one. She wouldn't be shot on sight. If caught, she would be kindly treated, at least at first.

The hall was empty when she arrived, and the door to the Munro suite was closed but not locked. Mrs. Munro had been in too much of a hurry to take many precautions. Adelia opened the door, backed into the room keeping an eye on the hall, then closed and locked it. She turned around. Mr. Munro was on the floor but not where she had last seen him. He was closer to the fireplace and now on his back. The fire poker was next to him, blood was splattered about, and a savage wound on the front of his head showed through to the bone.

Mrs. Munro must have hit him very hard. Adelia quickly looked away, recoiling from the gore. She'd seen innards before, of course, elks butchered and a bear bled out. But never a dead human. She conquered the revulsion and went to work, circling around the body and rushing into the master bedroom.

Clothes were flung around, doors and drawers open, a sure sign of hurried packing. Adelia straightened the room, replaced everything in the wardrobe, and shut dresser drawers. She refolded towels at the wash stand and set tipped bottles of hair oil and perfume upright again. Next, she did Ernest's room. When she was done, neither chamber looked like its occupant had run away. Instead, both were tidy, inviting.

Adelia returned to the main room, avoiding a look at the body. This area should appear chaotic as though people had been kidnapped and carried off in thin air by desperados. So she created chaos, tipping chairs and breaking two vases. She opened all escritoire doors and drawers, dumping their contents. An empty money wallet was tossed and landed under the table next to cushions and several books. Marbles still speckled the floor.

When she was done, it looked possible that a couple of blackguards had beaten Joseph Munro, stolen his money, and taken his wife and child for nefarious reasons all their own. As Adelia crumpled a Persian rug into a wad next to the door, a terrifying sound struck her from behind.

"You," the voice hissed.

Adelia yelped and spun around. Joseph Munro was not dead. He had turned his head away from the wall and was looking at her, eyes red with blood. Or fury.

Adelia was terrified by what she had to do next. But she did not hesitate. She picked up the fire poker and struck with all her considerable might. This time there was no doubt. Mrs. Munro thought the brute was dead, and now he was.

Adelia felt faint as anxiety consumed her. Her heart beat so loud her ears rang, and she crumpled onto a delicate occasional chair, its gilt wood arms carved with foliage. Her breath came in gasps and for a moment, she thought she would collapse as her vision blurred with dark spots. She thought of Ernest asleep with the cat, and the image calmed her. He needed her, and she him. He was her little brother now. A good brother. In time, her breathing slowed and deepened. The panic attack passed, leaving her weak, wobbly kneed.

She used the pitcher and wash basin to blot away a smattering of blood on the front of her frock before she left the room. Two guests dressed for tennis sauntered past her as she was shutting the door on the gruesome scene within. Adelia turned in the opposite direction, her hand on the wall for support as she weaved her way to the servants quarters.

Harriet was not in their room so Adelia left a brief note on her cot. She wrote that she would meet Harriet at the train on Thursday to go to the logging camp with her. She did not mention she would have a little boy in tow.

Adelia was exhausted when she returned to Hydrangea House in time to say good-bye to Mrs. Munro. Now on the sofa, she pulled the blanket closer to her chin. Zeus purred in a continuous rattle. Until Emma Watson returned from Astoria, Adelia was alone with Ernest, the cat, and her churning thoughts.

Mrs. Munro did not murder her husband. I did.

Chapter Eight

September,1893

George Wright didn't hate everything about life on Tillamook Rock Lighthouse. He was fastidious by nature so he liked keeping confined quarters clean. When he was Duty Man, up all night, he enjoyed sitting alone and reading in the kitchen. He took pleasure in watching the gray whales that scratched their backs on the rock's barnacles, and he got to know the birds as they nested and migrated, the murres, puffins, guillamots, and oystercatchers. In general he preferred having very little to say to very few people.

No, he didn't hate everything. But he did hate the trip off the Rock and away from the lighthouse. To make matters worse, this time he had a hateful task he must do.

George had received an answer to his advertisement in *The Daily Morning Astorian*. A lad who called himself Billy Bell had written that, for a fiver, he would provide the third assistant keeper with the circumstances and location of Adelia's employment. The deal was struck.

George left on his two-week leave. He started the day in a bad skin, ill-tempered over the inevitable dunking by the derricks, pulley and rope. He pulled on the canvas pants of a breeches buoy with its life ring around his waist. Once the bulky contraption was attached to the rope, the pulley swung him into the air, transferring him to the supply ship as he dangled above the sea.

Last time he crossed, the Pacific was so high, it flooded the rig and dragged him underwater. He nearly drowned before crew could lift the line again. But today was calm, and the tide was low. As George was pulled to the boat, he could see the slimy barnacles that low tide revealed around the base of the Tillamook rock. Bird droppings added a sour smell to the odor of the sea, and sunbathing sea lions barked at him for disturbing their rest. When he was hauled into the bouncing boat unharmed, he was dumbfounded by the lack of damage. He so seldom thought of himself as lucky.

From the Skipanon dock south of Astoria, George caught the stagecoach to Seaside. He usually bought supplies in town, hitched a ride down the Elk Creek Road across Tillamook Head, then walked to his cabin.

But this time, he diverted his course to Seaside House.

George did not feel at home on the grand verandah among the guests, so he waited in front until the doorman sent Billy Bell out to him. A fiver changed hands. Then Billy Bell led him around back to the servants entrance into the scullery. The lad was surprised that Adelia was not at her regular sink, wrangling pots and pans.

"This is Adelia's father," Billy Bell announced to everyone in the scullery. "You deal with him. I must get back to my station."

"And you'd be wanting her why?" Albin asked. "You'll not be taking her from us now."

Katja snapped. "Albin! The man is her father."

Harriet smiled sweetly and said, "She has been sent on a mission to Astoria, sir. There she helps make special soap for the scullery. For the fine china and silver. She is quite good at it."

The others stared at Harriet until the Ghostly Girl surprised them by joining in the fabrication. "She will not return for several days. She is a good worker, our Adelia. We are glad to have her."

"*Joo,*" nodded Katja in agreement. "She is ours to care for now. We keep her safe for you."

"I suggest you leave now, Mr. Wright, if you have no other business here." Albin leaned in to whisper, "A body was found in the hotel this morning, and there be lawmen everywhere looking for someone to blame.

Strangers such as yourself could be at particular risk."

And so George Wright left, convinced he'd done all he could and feeling greatly relieved. His daughter was working and secure. He need not worry about her. He gave no more thought to Adelia or to the murder of Mr. Munro.

* * *

"We are in hiding?" Ernest asked before lifting oatmeal toward his mouth. He made it although the spoon tipped sideways precariously.

"Yes," Adelia said. "Like Pinkerton men, we are undercover." She had marveled at the world's largest detective agency whenever a hotel guest left behind a *Frank Leslie's Illustrated Weekly* which carried exploits of actual Pinkerton actions. She and Ernest acted the tales out, sometimes on the side of good but sometimes on the side of bad which was often more fun.

"What's in there?" he asked, pointing to the wooden box, about a foot square, that Adelia had placed on the table. The lid's delicate floral design of inlaid wood was complemented by decorative brass hinges.

"Just you wait and see. We'll have fun indoors for a few days, then we will be off on an adventure."

Zeus sat on the kitchen table, staring down the cheese and egg on Adelia's plate. The very tip of his superlative white tail flicked. She took a final bite then pushed the remains in the cat's direction.

It was hard to eat when she was so full of turmoil. It felt as though her head might pop like one of those rubber balls on strings that they sold on the beach, the ones they called balloons. They faced so many problems, Ernest and she. Adelia inhaled a great breath and resolved to take them one at a time. In fact, she'd already faced one down. It made her feel stronger to have at least one dilemma under control.

She knew that if they were heading for a logging camp with Harriet, that Ernest's fine knickers and smocks were useless as codswallop. Other than his underclothes, the items in the satchel left by his mother were impractical. He needed hard-wearing clothes fit for a workman and something far warmer than beach wear. Ernest required his first pair of full length trousers to handle the wilderness, a visible sign of how fast he must outgrow childhood. Adelia needed clothes, too, and wished women wore trousers to keep blackberry whips and fir branches from scraping their legs.

Women in trousers! The thought was weak-minded enough to lift her spirits.

"First thing we do after cleanup is create undercover clothes so bad eggs cannot find us Pinkertons. Will you get me a pail of water from the pump out back? Leave the door open so I can watch. And let Zeus out with you." It was time her little brother started helping with chores. His young life was changing in ways even more vast than her own. He was no longer of the leisure class.

When the kitchen was back in order, and Zeus was asleep in the flower cave, Adelia said to Ernest, "Come with me." She picked up the wooden mystery box, and they climbed a narrow staircase to the second floor.

As they started up, Ernest hung back. "Are we allowed up here?"

Adelia laughed. "Yes, indeed. While you were asleep, I asked Mrs. Watson if she had fabric to make clothes. She said she could do better than that. And she brought me up here!"

They entered a back room that had wooden crates and furniture stacked all around its edges. Slices of morning sun cut through long narrow windows, providing all the light they needed. In front of an old iron bed frame, an enormous travel chest stood open. Its exterior was covered with rich red hand-tooled leather. Mrs. Watson had undone the belt-type buckles on the straps and left the rounded lid open.

"Just look in there!"

Ernest drew near and peered inside. "Golly!"

Next to folded linens were stacks of clothes including coats, shoes and hats. "Mrs. Watson told me these things belonged to her children when they were growing up. She said we could take what you need. And then she gave me this sewing box." Adelia opened the wooden box to display mother-of-pearl and silver sewing utensils in a velvet lined tray. She lifted out the tray so Ernest could see the area below that held trims, threads, and slips of fabrics. "I've never had anything so wonderful," said Adelia, stroking the lid as she might a fine horse. "I can tailor what you need."

"Things for you, too, Addy?"

"Mrs. Watson said her clothes would come close to fitting me. When we are done in here, I will go to her closet."

An hour later, they assembled their booty in the flower cave downstairs. A sturdy pair of shoes, waxed cotton jacket, thick moleskin shirt, and flat wool cap all fit Ernest, more or less. A pair of boots were too big, but Adelia took them anyway, figuring she could stuff them with socks. She also selected dungarees for a bigger boy. The pants were made from denim dyed with indigo. "These are called Levi jeans," she said. "Working men wear them. I can cut them down for you. And these brown ones are corduroy. They shall fit, too, when I am done with them."

"I'll look like the big boys!" Ernest was thrilled to graduate from short to long pants. Adelia was pleased that, for this moment in time, he was not thinking about his missing parents. He was like the coastal weather, squalls separated by stretches of sun.

Selections were sparse for Adelia. Mrs. Watson simply did not own many durable garments. Like Mrs.

Munro, her clothes were mostly silks, satins, and all for pretty. Adelia chose two dresses, one a winter weight linen and the other a fustian cotton weave. Mrs. Watson was so small, the dresses nearly fit Adelia. She could nip in the seams but leave the material intact to grow as she grew.

As Adelia basted the clothes to her own measurements, she realized her body was making life changes, too. Her breasts were getting bigger. Their new softness felt like marshmallows when she touched them, and her nipples were sensitive to the restraints of her chemise. She had questions for Harriet when they next met.

For two days, Adelia sewed. She showed Ernest how to rip out a hem and to thread a needle. Other than that, he spent much of his time retrieving spools of thread that Zeus batted under every chair. He also drew pictures of a fat white cat in a very dark universe.

When they were hungry, Adelia raided the kitchen for the supplies to make meals. She could not leave the house, so she made do with what she found. There were four eggs and more cheese. In the pantry she found two cans of salmon and another of condensed milk that had not exploded, so she thought they must be good. A hard sausage hung next to strings of dried apples, looking as though it only needed the green end removed. Dried beef or elk or venison - she couldn't tell which - was wrapped on a shelf. Mason jars of peaches and pears sat beside bags of dried beans, flour and sugar as well as small containers of seasonings. They ate, if not as well as at Seaside House, well enough to fill their bellies.

"What is this?" Ernest asked of the sausage.

"A man named Albin calls them bags o' mystery."

"This is good, Addy."

"A short cake I made from the flour, sugar and lard. Here. Try it with a drizzle of syrup on top."

"I cannot bite this."

"No. It's hardtack. And it is awful. Soldiers dip it in their coffee."

Off and on they played the name game, as Adelia dubbed it. "Pinkerton agents do it when they need to hide their identity. Your name is now mine. I am Wright, and so are you, not Munro."

"Why is Wright right now?"

"Because you are my brother now. That makes you Wright."

"Wright, right."

"Think of it like this: Wright is right. Munro is no."

"Wright is right. Munro is no," Ernie said to Zeus who apparently did not care.

Late on the third afternoon, Mrs. Watson returned. She was covered with dust and smelled of wood smoke. Removing her hat, she said, "I took the train home. I declare that open car is dirtier than the stagecoach and not a bit less rocky."

"Is everything safe?" Adelia asked, casting a sideways glance at Ernest who was dangling yarn for Zeus to kill once again.

"Yes. Yes. A lovely steamer to San Francisco, a place of great interest and where everyone is a stranger who has no interest in Oregon happenings."

"Ah," Adelia breathed. A knot between her shoulders released and for the first time, she realized how tense her body had been. But San Francisco. So far away.

"And you? Are your plans complete?" Mrs. Watson asked as she beat dust off her jacket.

Adelia felt that the less anyone knew, the less they could tell. "Yes. We take the Elk Creek Road then catch a ride to Tillamook. My aunt and uncle live down that way. They will take us in. It is a beautiful farm. We will be safe and well fed." She marveled at how easy lying had become for her.

"Oh, good. Good."

"Do you maybe have a note from...ah, anything for Ernest?"

"No. We thought it unwise to remind him. No contact for a while is best if he is to move on."

Adelia was not sure that Ernest would agree. She herself missed a mother she had never even known. Besides, Adelia did not allow herself to believe that this mother and child would be out of contact for long.

"I did bring you a newspaper, though."

Adelia looked at *The Daily Morning Astorian,* an issue now two-days-old. Headlines involved news of the millions visiting the World's Fair in Chicago and an overview of the lingering depression following the Stock Market crash last spring. Adelia cared about neither. What interested her was the small front page headline: *Seaside Woman/Child Disappear Following Death of Husband/Father. Search Intensifies.*

She read the short article then folded the paper in quarters and tucked it inside her sewing kit. So far, so good. The authorities weren't sure whether Florence Munro was victim or perpetrator. But the *Search Intensifies* part was devilish worrisome. Maybe she didn't have time to wait for Harriet. And even if she did, was it ever safe to go to the train stop? Adelia thought that Ernest and she, in their work clothes, could pass as Harriet's niece and nephew. Authorities would be looking for a mother and boy, not two children. They should be safe enough. But that might be wrong. The hotel would know she was gone, too. Maybe Mr. Stapleton told the lawmen she was a rogue, one of the kidnappers.

The next morning, Mrs. Watson went to the shops for a load of supplies and gossip. She came home, her face in a high state of color.

"What did you hear?" asked Adelia.

"Well, I was in the grocery, you know, and had just maneuvered the conversation to the missing woman, and her poor little boy, and how everyone was looking for her, murderess or victim, when we heard a bustle of excitement outside." She stopped to inhale and plunged on. "People were hurrying down the street. Three of us went out and stopped a man to ask. He said a whale has beached itself."

"Why would a whale beach itself?"

"Old age or illness or sharks, who knows? But this is a very big event. People will gather for days to take pieces of it."

"Whatever for?"

"Indians eat it. The bones have value, I am told, and they say perfume can be made. I don't know about that, but I do know loggers and fishermen will come from all around to cut off the blubber and render it for oil. That carcass is a gold mine. The whole town will stink of it for days. It is vastly more exciting than a woman who disappeared several days ago. You are not the news today, my girl. Such crowds can help you hide."

Adelia took it as a sign. "Then tomorrow we will leave. While Ernest is of little interest."

That night, Adelia slipped out of the Watson vacation house. She hastened through the dark toward the beach. The appalling aroma of decaying flesh made her stomach churn. Men had built driftwood fires around the massive carcass. She figured they were protecting it from predators of all kinds, coyotes to crabs, and most likely from each other.

One man yelled to others, "It's bloated with methane. If it blows, she'll cover the town with decomposed guts." The thought made Adelia's belly lurch again so she hastened on. The pathetic sight was not what she had come to see.

She walked through the sand to the far end on the beach toward Tillamook Head, away from the others, following the water's edge by moonlight and the sound of the waves. She got as close as she could to the lighthouse over a mile out to sea. It was invisible in the night, of course, but every five seconds she saw the steadfast pulse of its powerful beam.

Stay away. Stay away.

The light promised safe passage to some, but not to her. It was as if her father was telling her not to come near. If he had ever so much as looked for her, would she have gone back home with him? Had she hoped for a sign that he loved her?

Ah, well, it no longer mattered. She had another family now with a brother to love, not one to fear. She said her good-bye to George Wright, knowing she would not see the light again anytime soon.

* * *

The children left before daylight the next morning. "When you get to your aunt's, place an ad from Tilly in the paper so we know you are well," said Emma Watson as she handed a cloth bag of edibles to Adelia. "This should last you a couple of days."

Ernest fussed, not wanting to leave Zeus. Zeus fussed, as well, taking a swipe at Adelia as she plucked the cat from Ernest's arms and handed it to Mrs. Watson.

The little boy's tears hurt more than the cat's scratches. "It's okay to be mad at me," she said to Ernest as they walked down the narrow lane. She thought about her own loss of Shep. "But Pinkertons cannot take cats on their adventures. So I hope you forgive me soon."

His lips trembled, his nose ran, his eyes leaked. He let out a yowl that would have done Zeus proud, a yowl of elemental anger and fear. "Am I gonna have to say good-bye to you, too, Addy?"

She dropped the bags, got down on her knees and hugged him close. "No, Ernest. No more good-byes. I love you three ways from Sunday. I am here to stay. You will not be alone. I promise."

He cried until the bodice of her newly created work dress was damp. "Okay then," he finally managed. He took her hand, and she stood. They started off again, Ernest carrying the bag of food from Mrs. Watson and Adelia their two satchels plus her sewing box.

"We're going to see your Aunt?"

"No, that is part of our cover story. Pinkertons sometimes tell tales. We are on our way to surprise my friend Harriet. She thinks we are meeting at the Seaside train stop tomorrow."

"But today is today."

"Yes. We are going a day early to surprise her when she gets off the train at the other end, not here in Seaside."

"Will she be mad we aren't where we should be?"

"Maybe. But when she meets you, all will be forgiven. Now, do you think you can walk three miles with me? That's just two whoops and a holler to the next stop."

They turned from the shell-covered street onto the dirt road that would lead them to the next stop on the train line. As they walked, Adelia fretted. Leaving a day early made sense, right? To be gone while the town's attention was elsewhere. And it was smart to avoid the Seaside train stop altogether. Gearhardt was not quite three miles north, the first stop after Seaside. Ernest and she could board there where they were more apt to avoid searching eyes. That was smart, wasn't it? She missed the scullery crew who would help her know what to do.

The road they walked was maybe the worst in the state. It was the one used by the stagecoach, and she'd heard a man call it a bone-cracker. Stumps from the trees felled to lay the roadbed rose up through the dirt to break wheels that passed over them. Ernest and Adelia took care not to twist their ankles on the massive roots slithering across the surface and grabbing at their shoes.

They were both brightening even though the dawn was gray. They were warm enough in their sturdy new clothes and happy to be outdoors after hiding so long inside Hydrangea House. In some spots the road paralleled the single track of the Astoria and Southcoast Railway so Adelia knew they were heading in the right direction. A few wagons and carriages passed, but the children skittered off the road to hide from sight in the woods along the way. The greatest danger was a bull who rushed his rickety fence then snorted and bawled at them.

"Is that a *cow*?" Ernest had never seen a bovine other than a dairy cow. This was something altogether different.

"It's a gentleman cow."

"He is not very nice."

"Well, you'll see oxen on our adventure, too. They're, um, nicer to be around."

"What's oxen?"

"They are bulls trained to pull loads."

"What loads?"

"Logs. Lots and lots of logs. They work hard. You shall see."

"I like this adventure, Addy."

Adelia thought about it and realized she was liking it, too. So far, so good.

On their way, they saw elk whose curiosity about the young people equaled the young people's curiosity about them. Woodchucks chirped and whistled. Adelia could point these things out, but she didn't know the names of all the birds so their songs went unidentified.

They arrived at Gearhardt in time to hear the train puffing and belching its way from Seaside. The Westinghouse locomotive of the Astoria and Southcoast Railway ran on a single track slightly over fifteen miles from Seaside to Skipanon, hauling two cars at most. One was a box car with windows punched in its walls and benches around the inside perimeter. The other was a flatcar rigged with railings around its rim and benches in haphazard rows.

"Mrs. Watson took the flatcar," Adelia said. "I have never ridden the train at all. You can choose where we sit. It is about a four hour trip." She had to shout to her excited companion to be heard over the chugging engine.

As they waited to board, other people began to appear. Adelia gave Ernest a critical look. He was no longer a rich little boy. In his hand-me-down wool cap and shirt, rugged jacket and long trousers, he looked like a farm boy, or a whistle punk, or a truant from school. She was proud of the effort she'd made to hide him from prying eyes. It pleased her to see how he fit in.

But that pleasure was short lived. Before they boarded, a middle-aged couple detrained. The man lumbered on ahead, but the woman looked at them, then stopped to stare more closely.

"Little boy. Have I seen you before?"

Ernest dashed behind Adelia's knees. She said as calmly as she could, "My brother is very shy, ma'am."

"But isn't he...I met that Munro woman once...isn't he her child? The one they are all looking for in Seaside? We just came from there."

"No, ma'am. He is my brother and our name is Wright. We do not know any Munros."

"Nonsense. Step aside, girl." The woman reached for Ernest's jacket sleeve and pulled him forward. "What is your name, boy?"

"Leave him alone, ma'am, please," Adelia tensed, prepared to push the woman away and run like all-possessed.

"What is your name? Are you not the Munro boy?"

"I'M WRIGHT. MUNRO IS NO!" Ernest pulled away from the woman, turned his back on her, and clambered up the iron steps to the flatcar.

"Sorry, ma'am. We have to go. Hope you find the boy you're looking for." Adelia rushed up behind Ernest as she heard the woman's companion snap, "Whatever is the hold up, Winnie? Come along now.

No more of your lollygagging."

With a final glower, the woman turned on her heel and hurried to catch up with the man.

Adelia joined Ernest at his chosen bench, far from other passengers. "What a very smart Pinkerton you are, Ernest. Good job." She was thrilled he remembered the name game.

"I did not like that old bag," Ernest said.

"Ernest! Wherever did you hear such language. That is not a nice thing to say." Adelia could hardly blame him since she herself was thinking along the lines of skeery old goosecap. She wondered what his vocabulary might be like after a few weeks among lumberjacks. She gave a hoot of pure joy at the thought, the first in a very long time. "What an excellent team we make, young Mr. Wright!"

"We're both Wright now."

* * *

The next afternoon, Adelia and Ernest were at the Skipanon dock awaiting the train, the same one they had taken the day before. But today, Adelia hoped it would deposit Harriet before their eyes.

They had found a safe loft in a large dairy barn for the night. It was dry up there, and if anyone else approached the rickety ladder, Adelia would hear them coming. There was enough sweet smelling hay to burrow down in; even if somebody came they might well go unnoticed. They spoke quietly, often not at all as they listened to the squeak of the weathervane above the roof when the breeze turned it. Below them, cattle settled in. Ernest was delighted with the idea of hiding away.

The food from Mrs. Watson was an abundance of tasty buttered scones, jerky, creamy cheese, and two juicy apples. "And look, Ernest...fruit biscuits."

"What are they?"

"Well, they are bars of mashed fruit. Dried and cut like candy. Taste how sweet."

When they were full, Ernest took a final piece of jerky to pretend he had a chaw of baccy to complete his new, older image. "I love my new sit-down-upons," he said of his trousers. He promised he would not be afraid in the night; big boys weren't fraidy cats. Adelia hoped that would be the case after the sun went down, although he would probably be asleep long before then. The days were very long at this time of year.

She stretched out next to him, snuggling under her cape, and told him about the barn she'd stayed in on her way to Seaside. About the farmer who shot milk from cow to cat. She sang him the song about clams. It seemed like years ago. It had not yet been six months.

Chapter Nine

September 1893

Skipanon was a beehive at the bottom of Youngs Bay, on the lower lip of the Columbia's mouth to the sea. It was a place of transport for goods and travelers alike, where product from the farms and forests of Oregon made its way to the Astoria port and beyond. The bay itself was far calmer than the actual meeting of the Columbia and the Pacific, so small boat traffic congregated there while ocean-worthy trading ships went right into the Astoria port. The air smelled of grassland, mud, and wood fire from the dozens of steamers, ferries, barges, and log rafts. Adelia had never seen such a hodgepodge of vessels. Nothing she knew of the Oregon coast had prepared her for a large body of water so smooth.

With a tight hold on Ernest's hand, she watched the Astoria and Southcoast Railway pull in. The track ended just uphill from the dock, positioned there so ferry and train passengers could easily transfer from one mode of transportation to the other. A rough-hewn boardwalk linked the two.

The woman who accosted them in Gearhart the day before was fresh in Adelia's mind. "No more standing out in the open, Ernest. Pull your cap low. Look down at your feet." They waited at the dock, half hidden from the tracks by piles of crates and barrels. They could peer at passengers getting off the train, but were well hidden themselves. In the flurry of train passengers rushing to waiting ferries, nobody took notice of two ragamuffins.

"That's her!" Adelia said when Harriet stepped off the train and onto the wooden platform. "You can look now, Ernest! That's your new auntie!" She would have cried in relief but didn't want him to see such an obvious sign of weakness in his protector.

Pushing thirty, Harriet was not exactly the prime article in any room anymore, but her wine-colored wool jacket nipped in her waist, making her bosom pleasingly round and her wide hips alluring. Adelia had once heard Albin whisper to Ephraim that she was quite the saucebox, with a smile to level a man when she chose to unleash it. Adelia thought he'd better not say something like that within a mile of Katja's hearing.

The train conductor and a stevedore squared off over the opportunity to haul Harriet's suitcase from track to dock. Travelers darted around them in both directions, to and from the train back to Seaside. "Excuse us...outta the way...pardon me, ma'am." The conductor finally released the luggage to the dock man and went back to his duty.

Down the dock from the passenger ferry was a riverboat with no frills. Other than a pilot house, the deck of the old sternwheeler was open and packed with freight. At the moment, it was wooding up, loading the logs it would burn in its boiler.

"The *Inland Intruder,*" Harriet said, reading the name of the boat on its battered side. "That's where I'm bound."

"You go on ahead now with my things," she said to her wiry helper, making a shooing motion. Then Harriet saw Adelia. She exploded like a pheasant from a hedge row, pushed through the crowd, rushed to the dock, and enveloped the girl in a crushing hug. "Oh! I worried so when you weren't at the train in Seaside this morning. All in the scullery think Mr. Stapleton fired you, and I couldn't tell them what I know without breaking my promise to you, and I thought maybe the searchers had..."

At that point, Harriet spied Ernest, once again tucked behind Adelia's knees. She recognized him. All sound and motion stopped for a fraction of a second, before she cried, "Ohhh! Adelia, no!"

"Harriet, we must. He is my brother now. We are

your niece and nephew. Such a sorrow our parents went down in a shipwreck, and you had to take us in, good God-fearing woman that you are. Of course, I am a hard worker, a boon to any cook camp, and Ernest will help, too, with no expectation of payment, just a place to stay with his big sister and favorite aunt."

"But I can't be responsible."

"You can. Besides, he will be no extra responsibility for you, I promise."

"But the cook doesn't know about you much less him, and..."

"You said you knew the cook well. Surely he will abide by your recommendation."

"But what if he says no?"

"Then we leave, no worse for wear than we are now."

Their conversation was interrupted by a gruff shout from a squarely-built man onboard the *Inland Intruder*. "Hate to break up a family flapdoodle, ladies, but this here boat's leavin' with or without."

"Oh! This conversation isn't over yet, young miss. But we must run now. Ernest, I'll take your satchel. Here we go!" They bobbed and dodged their way through the farmers, fishermen, and Clatsop merchants who had business with the handful of steamboats at the docks.

"Welcome aboard," boomed the man, built solid and compact as a brick. His hair, that which was visible around his cap, was a pale blonde shot with gray and his fair skin was ruddy with cold. He held the boat in place as the three of them scrambled onto the tired-looking vessel, then he released the last mooring line. "I was expecting just one of you."

Harriet said, "These are my niece and nephew, accompanying me to the logging camp. More help for the cook, you know."

"Ah. I am Elias Jokinen, riverboat pilot and captain. That means I rule. You are passengers. That means you obey."

Adelia wasn't so sure Harriet's magic smile would work on this man.

The boat creaked and huffed its way along the rim of the bay, soon leaving inhabited land and passing thick forest along the southern bank. The water was marshy, and great blue herons croaked their disapproval at the intrusion. A weathered boatman, apparently the only crew, chopped logs stacked on the bow and loaded wood into the boiler. Harriet, Adelia and Ernest sat on three kegs, two stenciled with 'butter' and the smallest with 'nails' across their staves. All three passengers were fascinated by the unfamiliar sights and sounds.

"Is this safe?" Ernest asked as the sternwheeler gave an inexplicable shudder that lifted the port side then slammed it back down.

"Course she's safe, boy." the captain bellowed over

the noise of the steam engine. "I checked the load to be sure it's well-chained. But we musta hit a sea monster."

"Sea monster?" Ernest looked up past the man's furry beard into his laughing eyes.

Harriet said, "He's joshing with you, Ernest. I am sure it was just a log."

Adelia was none too sure she was right.

"Can be one and the same, ma'am, in these waters. Logs can capsize a boat less worthy than this 'un. True, the *Intruder* is an old gal but she's a sturdy one." He patted the railing with affection then headed toward the pilot house. "Come with me, lad, and I'll show you how to steer."

"Can I, Addy? Can I?"

Ernest had sobbed in her arms that morning before they left the barn where they had slept. He got through the previous day with the adventure of their escape and the excitement of the train, but in the wee hours of the morning, when all was still except cooing from a pigeon cote, he was shaken by a nightmare. After that, he crumbled. Ernest mourned for his mother and the life he had lost. His grief was so deep, Adelia began to doubt her ability to be his lifeline. This job might be too hard. How could she be his sole protector when she had so many doubts herself?

Against her own nature, she realized she could not just look for the bad in strangers around them. She had to seek out the good, if not for her sake, then for this little boy. She committed to helping Ernest conquer shyness and look at strangers as sources of help. They could hardly be worse than his father.

Now, seeing excitement emblazon his face delighted her. This gruff boat pilot might be today's hero. Tomorrow, she would look for another one. "Yes, of course you can, Ernest. But be sure to mind everything Mr. Jokinen says."

The big man looked back over his shoulder as Ernest hustled to go with him. "That's Captain, missy."

After they left, Harriet demanded, "Catch me up," and Adelia did. She called the death of Mr. Munro a self-defense measure, but she did not specify whether she or Mrs. Munro was the defender. Adelia didn't name Emma Watson either, just called her a friend of Mrs. Munro. The telling took on high drama with many 'we-are-in-dangers' and 'the-man-beat-thems' and 'what-else-could-I-dos' and 'you'd-do-the-sames.'

Harriet put up both hands. "Enough! I surrender. The boy can come to the cook camp with us. But if the cook says no, then you must go. And you must be sure to keep him out of the way of the loggers. And you must stay in touch with his mother."

"So many musts!"

"Adelia, his mother may be a bold woman, one who can take risks. But if she loves her boy, she will die each day without news of him."

"They will be together again. I know it, Harriet. I

promised it to them both." Adelia, encouraged by Harriet's capitulation, watched the wild riverbank slip by for a while. The boat huffed and steamed enough to frighten off deer, but she saw river otters wrestling in play and more herons, tall and thin as reeds. She changed the subject from past to future events. "Now I have questions for you, Harriet. Tell me about the logging camp. I have never been to one."

"You'll see for yourself soon enough. But I guess some of the sodbusters got bored at the end of the Oregon trail. They took off for gold rushes. Others stayed for the green rush."

"You mean timber?"

Harriet nodded. "Speculators have snapped up the land and hired tough men to fell and buck the logs, then haul them to rivers with teams of horses or oxen."

"But aren't you afraid to be among so many harsh men? And after such a fine hotel, the cooking in a camp must be beneath you."

"You might think so, but food is a logger's one true comfort in a camp away from family and friends. All he faces every day is strenuous, dangerous work. The good ones only work at places that provide the best grub and lots of it. The food in logging camps rivals the finest restaurants. "

"You are making light, are you not?"

"No, I am most certainly not. The camp with the top food gets the top workers. Being a cook in a lumber camp gives you stature, even if you are a woman. Men will look out for us. Keep their bellies happy, and we'll be safe there, Adelia."

Safe, Adelia thought. *Just imagine.*

Ernest soon came skipping back to Adelia. The captain gave her a doff of his cap then returned to the pilot house. "What have you learned, Ernest? What have you seen?" she asked the excited child.

"The *Inland Intruder* is fifty-six feet of muscle and bone, says Mr. Captain, with a sixteen-foot beam and a four foot draft."

"What a lot of numbers to remember!"

"She's flat-bottomed so she can go upriver without wasting a fart over snags, and her paddlewheel's on her ass so she can get right up to a riverside to load."

Adelia and Harriet tried to contain their amusement. Ernest, unruffled, continued. "Captain Jokinen says one day her old boiler will blow him to kingdom come 'cause that's how old pilots piss off, but he will not be slipping his wind today. I think he means he will not die. So I guess we are all okay."

Adelia and Harriet burst into laughter. "That's very good news, Ernest."

"Good luck washing that mouth with soap," Harriet said to Adelia.

"Yes, I was worried about the loggers, but now I see he may teach them a thing or two."

The boat puffed into the Youngs River heading

southwest until another tributary joined in. There the riverboat pulled up to a landing site, downriver from Youngs Falls. Trees had been cut back from the bank for a clearing large enough for the six-horse hitch and enormous freight wagon that awaited their arrival. The three passengers were hustled off the *Intruder* and told to stand aside while men unloaded crates and barrels, then reloaded them into the wagon under the teamster's instruction.

"It's the transition of power, ladies and lad," said the Captain. "You now be the responsibility of the Lucian P. Durand Lumber Company, and I be on my way."

"Thank you for our safe passage, Captain," said Harriet with a sunny smile.

"And for your kindness to my brother," added Adelia.

He stared at her for a moment, then said, "A brave thing you be up to, girlie, and nobody who would hurt you will hear nothin' from me. You will not be followed, I'll be sure of that. But be aware it is hard for such an honest lad to hold in so many secrets."

Adelia's blood froze in her veins. Her heart liked to stop. The big man put a comforting hand on her shoulder. "You need help, I deliver supplies here once a week."

He knelt and shook Ernest's hand, man to man. "You be a crack boatman, lad. You have a job with Elias

Jokinen, riverboat pilot when you outgrow the apron strings. In the meantime, mind your sister. What she says goes. Keep her secrets from now on."

He doffed his hat to all three of them this time and was soon aboard the *Inland Intruder,* heading downriver and back toward Skipanon.

* * *

Harriet rode on the freight wagon's spring seat next to the teamster. She took up the lion's share of the bench. While she tried to maintain a discreet distance, each jolt and bounce landed her squashed up against the driver.

Adelia would have laughed at her friend's predicament but she was still too miffed at Ernest to find much humor at the moment. She had told him and told him, but still he spilled secrets. At the moment, the two were burrowed amid the freight in the wagon load. Adelia would have liked a little distance to allow her anger to dissipate. She did not want to frighten him by throwing a crab. She thought, not for the first time, that motherhood must be terribly hard. Her authority had failed on day two of their journey.

And yet, maybe she was in the wrong. Hadn't she told herself she had to depend on help from others? Isn't that exactly what Ernest had done? He'd trusted a man who might very well be an ally in times to come.

Was Ernest any less capable of intuition, just because he was younger than she? How many times had she been paid no heed, just for the sin of being young?

She forced her mind away from philosophical issues she could not answer. Instead, she considered the journey they were on, and the fat rain drops plopping down on the canvas that covered part of the load. She watched Harriet's bouncing pulchritude and overheard the woman snap at the teamster, "Save your cupboard love for the next cook that you carry this way, good sir. I know tommy-rot when I hear it." Harriet made another effort to cling to the far side of the narrow seat.

The rain increased, and Adelia found a flap of the canvas to cover Ernest and most of herself. The ride from river to camp was slow as the six work horses labored against the wagon's weight, lugging it up a path of fir needles and slippery mud, a track too narrow to call a road. If there was a road, it was the odd-looking passageway that ran beside them. Logs cut to eight foot lengths were peeled and half-buried across it every seven feet, looking like wooden domes to clamber over.

"It's a skid road," yelled the teamster when Adelia rose up on her knees to call out a question. "The oxen come down it to the river hauling logs. Up to ten yoke at a time. Those bumps in the road keep the logs sliding down to the bottom behind the beasts. You'll see teams working if you're staying in the camp."

"Gracious sakes! Remember seeing the bull yesterday? Think of twenty big as him all hitched together," Adelia said to Ernest.

"You are over being mad at me?" His troubled eyes bored holes in her conscience.

"No, Ernie, no. Not mad. I was scared is all. What you told the Captain is probably exactly right. I just need to be sure you know when to open up and when to not."

"Of course I know, Addy. I am a Pinkerton man."

She found she could still laugh at her little brother.

The path grew steeper and the teamster yelled, "Giddup, yaw" to the laboring horses. The beasts reeked of sweat. At last, after a final turn of the muddy path, they emerged from the hole that was a thick dark tunnel through the forest. They were in the open where the ground had been cut bare. The light after so much darkness should have been blinding, but it wasn't. An overall gray sky melted into a sodden landscape of stumps, dead limbs and mud. Brown rivulets drained toward the river, carving even deeper ruts in the path they climbed. A sign nailed to a stump was hand painted with *Home Soggy Home*.

The first structure visible to Adelia through the misting rain was a windowless, featureless rectangle of hand hewn boards. It was jacked up on a pallet-like foundation to keep it out of the wet, and its one door was in the center.

"Bunkhouse for the loggers," yelled the teamster to his passengers. Then warming to the role of tour guide, he started pointing. "Privies...wash house...foreman's office...stock corrals down the hill over there...cookhouse." Here he whoaed the wagon. "Everyone out." Their destination was as bleak as the bunkhouse.

Harriet debarked first, slapping away any help from the teamster's eager hands. Adelia lowered Ernest to her then grappled off the wagon herself, sinking into a slurry of fir needles and mud. The hem of her skirt was soaked before they slogged onto a raised walkway of thick planks, four across, that connected the cookhouse to the other buildings. It lifted human traffic out of the spongy mess on days such as this.

After the beauty of the seacoast and hotel, her new place of labor looked nothing but dreary to Adelia. She was cold, mud-splattered, and near blinded by a fog that was descending so fast the other buildings were disappearing from view.

"Home soggy home," Harriet muttered. Then she climbed up three low steps from the plank walkway and opened the door of the cookhouse. The inviting aroma of wood fire, hot coffee, and baking pies burst free to overcome the outdoor scents of wet fir, pitch, sawdust, and horse manure.

On the outside, the cookhouse looked austere, but once through the threshold, the sodden threesome was standing in an enormous dining room heated with a woodstove and lit by overhead gas lanterns. Heavy log tables filled the room, each set for the next meal. It was rustic, but bright, spotless, and inviting. As Adelia lifted off her muddy cape, her spirits lifted as well.

"Hallooo," called Harriet, and people came scuttling out of the next room to greet her. Two were woman, one a large native man with long black hair, and the fourth a Chinese cook in an apron that dominated him chin to shoe top.

"Hello, Hai," Harriet said, beaming at the cook.

"You back! You start work tomorrow morning."

"Yes, sir, Hai. Good to see you, too." Harriet executed a mock salute and laughed.

The diminutive man maintained his deadpan scowl.

"I'll just go settle my niece and nephew. Adelia here starts her shift in the morning, too. Good worker. Strong."

Everyone stole glances at Adelia then Ernest, but nobody asked questions. One of the women said, "Follow me. You need to change into dry duds." She led them from the dining room through a huge kitchen and into a small room with six bunks, three small bed stands, and a well-used table with chairs.

As they followed her, Adelia saw that the woman's

expansive girth gave her the same barrel shape, front or back. She waddled in a rocking motion, like a sailing ship at sea.

"Addy, that lady is..."

Adelia shushed Ernest.

"Good to see you again, Harriet," the jollicky woman said. "Nearly saw Hai smile when he heard you was coming."

Ernest tried again. "Addy, that lady is..."

Harriet cut him off this time. "More bark than bite, that Hai. Glad to see you, too, Gerty."

Gerty indicated bunks along one wall. "Them's the empties. Take your pick. I best get back to work. We're servin' soon. Come fill your plates in the kitchen when the 'jacks been served."

"Addy, that lady is..."

"...being very kind to us, Ernest." Adelia gave him a flinty look. "And we will be very kind to her."

Ernest's lip trembled. "But..."

Gerty bent over to address Ernest eye to eye. "They say ain't nobody fat on a logging crew. But that doesn't apply to some of us in the kitchen." She patted her round stomach. "There's no harder work for men to do, and it's up to us to fuel them. They got twelve hours to run, long as it's daylight. Now then what do you have to say?"

"Addy, this lady is wearing spectacles! Like mama when she reads to me. Maybe Gerty will read to me, too!"

"Ha!" Gerty touched her wire frames. "That I am, lad. And that I will!"

Adelia blushed. Harriet snorted. They heard Gerty laughing all the way back to the dining room.

"You are a charming pippin, Ernest," Harriet said as she dropped her carpetbag on one of the bunks. "I'll go get my other cases from that crazy teamster afore he opens 'em to view my woolen bloomers."

When the two youngsters were alone, Adelia asked, "You want the bunk above mine, Ernest? See, you climb up the end of it like a little monkey and drop right in. It's fun." He did just that, giving it a good bounce as she unpacked his satchel and then her own. The two things she set on the little table next to their bunks were her sewing box and her lighthouse with its legend, *May Your Light Always Shine.*

"Is this where we live now, Addy?" Ernest called to her from the top bunk as it squeaked with each bounce.

"We shall see. We shall just have to see."

* * *

The autumn days continued foggy, wet, and chill. Adelia and Ernest settled into the rhythm of the camp, one of four owned by the Lucian P. Durand Lumber Company. Nobody actually said they could stay, but it was assumed that someone else had given their permission. So Adelia was put on the payroll, and Ernest received bed and board for helping with a handful of chores.

He excelled as an assistant to Adelia, Myra, and Gerty, the three flunkeys. One of his jobs each morning was to set out the crocks of sauerkraut and mustard, plus jars of pickles, jams, vinegar, and Tabasco sauce that lined the centers of the long dining tables.

"He's a joy to a lot of the men," Harriet told Adelia. "Reminds them of family they left to come here for the winter logging."

"Addy, did you know about this?" he shrieked joyfully one morning, having discovered a miraculous spread called peanut butter available for the cook camp tables. After that, a handful of the loggers called him Peanut.

Each night after dinner, he wiped down the crocks to remove hand prints and spills, then placed them back on the shelves he could reach with the help of a foot stool. He swept under the tables where only he easily fit. The flunkeys delighted in the four-year-old's help which he gave willingly, thrilled with his self-appointed status as a big boy.

"He has a knack for worming into your heart," Myra said to Gerty.

"A right genius at it, that boy," Gerty replied as she stoked the fire, her arms as sturdy as tree limbs. A white apron patched together from numerous flour sacks billowed around her.

The dining room held four enormous hand-hewn tables. Their heavy benches seated forty-eight loggers with just enough room for the flunkeys to duck and weave in between, each laden with massive platters of food or pots of coffee.

Adelia came to think of it as a balancing act. "I shall join the circus after this," she laughed as she danced around Gerty, one with a tray of pies and the other an equal burden of chocolate cake. The dining room was always blessed with the luscious aroma of baking bread, roasting meat, and root vegetables in butter, gravy, or cheese.

Adelia and Ernest found that their quarters at the far end of the building were warmed by the massive kitchen ovens that threw heat day and night. "Cook staff lives separate from lumberjacks 'cause we get up at 3:30 to start the breakfast baking," Gerty told them. "Loggers might murder us for disturbing their sleep at such an hour."

Ernest was considered young enough to stay with Harriet, Gerty, Myra and Adelia, although he was unsettled by the arrangement. On the one hand, his long pants and new chores made him feel like one of the men during the daylight hours. On the other, he was terrified to be separated from Adelia through the long cold nights.

The thin panel that cordoned off the women's

quarters did little to muffle the snoring of the long-haired cookee, Three Fingers. He was surely an Indian, Adelia thought, but not from the coast. Too tall for that. It was Ernest who learned Three Fingers was from the Dakotas. And that he was named Three Fingers following an unfortunate encounter with a butcher knife. The taciturn Sioux gave orders to the flunkeys, answered to Hai, but conversed only with Ernest.

Three Fingers had his own cubbyhole while Hai and his wife kept separate spacious quarters. Adelia didn't know if it was the respect due to the cook, or because Chinese of any stature were not allowed to share rooms with whites, or if Indians couldn't share with anyone.

Hai's wife and two helpers ran the laundry in a separate shack; it differed from other laundries only in that the helpers had to concentrate on removing lice from the loggers' clothes as well as unknown vermin that hitched a ride on men arriving from foreign places like British Columbia or Minnesota. Adelia never heard Hai's wife called anything but Hai's wife so Haiswife she became.

During the day, Harriet worked alongside Hai and Three Fingers. Like the two men, she became a snarling monster, ordering the flunkeys to scrub harder, peel faster, spill less, dish up more, and carry heavier platters as they danced between tables. Only in the evenings, after dinner was done and the kitchen was put to bed for a few hours, did Harriet have time for a smile at Adelia. "The bakin' and bitchin' is done for another day," she would say, rolling down her socks and wiggling exhausted toes.

At six in the morning and six at night, Hai hammered on an old crosscut saw blade which hung near the cookhouse door. It warbled a shrill song, telling the camp a meal was served. Men came running.

"They call those saws misery whips in the woods," Harriet told Adelia once as they backed out of the way of the stampede. "But not when it's calling them to the table."

Adelia had thought that Seaside House was a trencherman's paradise, but she'd never seen anything like the way lumbermen could eat. She would slap down a platter of steaks just to have it consumed three t-bones at a time. Even the smallest high climber could devour six pork chops.

To her surprise, meals were eaten in silence, other than "Pass the beans" or "Gimme another." Where she grew up, mealtime was about the only time her father ever talked. And in the scullery at the hotel, it was great fun to gossip and laugh around the table. But these men had to pack in their calories in under fifteen minutes; there was no time for chatter. Quiet as monks, they ate breakfasts of cornbread, pancakes, liver, onions, and doughnuts.

Meanwhile, Adelia and Myra lined up lunch buckets they'd filled with boiled eggs, slabs of meat on rolls still warm from the oven, fresh fruit if they had it or dried if they didn't, and cake or pie or both. When the loggers shuffled out to begin their workday, Adelia handed each a pail for the midday break in the woods. "Thank you," most of them said politely. Some seemed compelled to add, "sweetheart" or "honeycomb." Adelia could not decide if 'cute as a bug's ear' was good or not. But she was fairly sure bugs didn't have ears.

Mail delivery was surprisingly good although Adelia despised the wait. Several times a week someone went to Astoria for supplies, carrying outgoing letters and delivering incoming. In the first days, Adelia spent a bit of Mrs. Munro's money on a subscription to the Astoria paper which she received only a day or two late.

In the evenings, she scoured the pages. Stories about the whale in Seaside were the big news for the earliest days. The missing Seaside woman and child got less front page space, moved below the fold and finally to the interior. It disappeared altogether when no more news was to be had.

Adelia began to place ads that said things like, *Tilly and brother safe awaiting word.* It seemed a century - but was only three weeks - before an answering ad said *To Tilly: Sweet Violets in SF. Lonely for your brother. All love.*

Adelia floated through the day.

"You gonna get a face ache from that smile, girl," said Myra, whose own stern countenance would never make room for such a glow.

Chapter Ten

November 1893

Adelia had little time to think of herself. She took care of Ernest, and she worked. At night, long after Hai, Three Fingers and Harriet left the kitchen for their bunks, the flunkeys labored on with clean up. Ernest stayed with Harriet then and was asleep by the time Adelia came to their room. She worked steadily and willingly without complaint, so the rest of the kitchen staff found her agreeable. More important, the loggers saw no cause for criticism of the thirteen-year-old girl, or she would have been booted from the camp the very next day.

Adelia was warm and well-fed which was about all a child on her own could hope for, so she was content at the logging camp. But, oh, how she longed for news from Mrs. Munro. When *Sweet Violets bloom at 138 Flora* finally appeared in the newspaper's personals, Adelia wrote immediately, and from then on the two could communicate by mail.

> *" ...I am no longer Munro having gone back to my maiden name of Burlingham, not that anyone in San Francisco would care..."*
>
> *" ...he goes by Ernest Wright here, so he is accepted as my brother and everyone is kind..."*
>
> *"...the street has many hills that I enjoy walking. And the ocean reminds me of the Seaside town and people I love..."*
>
> *"...Harriet taught him how to gather eggs from under the chickens. He's very good at it and he appears to like Harriet..."*
>
> *"...I am lonely, of course. But I am making headway here in this discreet hotel where a woman of means can feel safe. A Mrs. Brodie invited me to play euchre with two of her friends..."*
>
> *"...of course he misses his real mother! He knows he will see you again so he bides his time and enjoys the life of the camp as best he can. But I warn you, when next you meet, you must provide him with peanut butter."*

Adelia did not fret about the future. She knew that Ernest would go back to his mother in time. But for now, his sunny nature rarely failed to lift her spirits. His hugs were a balm, something she'd had little enough of in her young life. She would miss him terribly, but he belonged with Mrs. Munro; she thought of his mother as that, never transitioning to Mrs. Burlingham. Adelia gave no thought to how it would happen. The future stayed in the future, and she was satisfied not to rush it.

Two things changed that.

First, Adelia become consumed by her own body. It was changing in ways she could not control. She already despised the dad-burned bleeding each month, and now something else was making her itchy in her own skin. She might giggle all day then swing to a severe case of the morbs in the evening. She covered her turmoil by working so hard nobody noticed. Nobody but Ernest.

"What's wrong, Addy?" he asked, hearing her sniffle. He swung from the top bunk down into hers to snuggle next to her warmth. She knew she was the one stable factor in his life. She was showing signs of distress, and that was scaring him. She must control this moodiness. "Nothing, Ernest. I'm fine. Just didn't sleep well, I guess."

Her breasts sent her weird signals all their own. The tips hardened if she brushed past a man in the overcrowded dining room. They tingled when she washed herself. As if that wasn't strange enough, soft curly hair was growing down there. Hair under her arms, too.

Can this possibly be right?

Maybe she would look like the wild man of Indian

legend before this hair stopped growing. The local tribes were terrified of a big-footed stranger; they warned against using its name aloud lest the monster hear and carry you away. Maybe this monster was just a woman whose hair spread everywhere.

She was aware that the men in the camp looked at her in ways that were somehow different from men's gazes in the past, especially when she leaned over one's shoulder to put a platter in front of him. It embarrassed her, this lingering assessment. But, what the dickens, she liked the attention, too. Sort of.

While she sliced two dozen apple pies one afternoon, she remembered Mrs. Munro's explanation of crushes. What had she really wanted from Ephraim? It wasn't sex, she was pretty sure. She recalled how her brother hurt her on the floor of that chicken coop. If that was an attempt at sex, how could it ever solve an ache instead of create one?

This was more like a hand to hold, soft lips to kiss, notes to pass, secret glances to share. Someone she could give the biggest piece of pie or the freshest cup of coffee. Adelia was thirteen and in need of romance. Ephraim was no longer her soul's desire, but another crush was sure to happen here where there were men behind every tree.

Without Mrs. Munro to confide in - and Adelia was far too mortified to write this sort of trouble in a letter - Adelia needed Harriet to explain what on earth was going on. But she was almost never alone with Harriet now. Ernest was always there, or worse, the entire kitchen staff gathered around. This was nothing she could talk to Myra or Gerty about, or Haiswife who spoke a variety of English that nobody understood.

The second event that changed Adelia's view of the future happened on the first sunny afternoon in November. It had rained so hard for so long, everyone was giddy about that bright orb up above. Adelia was given an afternoon off. She took Ernest to visit the animals in the camp. They kept chickens and pigs for fresh eggs and meat which augmented the game that local tribes sold to Hai. Down a short hill, the corrals held working stock. Two dozen oxen ignored them, but two of the gentle workhorses let them pet noses.

The camp was fairly quiet, a slight breeze in the trees. It was a Sunday, the loggers' day off. Many had gone to Astoria the night before and would straggle in late, broke and hung over, ready to start all over in the morning. Others stayed in the camp to play poker and cribbage, repair their equipment, write letters. They found places in the sun to sit and relax sore muscles.

Adelia could hear a fiddle and a guitar picking out a melody, and the joy of music lured her. Ernest and she neared a fire ring where several men sat, two playing instruments and others listening. One of the grizzled bullwhackers made room on a log for them to sit. Ernest, eying the men, crossed his legs, ankle on knee, like the other fellows

A young tenor was singing, his eyes on the guitar that he strummed. Adelia had seen him before at mealtimes but was too busy to examine him closely. His hair was the same burnt gold blonde as his beard. Every man in the camp had either a beard or a mustache or both. Adelia assumed the facial fuzz kept them warm. This boy had no gray, just shiny full hair. Was it springy to the touch or silky like her own? She saw the strong veins in his arms where his shirt cuffs were rolled back. His lean body bent over the instrument, circling and protecting it on his lap. She felt envy of the guitar. His voice was the smooth butter of an Irishman as he sang:

Come all you sons of freedom that run the Youngs Bay stream,
Come all you roving lumberjacks and listen to my theme.
We'll cross the wide Columbia where the mighty waters flow
And we'll range the wild woods over
and once more a-lumb'ring go.

With our axes on our shoulders we'll make the woods resound
And many a tall and stately tree will come tumbling
to the ground.
With our axes on our shoulders to our boot tops deep in snow
We'll range the wild woods over
and once more a-lumb'ring go.

When our youthful days are ended and our jokes are getting long
We'll take us each a little wife and settle on a farm.

We'll have enough to eat and drink, contented we will go
And we'll tell our wives of our hard times
and no more a-lumb'ring go.

When he finished he ducked his head then sat up straight, pushing hair from his eyes. Adelia was across the fire from him, but she was pretty sure his smile was for her. "That's a song from back East. I changed a lyric or two away from Michigan to fit Oregon."

"It was nice," Adelia said. After that, she was tongue tied. *Please, please let me think of something to say!*

The man who made room on the log for them saved the day. "Lotsa back East loggers follow the green rush to the coast. Too bad they know more about singin' than loggin.'" He chortled at his own joke.

The singer laughed and said, "We know better than to crack ourselves in the head with our own bullwhips, old man."

Adelia turned to see the scar that crossed the bullwhacker's head from ear to brow. Maybe it wasn't a scar from a whip but it surely looked like one.

"You work in the kitchen, right miss? I've seen you there, shufflin' out platters like a card shark deals aces. My name is Martin Driscoll." The tenor's talking voice had a brightness that replaced the softness when he sang. Adelia wasn't sure which she preferred. Either way he was what Harriet would call a real lally-cooler.

"I am Adelia Wright. And that is my brother, Ernest Wright." She had a hunch that society would frown on her sitting in this circle among men. But in a logging camp on a sunny day, society's opinion seemed very far away.

Ernest, fascinated by a whittler who created a bear from a stick of wood, inched toward him. Soon the two were having a chat of their own.

"Shall I sing another?" Martin asked.

"Oh yes."

And he did, then another until men began to move away to do chores for the workweek ahead.

The young tenor finally stood and stretched.

"Thank you for the songs," said Adelia.

"Pleasure, miss. Thank you for the fine grub day in, day out." He touched the brim of his hat. "See you this eve in the dining hall, I reckon."

"Yes, I will be there."

"Adelia!" She heard Gerty yell from the door of the cookhouse, waving at her.

Leaping up she gasped, "Goodness, I should be there now. Come along, Ernest. There is work to do."

She noticed Ernest now had the toy bear in one tight little fist. As he rattled on about whittling, Adelia answered with appropriate 'Ahs' and 'Reallys', but her thoughts stayed with the singer, Martin. She wondered if he could teach her how to romance.

As they walked toward the cook house, a rider passed ahead of them, aiming toward the building that housed the camp foreman's office. He was remarkable enough to pull her attention away from young Martin. And apparently, she and Ernest were remarkable enough to pull his attention away from the foreman.

The horse was unlike any she had ever seen, built more to run than to work. She thought it to be a fairy tale sort of horse, all tall and willowy, and it did not walk so much as prance. The rider was as majestic as a fairy tale as well. Unlike the loggers, he was clad in a fine wool suit and linen shirt. When he doffed his wide-brimmed hat his dark hair was as slick as his mustache.

He stopped, as if to assess the pair. Closer now, Adelia smelled the leather of his saddle, sandalwood from a barber shop, possibly a hint of liquor.

"By jove, my employees get younger by the hour. You are hirelings here?" he asked. His accent was like Mr. Stapleton's. English English. She tried not to dislike him for that, but Adelia felt his air of power and privilege. She had encountered wealth at the hotel, but had not expected it so far into the forest. "I am Adelia Wright, sir, and this my brother, Ernest. I work for the company cook, sir."

"Ah. Our Mr. Hai. And he for me. I am Lucian P. Durand, scallywag, remittance man, and owner of the Lucian P. Durand logging company. At your service, my young friends."

Adelia had never curtseyed. She stared, mouth and eyes wide open. It was Ernest who reached up with his little hand for a shake. "How do you do, sir." Wealth and privilege were more his world than Adelia's.

To Adelia, the future had become something very much to think about.

* * *

"Adelia!" yelped Gerty. "Careful with that pail. Yer spillin' it."

"Sorry, Gerty. I'll get the mop."

"Right, girl. And where is your head this fine Monday morning?"

Adelia's head had been visualizing signatures of 'Mrs. Martin Driscoll' and 'Adelia D.'

"I saw you yesterday makin' cow eyes at that handsome Eastern feller. Might be time Harriet talked to you about mother's friend."

"I was not making cow eyes at the Easterner, whatever that means. I was merely listening to him sing. And who is mother's friend?"

Gertie leaned in close. "Mother's friend. You know, female medicine. Prevention powders. Be asking me no more about it now. And no more sassin' neither."

Adelia had no idea what Gertie was on about. But the men were bursting into the dining room, and there was no time to ask.

After breakfast was served, lunch pails

distributed, and clean up was done, the flunkeys and cookees had a moment to slow down before dinner prep began. Adelia figured she could take Harriet aside then. Instead, Hai said something in his thick accent that she didn't understand. It was the first time the cook had spoken directly to her, and she didn't want to appear to be a brainless foozler.

"Pardon, sir?"

He said it again, this time faster, louder, and with hands flailing in the air as though bees were on the attack. Harriet scurried up with a bucket of lye soap and water, brushes, rags, vinegar and a broom. "He says go to the foreman's office. And take along your cleaning things. And it's not his job to provide cleaning staff to the loggers."

"What is happening?"

"I do not know. But go."

Adelia scooted along the plank trail to the foreman's office, carrying the tools of her trade. This was foreign territory for her, so near the living quarters of the men.

She took a deep breath, then peeked inside the open office door. The man she saw was not Mr. Koskinen, the foreman. Instead, it was Lucien P. Durand, leaning on one of three desks, staring at precarious piles of papers.

"Damnation," he growled to himself.

When she tapped on the doorframe, he looked up

and brightened. "Ah, the cavalry has arrived! Come in, my young friend."

Adelia walked to the side of the desk, laden with cleaning equipment, feeling terribly awkward.

"I remembered seeing a young bub and his sis on my way in yesterday. So I asked Hai if I might borrow you to help clean up this office. You up to the employment?"

Adelia took a look around. Clearly, Mr. Koskinen was no housekeeper. The desks were coated with sticky grime, cigar butts, and dirty cups, the beleaguered shelves with machine parts, tools, and sawdust, the floor with dried mud, footprints, and fir needles. When she set the heavy bucket down, fluffy puffballs of hair, lint, and dust floated out from under the desks, swirling in clouds around her worn boots and Mr. Durand's fine shoes.

"A house is none too clean when the beggar's velvet amasses under things to such a degree," she muttered, then put a hand over her mouth. This was no way to speak in front of a boss.

"Is that what you call those dust balls?" Mr. Durand asked with a grin. "My mother called them ghost turds, but I suppose that may be nothing to say in range of a young girl's ears."

She couldn't help but giggle at the phrase. "Not so young, sir. And to answer your question, yes, I am up to this employment."

"Then while you clean, I shall cut down this forest of paperwork."

They worked for over an hour before another word was said. Mr. Durand sat at one desk and never moved, except to write a note and mutter to himself now and then. Adelia started with the shelves, removing the items on them, scrubbing until the filth was gone, then replacing the arcane tools in a tidy row. Next, she removed all the clutter from the other two desk tops. She snuck peeks at her boss, admiring his demeanor and the look of concentration on his fine face as he read, scratched his signature with a pen, and occasionally whispered an oath so low she could not truly hear it. He was a handsome man, she decided, although an old one. No doubt at least thirty. He had called himself a scallywag, and she knew what that meant. But a remittance man? Her curiosity itched like poison ivy.

She climbed on a chair then stood on a desktop to wash the lantern hung above it. When she jumped from desk one to desk two, she realized that Mr. Durand was watching her.

Finally he spoke. "Gosh darn it, girl. Take care there. Cannot lose a good high climber from my logging crew."

"I shall not fall, sir. I am quite sturdy."

"I shall not watch then."

When done with two desks and lanterns, she went

for clean water. On her return, Mr. Durand was putting on his hat. "I remove myself from your way now, Adelia. Be sure to return these papers exactly as they are now piled." He tapped the newly straightened stacks.

Her curiosity burst free. "A question, sir, before you go. What is a remittance man? You used the term yesterday."

"Ah. An English term, actually. It means I am the black sheep in the homeland of my family. I have been booted out for my dubious conduct. Lucky for me, dubious conduct makes me quite successful here in America."

"I am the black sheep in my family, as well. Nobody wanted me at home either."

"Clearly we are meant to be brother and sister."

Adelia laughed. "I will not give you orders as I give them to Ernest. Sir."

"Maybe. But a little bird told me you are taking very good care of that child, a boy who is sought high and low."

Adelia had until this very second been happy. She liked his English accent, so much finer than Mr. Stapleton's. He made her laugh. He did not patronize although both rich and grown up. He answered questions and soothed her curiosity.

But now, he revealed himself a dangerous bounder.

With all the might she could muster, she snarled, "You will not hurt Ernest. You will not take him." She turned to the door but he was quick and caught her arm.

"My girl! No. It is not my goal to steal the boy."

She pulled at her arm, but so did he. She gathered wind for a shriek, but he got his hand over her mouth. She bit the pads of his palm.

"Ouch! Now stop that. Listen. You are safe here. A friend told me the truth of your situation. Because of that, I will protect you here. You have my word. Will you cease your attack?"

She quit squirming but turned on him an evil eye.

He slowly removed his wounded hand, shaking it like a pup with a sore paw. "No unauthorized stranger will be allowed in this camp should one come looking. Although a hellcat such as you might be more danger to the authorities than the likes of me." He doffed his hat and went on his way.

She stood, surrounded by the grime she was meant to scrub, wondering just what the hell to do next: clean up or clear out.

She could grab Ernest and run. But where? Into the wilderness in hopes a wolf pack would raise him? Or she could stay in the camp where the owner appeared to have joined Harriet on her list of protectors. Besides, there was still that tempting Irish tenor to be dealt with.

"But who told the boss about us?" she asked herself as she carried her cleaning tools out of the office. It took little time for her to work it out. "Of course! The riverboat pilot, Captain Jokinen." He must have told Lucien P. Durand on the ride from Skipanon to the lumber dock. The two men were looking out for her. Or so it seemed. Even so, she wasn't really sure she liked being talked about when she wasn't part of the conversation.

Adelia sighed and made her choice. She had told Ernest that sometimes you had to trust people. It was true for her, too. The Captain and the lumber man were allies. She had to believe it was true. With a determined set to her chin, she gave a nod, then got on her knees to wash the front steps.

Chapter Eleven

November 1893

November continued to astound the logging camp with a series of sunny days. In the lull before dinner the next afternoon, Ernest sat on a keg in front of the cookhouse. He was getting a lesson in whittling from the man known as Witless to all in the camp.

"He is very young to hold a knife, you know," Adelia had said to the man, wondering just how worried she should be.

"Have no fear of my nickname, miss. Just a logger's joke about how much I whittle, not how poorly I think. I will watch the boy and hold his hand during the cutting."

Adelia, Harriet and Gerty sat inside, sharing a pot of tea and cracking a huge pile of walnuts into an enormous bowl. The door was left open for sun as well as the surveillance of the woodcarving.

"Harriet," Adelia said, "Gerty suggests I ask you about mother's friend."

Harriet nearly slapped the cup into its saucer. She stared arrows at her co-worker who was contemplating which nut to shell next. "Gerty!"

"You know it is time to have the talk with the girl, Harriet." Gerty chose then cracked down with the forged metal tool. "Just look at her."

"I suppose you are right." Harriet sighed with a tone of resignation. "Had you a mother, Adelia, she would share this with you. Or maybe not, as it is difficult to speak of. My mother prepared me not at all." She stopped to nibble a sweet biscuit and sip her tea.

"Yes, Harriet?" Adelia felt impatient with the delay.

"Yes, Harriet, do tell," Gerty said. The jowls of her beefy face jiggled a bit.

"As you know, Adelia, women are to be praised for their roles as mothers. Many people believe it is our only reason to be on this earth. I myself do not hold with that notion, but that is another story. Now then, I make the assumption you know how a woman becomes pregnant. The amorous congress between a man and a woman down there?" She pointed at Adelia's crotch.

Adelia thought she might faint in humiliation. Did women actually speak of these things? She certainly was not going to say a word about her brother, that was for sure. But still, her need for information burned.

Gerty goaded Harriet on."The man inserts himself into the woman, right, Harriet?"

Harriet nodded. "It is an act that causes pain at first, but becomes tolerable as time goes on."

"Even leads to most convivial society or at least some women say." Gerty's smile broadened.

So The Act must not always be brutal. Mortifying or not, this talk was proving illuminating. Adelia ventured a question that had been on her mind a great deal lately. She wanted to kiss Martin. But she certainly did not want to have his baby. "Babies do not result from kissing? Only from the...other thing?"

"That is true, my dear, but kissing can lead to games of pully hawly which can lead to a wee bundle of problems for the uninformed girl."

Better she heard the truth than hide from it. Adelia confessed, "I have watched the beasts, Harriet. I know about The Act that causes babies."

"Then what I have to say is not about how to become pregnant. It is how *not* to become pregnant. Even though church and state tell you it is wrong, there are ways of, ah, family planning that are important for you to know now that you are...maturing." She made fluttery hand gestures toward Adelia's body. "You are interested in men, and men are interested in you. This will continue for some years into your future."

Harriet next revealed a dark universe to Adelia. She spoke of *coitus interruptus,* the rhythm method, new condoms made of rubber, vaginal suppositories, pessaries, acidic douches, and syringes of antiseptic spermicides. "Some are dangerous, most don't work. But they are all called mother's friends and are legal if used for a woman's health, but not to prevent pregnancy."

Adelia's head fairly reeled with the inscrutability of it all. "But..."

"I know. It is dancing on the point of a needle. And in truth, other than abstinence, there is only one method that works very well." Adelia had thought things could get no more astounding, and then Harriet explained abortion.

This was all too much! Adelia felt in turns dismayed, intrigued, appalled. But the worst of it was when Harriet, at the end of her lecture, took a sip of tea. Without warning, her lip commenced to quiver, her nose to run, her eyes to water. She picked herself up and ran from the room.

"What in the world?" Gerty exclaimed, then lifted herself with the grace of a cow to shuffle away behind Harriet.

Adelia was left to contemplate the wonders of womanhood and to question what horrors boys must face. Finally, she cleared their dishes and called to Ernest. "Time to come wipe down the salt shakers for the tables."

"Thank you, Mr. Witless," she heard the boy say. She wondered if the nickname might be better applied to her at this point in time.

* * *

The following week, Adelia asked several times what had upset Harriet. Had she felt unwell? Was something said that angered her? Harriet refused to answer, merely saying she was fine. In time, Adelia let it go. Harriet was a woman of mystery in many ways. Adelia knew little of her background before they met at Seaside House. She finally accepted that everyone has secrets and some were impervious to her curiosity.

Lucien P. Durand visited the camp in a week, then again two weeks after that. Each time, Adelia cleaned the office while he worked. Only when Mr. Koskinen, the foreman, was not there did she venture a conversation with the boss.

"You do not seem like a lumberman," she said at one point. "You do not wear braces and swing an ax."

"That I do not. But a superlative poker player I am. I won these camps at the tables in Astoria. And I find I can make even better money from wood chips than poker chips."

"Do you live in Astoria, then?"

"I have rooms there. But it is not my home."

"Where is that?"

"I wish it were England, my nosy friend. But as I am not welcome there just now, I live in San Francisco most of the time. Close to my business here and to interests I have in the new railroads pushing fast this way from the south and the east."

San Francisco!

Adelia's fruitful brain put this and that and the other thing together. Her plan for the future took shape. But her plotting was interrupted by a question from Lucien. "I am told you have a new protector."

"Sir?" Could he mean Harriet? "Harriet has been my friend for months."

"I mean a bucker who happens to sing a fine song."

"Who has been saying such?"

"Goodness, girl. That frown eclipses your dimples."

"I do not enjoy gossip when it is about me."

"Be careful of the Irish, Adelia. They are an untamable breed."

"Am I not untamable myself, sir? And is this business of yours?"

He laughed. "Your temper has bitten me before. But you are little more than a child. If that lad were to misuse you, he'd find there would be hell to pay."

Adelia was shocked. How dare he butt in. He sounded like a father, for pity sake. Or how she'd been told a father should sound. She clenched her teeth lest bitter words escape, and she scrubbed a little harder, working the potent soap deep into the rustic floor.

To be fair, her interest in Martin could have been on the tongues of the camp at large. It was true they had taken walks together over the past weeks, but always with Ernest tagging along or at least in sight of other camp denizens. And the weather was no longer conducive to romance as it had turned sullen once again.

But there was that one time, a moment of all backs turned. Ernest was occupied with Witless, and others were tending to their own rat killing. It was not long after Adelia's talk with Harriet. With the assurance that kissing was no baby-maker, Adelia had been looking forward to the notion of a canoodle. Masked from the camp by a lush Sitka spruce, Adelia and Martin sat on a curved limb while he picked out melodies on his guitar.

"You know so many songs," she said.

"I know a special one, an ancient Irish ballad, that makes me think of you. It is about a nymph in the woods. May I sing it for you?"

A song sung for her? Surely no female could resist such a gesture.

He sang. She felt every strum vibrate through her body.

Oh I was walking by a ride
When from the glade I passed beside
Came a nymph, a sylph from the trees in the wood.
She filled my arms and danced with me,
and filled my arms and danced.

And then she rose and faded fast
Amid the green her body passed
And she cried Farewell from the trees in the wood
My eyes are wet with tears and still,
my eyes are wet with tears.

Oh I've been searching everywhere
To find a maid who can compare
With the nymph I met in the trees, in the wood
While I was tramping homeward bound,
while I was tramping home.

So hold me, kiss me, darling maid,
Be like my sylph in that fair glade
Be the love I kiss in the house, in the home
And then you'll hold my heart and hand,
and then you'll hold my heart.

He leaned the guitar against the limb of the spruce tree, stood to face Adelia, took her hands and pulled her up to stand. He put his arms around her. Martin held her not tight, but tenderly. "Did you like my song, little maid of the woods?"

"It is now my song," she said, aware he was kissing the top of her head. She had never known the top of your head could feel such a fine thing. *Imagine what might come next!*

He moved toward her ear and his beard tickled as he whispered, "Of late, you have taken up all my thoughts."

She looked up and felt his breath on her face. So strange, this closeness to a man, this exhalation a wave of warmth on the cold November day. She smelled the saltiness of his skin, felt the muscles of his chest.

Martin cupped her face in his hands. He touched his mouth to hers, pressed, pulled back, and did it again. Next he whispered, "It is better if you close your eyes." He kissed her chin and her throat. It was slow and sweet, but insistent. She felt unsteady so she put a hand on his shoulder. Her other hand circled around below his arm, and she pressed it against his back.

His lips were larger than hers and rough from working in the wind and sun. But they were soft, as well, and the pressure he applied caused her own mouth to answer back. Was she doing this right? She pulled away enough to run her tongue along his lips, offering a balm from the drying weather. Adelia turned her head to a new position and they met again, this time with her own lips slightly parted. When she felt his tongue, she pulled away in surprise.

"Too much too soon, dear one?" he asked. "Then I shall stop for now though it is devilish hard to do."

"I did not...it was a surprise. I did not know kisses ended so."

"Kisses go on and on, I am told. I am thrilled you do not know. We shall experience it together."

She pulled in a breath and pushed away. It was time to remember who she was. "But school must end for today. I have cream to churn and bread to slice."

"As long as you do nothing like that to my heart."

In the following days, Adelia and Martin had no more time alone, but they managed a touching of hands, lingering glances, secret smiles when their paths crossed within the cookhouse. Adelia could not stop Harriet and Gerty from teasing her, calling her spooney when she dropped a dish or rag.

* * *

Lucien P. Durand came and went from *Home Soggy Home*. As Adelia worked in the cookhouse and in the office, her liking for - and more important, her trust of - the boss grew. She schemed. He did not know it, but he was to be the way that Ernest would reunite with his mother.

"Ernest," Adelia said, "would you like to make a present for your mother?"

It was only when the two were alone that Mrs.

Munro was mentioned at all. Adelia read him pieces of her letters, helped him write back in hers. They talked about the fun all three had on the beach at Seaside last summer and how that would happen again someday in the future. Ernest would cry at these times, holding tight to his Addy. It was important that he grieved from missing his mother, not from losing her altogether.

Ernest's excitement gleamed. "Could I? Make her a present? Is she coming for me?"

"No, not here, not yet. But it will soon be Christmas, and Mr. Durand will be going to San Francisco. Maybe he would carry a gift for her from you."

"Yes, Addy! How?"

"Time to be a Pinkerton man again and keep a secret. We will go to Mr. Witless tomorrow and ask for his help. Tonight you think about what you would like him to help you whittle. Something your mother might like."

"But, Addy, I already know."

"Oh? And what is that?"

He pointed at Adelia's replica lighthouse. "Mama needs a light of her own."

Chapter Twelve

December 1893

In early December, Lucien P. Durand announced to the foreman of the camp that he would be gone for at least two months, leaving for San Francisco the very next day. He would be back in late winter or early spring. Adelia eavesdropped while removing ash from the office woodstove. When she heard the news, she was ready.

She'd watched the old whittler work with Ernest. Of course, Witless did most of the actual carving, but he held Ernest's hands to make the final cuts on the tiny lighthouse. Ernest then selected carefully from his paint pots, coloring the trinket an overall sky blue with white squares for windows. At each window he added a blob of purple for Sweet Violets, and he painted the base a brilliant orange for the tiger lilies his mother loved. It did not resemble Tillamook Rock or any other lighthouse in Adelia's ken. It was a happy place from a little boy's imagination, just for his mother.

Adelia wrapped it in clean flour sacks, addressed it to 138 Flora in San Francisco, to the attention of Mrs. Burlingham. She told Lucien P. Durand that this was the name used by Ernest's mother and asked if he would deliver it in time for Christmas. He told her he would oblige, knowing the street well, located halfway up Nob Hill away from the seedier part of town.

Adelia could have mailed it, just as she mailed letters. But that did not suit her plan. She did not tell him, or anyone else, what she hoped would result from this mission. It was a secret too fragile to share. But if Lucien P. Durand was willing to deliver a package directly to Mrs. Munro, then the day might come when he would do the same with Ernest. And maybe, just maybe, he would deliver Adelia, too.

The thought thrilled her with a joy even greater than Martin's kiss. *Imagine!* A real city, the Paris of the West, with theatre halls, libraries, cable cars, and dozens of stores with thousands of pretty dresses and shoes! Even the opera that Mrs. Munro so enjoyed. Think of the candies, the books, the fabrics Adelia could buy for designs she'd create from the magic in her sewing box.

But at the same time, there was a cloud that darkened her gray matter.

Harriet was becoming a worry. The cookee fainted

in the kitchen one afternoon next to the cauldron of beef barley soup that she was seasoning. Three Fingers lifted her up and to her bed. She stayed still for the rest of the day, emerging the next morning to resume her role in the kitchen.

Harriet claimed to have merely been overtired from a restless night and overheated from the enormous stoves. She carried on, refusing to answer Adelia's questions. If she confided in anyone it must have been Gerty. Adelia was aware the rotund woman stayed as close to the cookee as a loyal dog, a shepherd as attentive as Shep.

In the evenings in their room, Adelia spread open a map of the West Coast that the boss had given her before he left. Ernest and she crouched over it on the floor next to an oil lamp, and she guided a finger down the coast as he asked his nightly question about his lighthouse. "Where is it now, Addy?"

"It is in Mr. Durand's valise as the steamer leaves the Columbia River for the Pacific Ocean, heading south with Tillamook Rock Lighthouse guiding her way..."

"...racing the gray whales south to where the weather is warm..."

"...weaving through the lumber freighters entering the sea at Coos Bay..."

"...steering clear of the military prison at Alcatraz..."

It was a happy activity for them both. But a week after Lucien P. Durand left with Ernest's gift tucked in his saddlebag, their world tipped once again.

* * *

Three Fingers awakened Harriet and Adelia, holding a lantern in the gloom of night. He shyly averted his eyes as he shook their shoulders. "There's a man. Says he knows you. Come."

The two wrapped themselves in blankets against the chill and went to the dining room while Gerty, Myra, and Ernest slept on. Three Fingers had given the man coffee kept hot every hour of the day, then gone back to bed.

Captain Elias Jokinen, owner of the *Inland Intruder*, sat alone. He was not tall, but a big, stocky man, yet the scale of the enormous dining room made him seem small. He'd removed his hat, and his thick blonde hair in the light of the lantern looked like a puff of cotton.

"Captain Jokinen! What is it?" Harriet asked putting a quavering hand on his arm. Whether she was ashen from illness or fear, Adelia could not tell.

"Gladified you remember me, ma'am," he said with a smile before turning deadly serious. "What is wrong is this." He smoothed out a crumpled poster on the rough surface of the table.

Adelia gasped at the heading '$100 REWARD'

even before she read 'for information leading to missing woman and child.' The photo of Mrs. Munro was dark and blurry, a bad reproduction of the picture Adelia had seen in the hotel suite. Why hadn't she thought to remove it? There was no need to read details of the reward. She knew they were in trouble.

"The men here may keep their bone boxes shut since none of them much likes the law. They may know about Ernest, maybe through the boy himself, maybe through the wind in the trees, but they haven't seen the need to flap their yaps." Captain Jokinen shrugged. "But now money is on the table, and that changes a man. I fear the announcement could be in the newspaper next."

"How long do we have?" Adelia asked around the lump in her throat.

"No time at all. We must leave before dawn. I will take you. Get the boy. Pack light. Hurry."

Harriet and Adelia hustled back to their room. Harriet shook Gerty awake, whispered to her, and the old girl gave no guff but left for the kitchen.

"I am coming with you," Harriet said to Adelia. "No arguments."

"But Harriet..." Adelia protested as she forced possessions into valises for Ernest and herself.

"I dote on the boy, too, Adelia. And you. I must know you are both safe."

"But you are not well."

"The subject is closed."

Adelia wouldn't admit it, but she was relieved. Harriet's presence was as much solace for her fears as Adelia herself was for Ernest.

While they packed, Gerty made them sandwiches from thick slabs of ham and warm sourdough. They left with the Captain carrying a quarrelsome Ernest on his shoulders, the boy's bag under an arm, and a lantern he held high. Harriet followed with the food and one small case, leaving most of her possessions behind. Adelia was last in line with a second lantern, her valise and sewing kit. The night was cold but thankfully dry. Adelia's mind flitted from place to place like a lightning bug.

What will Hai think come morning when we have disappeared? Will we ever return to Home Soggy Home? Who in the camp might try for the reward? How will Martin feel when he finds me gone without a trace? Martin! How will I feel?

The Captain tramped down the trail that paralleled the skid road. They moved as quickly as possible, but each stumbled over the roots in the road, hidden in the darkness. They maintained silence until they were far from the camp, and then Adelia heard the Captain soothing Ernest with a tale of the high seas, one that involved him killing a sea monster called the Kraken. In time the little boy leaned forward, put his arms around the Captain's neck, and placed his cheek atop the man's hat. Adelia thought he must be deep asleep.

When Harriet fell, the Captain turned back to help her up and added her suitcase to his burden. "Thank you, Captain Jokinen," she said, sounding weak to Adelia.

"The name is Elias to you, ma'am. Now grab my elbow and hold onto me."

As the dawn to the east turned the cool, damp forest from ebony to emerald, Ernest stirred.

"Mornin', boy. We've traversed the night and are out of danger," the Captain said, "but it were close."

"We were in danger?"

"It was the hidebehind, lad. A fearsome critter who wanders the woods at night. It sucks in its big belly to hide behind a tree, then pounces and consumes yer innards. But see that bit of sun? It skeered him away. We're all safe and sound now."

"That isn't true, is it? Mr. Witless would have said. You're telling a thumper." Ernest's suspicion brought smiles to his traveling companions' grim faces.

"Well, it could be true. It could be, Peanut," Harriet said. "Although I believe the Captain is inclined to exaggerate."

"Always good to question what you are told, Ernest, if it sounds like so much moonshine on the water," Adelia added.

"Ah! The cruel tongues of womenfolk, flapping

like red rags! They surround us, boy!"

Soon thereafter, Captain Jokinen pointed out his boat on the Youngs River just ahead of them, waiting to take them away.

"Are we going back to Skipanon?" Harriet asked once he helped her seat herself on a barrel. The Captain opened a weathered chest and handed out bedraggled blankets to tuck around his three passengers.

"No, ma'am. It was there I saw the reward poster and shipped out alone to find you, too hurried to gather a crew. We're for Astoria, if you all agree. I have a load of canned salmon awaiting me there."

"I know nobody in Astoria. But I have money to pay for the passage," Adelia said. Even Harriet looked surprised.

The Captain said, "Do you now? Best you keep that nugget to yourself, my girl. There be rogues around these waters whose pockets are at low tide."

"But I owe you for..."

"We will bargain later. A Finnish woman named Raina Borg takes boarders into her home. It is clean and respectable, as is she, well, up to a point. Last I knew she had a room. For a reasonable price, she will take in a recently widowed woman with a niece and nephew to feed."

"How do you know I am a widow?" Harriet asked, arching a brow.

"I confess I do not know. But I believe it to be a

reasonable explanation to cover your current condition."

"What? What do you mean, sir?"

He gave her a long look. His voice, when it came, was less boisterous than before. "If you would be willing to consider a humble bachelor such as myself, I could take on a different type of cargo altogether. I could take on a wife."

Harriet stared at him, as he had at her. She finally spoke. "Elias. You may call me Harriet."

Adelia realized some kind of a bargain had been struck, but she couldn't figure out what or why. Fear and flight and exhaustion dulled her brain. Maybe later she would figure it out, when she was not so tired.

She had heard tell that Astoria was the greatest city on the West Coast north of San Francisco. Treacherous, yes, but full of riches and hope for the person tough enough to mine it. It was invigorating just to think about. But for now she curled her arms around Ernest, and they slept as the little riverboat worked its way along the shore of Youngs Bay in the dawn light

* * *

Maybe if they had approached Astoria by road, it would not have seemed such a brawling, godless place. But their arrival from the water was like nearing a dragon that reeked of rot and belched out smoke as it rested on the riverside awaiting fresh meat.

"The most wicked place on earth, this town be called," the Captain said to Adelia.

She was standing next to him in the pilot house in the morning gray, wide-eyed and amazed at the smoking stacks and dozens of masts in front of her eyes. Never had she seen so many fishing boats, sailing ships, ocean steamers. The *Inland Intruder* weaved its way between them like a shuttle across a loom. This was certainly no Paris of the West.

The worst odor came from salmon canneries, dozens of them pockmarking the docks. Adelia caught the scents of sewage and sawmill runoff along with the salmon offal.

"It is stinky, Addy!"

"Hold your nose, Ernest."

In the marshy caverns under the docks she saw rats so big she mistook them for tomcats. "It would be well to shut your eyes, too, Ernest, if what you see concerns you."

Nearly all the people up on the docks were Chinese men and women coming and going from canneries. Fishing boats gathered outside each cannery, disgorging their catches of salmon. The fishermen all looked like one breed of immigrants, too, uniformed as they were in pea coats, denims and curved billed hats. They shouted at each other, laughed and sang in a language new to her. But it reminded her of Katja.

"Finns to catch the salmon. Chinks to gut and pack in the canneries. Keeps the work getting done by the folks best at it." The Captain pointed in the direction of the fishermen. "Finns be my people, born to fish. Brokers bring Chinks and Finns from our homelands by the boat load."

The riverboat arrived at the waterfront and docked parallel to it, between two big freight steamers. The street in front of Adelia was raised high over the water. The whole town seemed to stand on pilings.

"Big fire a decade back. Started in a saw mill and burnt a chunk of the downtown. Still, the fopdoodles rebuilt on sticks again. To avoid the tides."

Commerce around them was brisk with other boats loading and unloading kegs of nails, barrels of butter, sacks of flour, sugar, coffee, salt, and stacks of cordwood.

"Why all that?" Adelia asked, watching stevedores carry hundreds of pounds of bacon into the engine room of a riverboat far sleeker and fancier than the *Inland Intruder.*

"Ah. She be a steamer takes passengers from here to Portland. Captain adds bacon to the fire box. Hottest fire for fastest speed. Nincompoop will blow the boiler one day, mark my words."

Harriet, Adelia and Ernest followed the Captain as he climbed up wooden stairs to the street level. He stopped a horse-drawn cab and spoke briefly to the driver as the females loaded their possessions into the back. Elias handed a letter to Harriet. "The driver knows where to go and this is a letter of introduction to Raina Borg who runs the boardinghouse. Do not set foot on the waterfront here or anywhere as you cross Swilltown onto the hill. "

"Swilltown?" Adelia asked.

"For all the booze and boozers, as you will see. Stay in the wagon until you get to the house on Eighth. I'll be by this evening to be sure you are settled." He stopped talking long enough to touch Harriet's cheek, then he went on. "Now I'm off to find my load of salmon."

The waterfront was crammed with ramshackle storefronts and warehouses on one side, open to the wide river and its traffic on the other. The steady horse pulled the cab carefully along the wooden road, negotiating around the tracks of horse drawn trolleys and dozens of pedestrians. The Chinese men all looked like Hai to Adelia, and the women like the one her father had brought home. She recognized Clatsop and Chinook natives, selling berries, baskets and small pelts along the road. But for the first time, she saw dozens of rough seamen loiter in front of sailors' boardinghouses, three cowboys with guns in their holsters riding hard-mouthed horses, Negro dancers in top hats, one enormous tattooed South Seas islander.

There were no ladies down here at the docks, except maybe those two in another horse drawn taxi, no doubt on their way to an outgoing ship.

Dozens of ramshackle doorways interspersed with saloons, seeming to be the entrances for housing above them.

"Why are all the curtains red?" asked Ernest. "You could have asked the captain that, Peanut. I am quite sure he would know." Harriet whispered to Adelia, "Bawdies and cribs. The better trade is still to come around the corner, or so I am told." It was Adelia's introduction to the brothels, the biggest land-based business in Astoria.

Adelia could hardly take it all in. Astoria was filled with stench, noise, grime, excitement. It was at once the most evil, exhilarating place she'd ever seen. She had heard the term electricity, and she felt as though such magic sparked through her. For better or worse, her curiosity was energized by all she saw.

As their cab turned south and uphill toward yellow clay banks, saloons continued to line the street but other stores mixed in. Grocers and eateries and tailors. The higher the horse climbed, the better the neighborhood. Ahead of her, Adelia could see squares of color where houses dotted the ridge. The big trees were gone, cut to build Astoria's Douglas fir plank streets, timbers for ships, and packing crates for millions of cans of salmon.

As they crossed Commercial Street, Adelia turned back to the west, hoping to see the mouth of the river where it met the sea and the new jetty that was reaching completion. She wondered if it would join Terrible Tilly in making the Columbia a safer place to enter, a place no longer given the nickname Graveyard of the Pacific. But fog was rolling in, climbing the hill faster than the horse could make the same journey.

The house at the address the Captain had given them was square with a low-pitched roof. It was constructed of wood, the most readily available building material. For all its sturdy squat shape, it was anything but plain. Decorative brackets and towers and curlicues disguised it with splendor from its broad eaves to its wide porch. A two-tone paint job added to the festive feel. A cupola plopped on the roof, like the cherry on the ice cream sundae Mrs. Munro had bought for Adelia last summer. The sharpness of the memory cut like a knife.

"Butter upon bacon," Harriet muttered. The three tired travelers stood on the sidewalk where the horse cab dropped them, and they gawked at their new surroundings. The houses in this neighborhood were as much a surprise for their glamour as the hovels along the waterfront were for their lack of it. Only with a closer look was it clear that the homes were not at their best, their glory years behind them.

"I've seen house pattern books," Harriet said. "I

think this is called Italianate."

"I think it should be called foolhardy," answered Adelia. "Who needs a porch like that with nothing but fog to look at?"

"I am hungry, Addy. And tired."

"Then let us go in and take care of all our problems."

* * *

Since leaving her father's home, Adelia had learned women were in general less formidable than men. The imposing presence of the Finn, Raina Borg, argued against that. Her hair was stretched into a tight little knot at the back of her head, seeming to pull her features into a pained scowl. Not one strand was allowed to slip free and soften her demeanor. Even at her advanced age - Adelia guessed maybe in the forties - Mrs. Borg appeared as inflexible as an artillery shell, wrapped chin to toe in an iron-willed dress. It did not flow as she walked, comporting itself as a stiff outer casing. Adelia wondered what sort of corset stays and ties would produce such armor. It was something to discuss with Harriet later in privacy.

Mrs. Borg's expression lightened slightly around her mouth and eyes when she read the letter from the Captain. "So Captain Jokinen would have me believe you are a widow of fine virtue and breeding, along with your niece and nephew. Is that correct, Mrs.

Wright?"

Adelia wondered about Harriet's use of her last name. Then she realized she had never heard Harriet's own. Maybe Harriet thought it would be easier for her to change her name than to ask Ernest to do it again. Something else to talk about when they were by themselves.

"Oh, yes," said Harriet. "I am a quiet lady, used to hard work and clean living."

"Have you skills?"

"Of course. I am a cook with fine references, should you need assistance in the kitchen."

"I clean and sew," Adelia added. "I will give you no trouble, ma'am. Neither will my brother."

"I am hungry," said Ernest.

"Hush now, child. Seen but not heard, you know," Harriet smiled at Ernest. "And, yes, Mrs. Borg, it is the case that my husband has passed. Widowhood is not an easy state of affairs. I see by your own somber dress you might agree."

Mrs. Borg stiffened once more. "No. My husband is quite well, thank you. He is a bar pilot on the river which is where he met Elias Jokinen. I simply prefer a less frivolous color in my attire."

"Ah. And a fine deep shade of purple it is," Adelia cut in. "Done by a seamstress with true talent at manipulating heavy linen." She bit back a smile.

"Addy, will this lady feed us?" Ernest insisted. He

had not been raised to have his desires put on a burner at the back of a stove.

"Yes, boy. For the proper price, I shall. I do have one room available, as it happens."

They toured the house then. The front living area had been changed into a sitting room with enough chairs for boarders. A huge bookcase held an eclectic collection along with back issues of several magazines.

"I serve two meals on the hour of seven, morning and evening. Miss a meal and there will be no reduction in your rate. The front door is locked at 10 o'clock, as I maintain the safeguards of a good home. If you are late, do not bother knocking. Find accommodation elsewhere."

The room for the three of them had no doubt been a family bedroom in the original house. It had a small fireplace, a window onto the street out front, and held a large bed for Adelia and Harriet, as well as a time-worn settee large enough for Ernest. There was no closet but the room had pegs on one wall and a dresser with a mirror, a wash stand, and basin.

"The curtains are not red," Ernest said. "I thought they all were."

The corners of Mrs. Borg's stiff lips turned upward. A low rumbling sound escaped from her inner regions. Adelia thought it might be a chuckle. Then the lady stiffened again and said, "No, young man, and we will hear no more about that."

She marched them to the bathroom which was just two doors down. "Bath rules are posted on the wall. Do not break them," said Mrs. Borg.

Adelia handed over enough to pay for a month. "I keep the money for my aunt," she explained when she noticed Mrs. Borg's raised eyebrows. "Thieves are less likely to expect such an arrangement when we are traveling."

"Clever," said their new landlady. "Now bring the boy to the kitchen. To tide you over until dinner, I have *korvapuusti.*"

All three were relieved to discover it wasn't some sort of torture device. It was the Finnish word for cinnamon rolls.

Chapter Thirteen

December 1893

That night, in an unfamiliar room in an unfamiliar city, Adelia was at the bottom of her emotional resources. The escape in the night, the boat to Astoria, the amazing arrival, the new place to live. None of this was foreseeable less than twenty-four hours before. Her feelings were one big knot of snakes: fear of flight, sorrow to leave the cook camp, confusion about next steps, a sharp loss over Martin, worry that Mrs. Munro did not know where Ernest was tonight. Adelia felt drained, entirely too exhausted to think anything through until after she slept.

Captain Jokinen had come to check on them as he said he would. He'd stayed for dinner and even drew smiles from the stern Mrs. Borg. Mr. Borg said not a word the entire evening, so Adelia had no immediate opinion of him. Maybe his English was impossible.

Maybe he was overwhelmed to find himself married to Mrs. Borg.

There were three other boarders. One was a girl not much older than Adelia. The others were a couple so wrapped together in their own world they were hardly present at the dinner table at all. They had eyes only for each other, floating in a cloud of new love.

"Must be like dining with Romeo and Juliet," Harriet muttered. But Adelia's curiosity was already asleep, and the rest of her would be soon. She'd consider all these new people the next day.

When Harriet and Ernest both settled for the night, Adelia gave her new living quarters a final inspection before turning down the oil lamp on the mantel. This was the fanciest bedroom she ever had, shabbier than the Munro suite in the hotel to be sure, but far nicer than she'd ever hoped for herself.

The dresser was a great joy. Harriet had claimed two drawers, leaving one for Ernest and one for Adelia. *Imagine having a large drawer of your own!* Before dinner, she'd unpacked the extra knickers and camisole from her valise, then placed these dainties alongside her sewing box. She rolled Mrs. Munro's money inside her extra pair of stockings. In the large mirror above the chest of drawers, graying and wavy with age, she could see her whole upper body at one time. Scraggly hair surrounded a freckled face far thinner than she imagined. This would take some serious contemplation when she wasn't dead on her feet.

The place was so swanky that the chamber pot was even the same pattern as the basin, ewer, and soap dish. Matching toilet-ware had been used in the hotel, of course, but she'd never imagined such luxury for herself, even though fine crazing webbed through the surface glaze of the porcelain. There was even a large copper can to carry hot water from the bathroom when they needed it.

Best of all, the room was immaculate; neither she nor Harriet could be fooled on that score. The carpet was faded and old, but still serviceable. She wondered if it had graced the sitting room at one time. There was no hint of vermin, fleas or bedbugs, in either it or the bedding. And there was little trace of dust or ash from the fireplace. Mrs. Borg rose a peg or two in Adelia's estimation.

It was almost enough to make her stop worrying about Lucien P. Durand, Mrs. Munro and, yes, Martin, at least for this one night. But after she hopped into bed, she allowed herself a quiet sniffle.

It happened that Harriet was not asleep. She reached over and cradled the girl in her arms. "Adelia, you are only thirteen, but you are called upon to be wise beyond your years. Ernest's mother could not have chosen anyone more dependable than you."

This bit of sympathy opened Adelia's tear ducts to

full deluge.

Harriet continued to comfort in a low voice. "It is asking a lot of a girl to care for a little boy, especially when it means she has to stay on the run."

Hiccup. Sniff. Blow.

"We all are tested, some earlier or harder than others. I am so impressed by your ability to handle adversity, come what may."

Adelia had never been so praised before. Nobody had made her feel this proud of herself. As her storm subsided, she thanked Harriet. And she fell asleep realizing that tears of sorrow and tears of gratitude were not so very different. Both came from the heart.

* * *

The next morning, Harriet, Adelia, and Ernest stayed at the breakfast table after the other boarders left for work. Mrs. Borg gave them permission, as long as they cleared the table when they were done. Ernest was happily eating banana slices off his cream of wheat. He was enthralled with this funny-looking fruit with the funny-sounding name that was a new import into the country.

Harriet and Adelia perused the help wanted ads in the newspaper they spread open in front of them. Adelia was a careful shepherd of Mrs. Munro's money, feeling it was meant only for Ernest. She did not presume that she should spend it on herself, so finding employment was an immediate need. "I cannot leave Ernest unattended. So I must find sewing projects that I can do here," she said to Harriet.

"I will watch him when I can, you know that. But I have to locate work to pay my way, as well."

"No shortage of jobs for honest women willing to work," said Mrs. Borg entering the room with a stack of table linens. "You mentioned yesterday, Mrs. Wright, that you are a cook."

"Yes. Most recently, for large parties of loggers," Harriet answered, not mentioning at which camp. "But can these ads be trusted? Hard to tell what a man means when he's looking for a 'healthy young woman of pleasant aspect' just to feed him."

The landlady placed the linens on the table and sat down. Adelia thought she heard the starch in the dress actually crack. Mrs. Borg said, "Cooking for loggers is a fine reference in Astoria. We know how exacting they are about their fixins. I believe you should speak with Mr. Borg this evening. He may have something for you."

"I thought he was a bar pilot. How does cooking fit into that?" Harriet asked, cocking her head.

Adelia wondered the same thing.

"He is. But he has another business, too," Mrs. Borg said after a slight pause.

"And what might that be?"

Mrs. Borg began folding napkins. Adelia reached for a half dozen and folded as well. Her curiosity leaped at the chance of a good bit of eavesdropping.

"Mr. Borg is a pilot, to be sure. A well-paid and dangerous job, getting sailing ships to and from the Columbia safely. It has allowed us to raise four sons in this home, all now on their own." She appeared to choose her next words with a certain amount of care. "Mr. Borg invested in property around the port, as have many of the leading families in Astoria. He built a fine saloon, not one of those filthy sin holes you saw on Astor Street. His is a gentlemen's club, with live theatre, billiards, occasional boxing matches and other *entertainment* for a high grade of patron."

"Mrs. Borg, I am far too old to be a...a...damsel of the evening, you know."

What the darnation was a damsel of the evening? Adelia wondered. *Could Harriet possibly mean...*

"Of course, Mrs. Wright. Nothing like that! But even high born men need to eat, do they not? Mr. Borg's saloon serves evening meals, and he could use a really good cook. If you are as you claim to be."

"The name of this establishment?"

"Ambrosia. You will find it down the hill on the corner of Bond."

"I am most grateful for the suggestion, Mrs. Borg. We women must always have each other's best interest in mind. I will remember your kindness." Harriet turned to Adelia. "Shall we take a walk about town this morning?"

That evening, Harriet prepared the meal for the Borg household. "Won't hurt to sound hoity-toity if I'd be cooking in a fancy gent's saloon," she said with a wink to Adelia who was lending a hand. So her luscious beef vegetable pie became *Boeuf en Croute*. And her apple cobbler was a *Tarte de Pommes*. The meal was a great success, and by the next day, Harriet was employed noon to midnight as the new chef at Ambrosia. She was even given a key to the back door of the boardinghouse, to allow herself in long past the evening curfew.

* * *

Adelia and her sewing kit were in the sitting room. The large front windows might have let in sun if it had not been raining again. She had written to Mrs. Munro that morning, passing on their new address and asking her to share the news with Lucien P. Durand, if they happened to still be in communication. Now, Adelia was lengthening a pair of Ernest's trousers. "We'll have to call your long pants longer pants. You are growing tall."

He looked up from the picture book of ships that he had found in the old bookcase at the far end of the room. Its shelves contained marvels for them both, a treasure trove of dime novels with titles like *Frontier*

Captive and *Gunfight at Deadman Creek,* back copies of *The Ladies' Home Journal* and *La Nouvelle Mode,* numerous volumes on domestic arts, strategies of war, Grecian gods, etiquette for gentlemen. Adelia could not imagine that any of this was to Mrs. Borg's taste but had been left behind by boarders through the years. And any astute landlady knew the benefit of offering free entertainment to her flock.

"Will I be tall as my father?" Ernest asked.

Adelia was startled. He rarely talked about his father. When he did, it was without a hint of anger or joy or loss or regret. She often wondered what he thought of the man. "You'll be taller, I reckon. And you are even now more handsome."

Ernest quietly turned one page of ships and then another. Finally he said, "I like the Captain. Mr. Lucien, too. And Mr. Witless."

"They are all good men, Ernest. It is okay to like them more than your father. He does not have to be your favorite. I know I prefer them to my father, too." In this regard, Ernest and she really were like brother and sister.

A cheerful voice startled them. "I do hope your name isn't something awful like Clara or Maude."

Adelia looked up to see the other young boarder stroll through the archway into the sitting room and reshelf *Girl Tenderfoot Saves the Day*. They had only been introduced by last names at the dinner table yesterday. She said, "This is my brother, Ernest, and I am Adelia. Is that too awful a name?"

"No. Adelia is nice. A little overused, maybe, but nice. I am Suzette Juliette."

"Golly. That's beautiful."

"Yes. But here is my secret. My real name is Bertha. Like a goldarn milk cow or something. So I changed it to be highfalutin and French. Much better for business."

Adelia wondered what business a girl who called herself Suzette Juliette might be in. Especially one whose hair seemed entirely too red for the real world. The girl answered before the question was asked.

"I am a hairdresser."

"What is that?"

"I help ladies look their very best by making their hair soft, supple, and something to be envied. My styles are the best in Astoria. Very creative, very look-of-the-day."

"I had not thought of the ladies of Astoria as quite so fashionable," Adelia said, thinking about the tight topknot and stiff bombazine chosen by Mrs. Borg today.

"Not just the uptown ladies. The ladies of the night, as well. They are the ones who know a thing or two about fashion and attracting a man's eye."

Adelia was taken aback not just by the thought but the courage to say such a thing aloud. "But...but, do such ladies have means to pay for a service like the dressing of hair?"

"Oh my yes! In Astoria? It's big business here, my new friend. I heard Mr. Borg say good prostitutes often make good money. More than women in other professions. More than many men, for that matter."

"Can they afford another service, too, do you suppose?" Adelia saw an opportunity and pounced on it.

"Have you one to offer?"

"I am a seamstress. I could help with their attire, to hem and alter as they wish."

"What an idea!" Suzette Juliette clapped her hands. Her golden eyes sparkled and her red locks bounced. "We will work together, you on clothes, and I on makeup and hair. Oh, what a team we shall be!"

"Team?"

"Yes. And to start, we both must appear smart. How we look determines how we are treated in this world. I have a dress you could alter for me in the waist and bodice, and you could use my touch on your hair. I'll get my things and meet you in your room."

And that was that.

* * *

Adelia's hair was long, never really cut although she sometimes trimmed off the ends. At work in the hotel or logging camp, she wore it in a long thick braid down her narrow back or pinned up high to keep it out of dishwater or pie plates. Nobody had ever done the things that Suzette Juliette was about to do.

"What is she going to do, Addy?" Ernest asked, playing on the carpet of their room with his toy horses that seemed to be racing around her lighthouse.

"Well, I cannot be sure," Adelia said, unbraiding her hair in front of the mirror.

Soon Suzette Juliette arrived with an armload of bottle, combs, and arcane items. She dropped everything on the chest of drawers.

"Is that a torture device?" Adelia asked, staring at a vicious weapon with wooden handles and metal blades.

"It is a curling iron. And yes it is a torture device if I burn either of us after heating it in the fire." Suzette Juliette reached over to run fingers through her new friend's mane. "Beautiful. But far too long for the modern woman. Sit."

Adelia did so on the room's one straight back chair. Without hesitation, Suzette Juliette picked up her scissors and sliced through the thick fall, shortening it to shoulder blade length. Adelia could not see the mirror, but she felt the lightness of her head and neck as great piles of ash blonde hair rained down around her.

"Suzette Juliette, what have we done?" she asked,

feeling as though she'd had a sort of amputation. "Is my head a skating rink now?" She lifted her hands and patted herself.

"Oh twaddle! You are not bald. No looking back. Customers will love you. It is the price of getting along. Now we must wash it. Ernest, if you will stay here while we are gone to wash Adelia's hair, I will give you this candy." She picked a piece of horehound from her pocket.

"Do you have two?" Ernest countered.

"Ha! Such flimflammery! Yes, young scallywag, you may have two."

"One is for Addy when she gets back."

The two girls moved to the bathroom, and Adelia was soon stripped to her camisole and bloomers, kneeling over the tub as Suzette Juliette washed her cropped hair and pronounced, "Glorious! The whipped egg will make it brighter, glossier." The hairdresser picked carefully through the wet locks. "You have brought no nomads from forest to town. Let us hope you avoid nits here as well, although it is nearly impossible."

Back in the room, they sat for an hour next to the fire waiting for Adelia's hair to dry. Ernest grew bored with hair and climbed onto his settee to nap. Adelia realized Suzette Juliette and she were actually chatting. She had never had a girlfriend her own age. The closest thing to it was the Ghostly Girl at the hotel. This was such fun.

As her hair dried, it began to curl. "You cut it curly!" Adelia marveled when she felt it lifting off her shoulders.

"Well, I shall take the credit. But the curl is yours. The weight of your braid was pulling it out. You are lucky. A nice new style will last for days with this much curl."

While Ernest slept, Suzette Juliette slipped on a dress which was too large for her hourglass waist. Adelia pinned it. "I can make it work for you, but I do not have thread this shade of yellow. I will need to purchase a spool." The dress was set aside while the girls looked through the lady models and clothes in the Sears and Roebuck catalog.

"I like this girl's hair. And this. Don't you? You will need a better dress if you are to present yourself as a seamstress. Do you have one?"

"Yes. I have one," Adelia said pointing to the one dress from Mrs. Munro that the hotel maids had not cut to bits. She wondered what had happened to those two gibfaces. Nothing good, she hoped. Her own plans for them had been interrupted by her flight.

"You will need at least one more frock which I suppose will be easy for you to make." Suzette Juliette flipped to the pages buried deep in the catalog. "And your underwear? Time to grow up a bit, I think. We will shop in the morning for thread and fabric and petticoats. But now let us dress your hair."

She used a pomade she had made from palm, rose, and jasmine oils plus a touch of bear grease. Then she manipulated the curling iron with no burns to her fingers or Adelia's ears. Suzette Juliette layered the top strands into a loose chignon but let the natural curl fluff the loose hair in the back and at the sides. "There now. Up in a bun or down, it will look fine for days. And I can always touch it up."

Adelia went to the mirror. This was a different girl from the last time she looked. She had slept, so the fragile skin under her eyes was no longer dark. And her eyes were more blue than bloodshot. But mostly, it was this new hair, a swirling, sweet-smelling cloud. A crowning glory. She did not look like a girl. She looked like a young woman. "I look...I look..."

"You look beautiful, my new friend."

* * *

Adelia had things to think about. Personal things. Everything felt like one big problematic pile. She needed to find compartments in her brain, like pigeon holes in a roll top desk. Each would contain an item. For that, she wanted time alone. Right after breakfast the next day, she went for a walk while Harriet kept an eye on Ernest. Adelia would be back soon to go to a dry goods store with Suzette Juliette before Harriet left for work.

It was clear but cold. "Here, wear this," Suzette Juliette called, stopping her at the door.

"Oh!" Adelia took the proffered cape and wrapped herself in downy blue wool which reached nearly to her ankles. Her own cape was only waist length. She instantly loved the drama of this one. She felt like twirling. And so she did, calling a fond farewell to her friend as she spun out the front door, onto the wide porch, and banged into a man with enough force to knock him down the top step. She landed beside him.

"Nice to meet you, miss. Are you okay?"

"Never better." Adelia stood and shook herself out, already feeling the bruise on her butt which was nowhere near as painful as the bruise to her pride. She covered her embarrassment with a huff. "Why were you loitering here on this porch?"

The young man stood, as well. "I was not loitering, miss. I was about to knock on the door when you knocked into me."

"Well, do not let me stand in your way any longer." She noticed that his eyes looked entirely too jolly at her expense so she flounced on down the steps, swishing the cape.

"I am very sorry, miss," he called after her.

"I am sure you are," she snapped over her shoulder.

"Maybe we could start again?"

"Sir," she said, stopping on the walk to look back. "I have so many things to think about now, I have no room for another one." She turned and hip-switched on down the sidewalk.

The near miss with a young man put her in mind of Martin Driscoll, Irish tenor and fine kisser. She wanted to write to him. But, really, could she? Nobody at the logging camp knew where she had gone, well, except Lucien P. Durand who may know soon, if Mrs. Munro told him. But no one else, not Gerty, not Hai, not Witless. And if they didn't know, they couldn't be tempted by a reward as big as the one that hung over Ernest's head. She liked Martin. A lot. She thought kissing was a sorry thing to give up. But. Who knew whom Ernest might have told? He was just a little boy. Maybe the whole camp knew their story. And a letter to Martin might well get opened by someone else who might tell someone else.

She knew the truth of it. She could not write to Martin, not ever. Ernest's safety was her primary responsibility. She had committed to Mrs. Munro. She did not give any thought to how Martin might feel, that a boy older than herself might well have seen their relationship as far more than a crush, that he might be grieving. Instead, she placed him in her first mental pigeon hole and sealed it shut.

Another pigeon hole was opened for whoever might still be looking for them. The Captain, Harriet, and Mrs. Munro knew where they were. The Borgs had no reason to question them, nor did anyone else in the boardinghouse or at Ambrosia. Her father would not care that she had disappeared. And if her brother was looking for her, well, she had friends now, people who cared more about her than him. She felt safe from Wiley, although she wasn't so sure he was safe from her, if and when he crossed her path again.

Now about Mrs. Munro. She belonged in more than one slot so Adelia tried to separate out the issues involving her. First, about money. She did not spend Mrs. Munro's money unless it was for Ernest. But was Adelia being a bit too narrow in her self-imposed definition? Since she was Ernest's lifeline until his mother returned, wouldn't Mrs. Munro want Adelia to be as strong a lifeline as possible? She had to work, of course. And wouldn't it be better to be a seamstress than a dishwasher? She could sew right here in the boardinghouse where she could stay with Ernest. Mrs. Munro would surely agree. But to be a seamstress, she must spend seed money for more needles, threads, measuring tools, bindings. Adelia had never really created a whole dress from scratch; all her clothes had been hand-me-downs that she had altered to fit. She needed fabrics with which to practice. She must upgrade her own look in order to upgrade the look of others. Adelia decided to take $8.00 of Mrs. Munro's money to the dry goods store to fund her fledgling business. Pigeon hole number two.

The third involved Mrs. Munro and Ernest. When would the two unite? Adelia had hoped that Lucien P. Durand would deliver the boy to San Francisco. It was possible that could still work, but the man may well be gone from her life now that she was gone from his camp. She sighed and kicked a pebble next to the sidewalk. She was growing up herself. As much as she loved Mrs. Munro, Ernest was becoming a harder issue to handle. She would never let Mrs. Munro down, of course. But she had to admit that sometimes having a little boy to protect was very hard on a girl. No, on a young woman, she corrected herself. She would miss him terribly if he was gone, but wouldn't it be fun to go out with Suzette Juliette without a child in tow? Ah well. This pigeon hole would have to stay open for a time until an answer happened along.

She turned back toward the house to meet Suzette Juliette. The fourth slot in her brain also involved Mrs. Munro. Adelia had killed her husband. There had been no opportunity to explain to Mrs. Munro, who still must think she herself was the murderess. This kind of confession could not be put in a letter. And when would they ever be face to face?

Adelia sighed. On her journey away from the home of her father, she had broken many rules of behavior. First, she had turned her back on family. She stole money and someone else's carrots. She hid in other people's barns where she did not belong. She begged for food from Ida Rose. She had told lies. None of that rivaled the breach in conduct of actually smacking someone with a fire poker.

Had he lived, Mr. Munro would have seen his wife and Adelia both imprisoned at best. He would have done heaven knows what to Ernest. Nonetheless, revenge was not her business, or so she had been told. This was another pigeon hole she would need to leave open, at least until she had opportunity to speak with Mrs. Munro. In the meantime, she was not sorry the man was dead. *Oh, what a bad girl I am becoming!*

The final slot in her brain was for Harriet. The new chef of Ambrosia had asked Adelia to let out her three dresses. She was gaining weight. Was the food at the camp and now the restaurant really that good? Or was something else going on with Harriet? Adelia began to suspect.

By the time she returned to the Borg home, the young man she had flattened was gone. A pity, that. She really should apologize. Besides, she'd like another look at those laughing eyes.

Chapter Fourteen

February 1894

The next two months passed in a flurry. Christmas came and went, as did the New Year. Ambrosia as concert hall, game room, gentlemen's saloon, and purveyor of first-rate daughters of sin, was already a popular club. Now its restaurant experienced a boom in business under the tyrannical new cook.

Adelia, from her recent past as a flunkee, knew Harriet was a she-bear when it came to a kitchen. But she was tickled how it surprised Mr. Borg.

He voiced a slight complaint one languid afternoon in the boardinghouse sitting room, on a Sunday when Ambrosia was closed. The dreamy young couple was out floating about in a bubble of love, Ernest was in his room for a snooze, and the other boarders were reading or chatting.

"My cooking staff has made mention of your, ah,

management techniques, Mrs. Wright," Mr. Borg ventured. "They say you can be, ah, shall I say, very direct."

Adelia tensed. He had actually criticized Harriet! *Oh dear.*

"It is *my* cooking staff, Mr. Borg. And I shall hire and fire until the entire group knows pan handles from their own talliwags."

Adelia tried very hard to concentrate on *The Sinners and Saints of Big Gulch Spread,* but a giggle bubbled out anyway. "Oh how funny this book is," she said weakly.

"Leave it to me, Mr. Borg, and your kitchen will run smoothly with a superior level of cuisine, " Harriet told her employer. Then she dropped a bomb. "I have also hired new waitresses. They may look like gorgons, but they can juggle trays of food as they cut through crowds."

Mr. Borg sputtered, "But! But! My wagtails should be able to serve tables while they, ah, display their wares, Mrs. Wright."

"Well, they cannot. My good food gets cold while they wink and wiggle at the customers. Let them do what they do, and my staff will serve the kind of meals that live up to the Ambrosia name. We will make men cry mercy for their bellies, and then your girls can work on their bollocks."

Mr. Borg, a taciturn man at best, gave in. He left

the room shortly thereafter.

Mrs. Borg explained that he was frightened of his new cook. "He'd rather pilot ships through wild waters than confront you," she said with a jolly laugh. "But I'm the bookkeeper, and I say you are a miracle to Ambrosia coffers as well as our patrons' bellies!"

"I am glad you approve, Mrs. Borg, as I have a favor to ask."

"What might that be?"

Curious herself, Adelia gave up all pretense at finding out what was happening in Big Gulch. She put the book down.

"I am so at home in my Ambrosia kitchen, that with your approval, it is the perfect spot to hold my wedding to Captain Elias Jokinen."

* * *

Harriet had never actually told Adelia she was pregnant. It became so obvious that any kind of announcement or confession was irrelevant. But she did ask Adelia to make her a dress for her wedding, one that could be altered after her belly collapsed again. Adelia took it on as her present to the bride.

Adelia had been her own first customer as a dressmaker. She carefully disassembled the adored dress from Mrs. Munro, then laid all the pieces out on the dining room table. Using them as a pattern, she cut into a new length of cloth from the dry goods store. Then she reassembled the original dress as well as the new. Next, she repeated the process with one of Suzette Juliette's far frillier frocks. She measured her own body and Suzette Juliette's to see how clothes inches related to body inches. At last, she measured Harriet and began the wedding dress from a lovely rose wool that Harriet selected.

Adelia based the design loosely on one of her two patterns, but instead of cinching the middle, she pleated the fabric so it flowed from the empire waist. It would grow as wide as a woman with child would need.

"It is lovely," Harriet said, standing on a stool.

"The color suits you. All colors suit you," Adelia said then got to her knees. She put pins in her mouth and began working on the hem.

Adelia had never really considered how handsome Harriet was, but she did now. When the dress was done, and Suzette Juliette had worked her magic with a rose and pearls in Harriet's dark hair, the Captain would see that the competent, tough woman he had claimed was also a beauty.

"I hope you will help with this baby as you have with Ernest," Harriet said, surprising Adelia with this reference to the child within. Harriet placed a hand lightly on the top of Adelia's head. "I know you have always longed for Mrs. Munro, would choose her as your mother. But I would be proud if you thought of me in that role, as well."

Adelia looked up, mouth full of pins. She hoped they were subterfuge for how truly speechless she felt. Mrs. Munro was flashy fun, elegance, light. Harriet was proficiency, ambition. If you couldn't have all these characteristics in one mother who didn't abandon you, surely it was splendid to have two stand-ins.

"My life has not always been easy. I have paid the price many times." Harriet patted her round belly. "This little bundle is a gratuity from a guest at the hotel, and that is enough to say about that." Her voice broke but, being Harriet, she muscled on. "But you, Adelia. You have added a softness to the months I've known you. I have grown a new nerve where you are concerned. It feels very fragile, could be hurt so easily if you turned away."

Adelia removed the pins from her mouth, replacing them in the cushion attached to her wrist. Still on her knees, she put her arms around Harriet's girth and placed her head on the baby compartment. "I will love this tyke as a sister or brother. And that means loving you as a mother."

The wedding was a delightful celebration on a week day morning before Ambrosia opened for business. The pastor presided in front of the enormous wood stove. Afterwards, he sampled the Ambrosia's wares in the private rooms upstairs. The Borgs, Adelia, Suzette Juliette, and the kitchen staff were all quite tippled, but nobody mentioned how soon it appeared the Captain would be a father.

At the boardinghouse, Adelia and Ernest moved to a smaller room, so the Captain could share the larger space with Harriet. He was rarely there, as his boat kept him on the river. She was rarely there, working a noon to midnight schedule six days a week. Absence indeed made the heart grow fonder as the bouncing walls would report when the two were both at home.

"What are they doing in there?" Ernest asked one day. It made Adelia think of her father and Lilac. "Is it a game?"

"Yes, it is a sort of game," Adelia said.

"Can I play?"

"No, it is a game for only two older people. But let's go look at the book with the pictures of Golden Gate Park. It has things called swings and slides. And even a carousel." She hoped Ernest would one day visit the park when he lived in San Francisco with his mother. And he would remember staring at the pictures with his Addy.

* * *

In the back of the Ambrosia kitchen, there was a storage cubbyhole with barrels of sugar, flour and other dry stores. At dinner one evening, Mrs. Borg suggested that Mr. Borg clear this area and install a daybed for Harriet, one brought down from the bordello rooms upstairs. "We must make her comfortable as long as we can until the baby comes. Give her a place to rest during the day whenever she needs it."

Adelia and Suzette glanced at each other. Adelia knew this was not mere kindness on the part of Mrs. Borg, but fear of the hours that Harriet would be gone from work. The couple who rarely spoke to anyone but each other appeared to have no opinion of the plan.

Later in her room, Adelia organized her small collection of buttons which Ernest had found most amusing. Suzette Juliette, scrubbing combs and scissors in the basin, observed, "Mrs. Borg finds the increase in Ambrosia restaurant profits as delicious as the food."

"Yes. Besides, if Harriet is gone, Mrs. Borg might have to do the cooking herself, perish the thought." The two friends giggled.

"Adelia, I have an idea for that storeroom." Suzette Juliette was far the better schemer of the two.

The storeroom, when cleared, was large enough for a table and chairs, along with the daybed. As well as a place of rest for the cook, it soon became a field office for the Dresser Girls: Adelia, the dressmaker and Suzette Juliette, the hairdresser. At times during the day, Ambrosia prostitutes met Adelia in the storeroom. She pinned dresses for alterations, took the articles home to sew in order to spend the day with Ernest, returned repaired items, and picked up whatever else the ladies wanted put to rights.

Suzette Juliette did Ambrosia hair appointments in the space, as well. The prostitutes washed their hair in advance, using potions and oils and scents she provided so their locks would be ready to style when she arrived.

The Dresser Girls learned techniques for the prostitutes that were not necessary when they worked with ladies of the upper town. Adelia developed a knack with the wispy silken togas which the Ambrosia girls wore when on duty in the saloon.

"Why this toga tommy-rot?" groused Suzette Joliette, while Adelia pinned a right shoulder seam to keep Pretti Patti's left breast from flopping out altogether. "Why not something classy, you know, French-like. Maybe can-can outfits."

"Because the place is called Ambrosia, you silly goose, and we are the scrumptious Greek treats," Pretti Patti replied, striking a scandalous pose. "Nectar of the gods!"

"Hold still," said Adelia.

Pretti Patti froze in place but added, "Men are honey-fuggled by our costumes, think us goddesses at their bidding. They soon need a trip up the stairs to pay for that fantasy. Some of them nutters even think I can really play a lute." The Dresser Girls knew this wagtail stretched out on a divan in the saloon, strumming an instrument until a gentleman chose her company.

Scarlet ladies, whores, strumpets, daughters of sin, wagtails. Adelia heard all the terms from the girls themselves. She found them to be appreciative and lucrative clients. They often experienced amorous congress that was a little too aggressive, so rips were common. Adelia could mend with stitches so tiny that patches were invisible.

Many men did not visit the saloon but went immediately to the girls upstairs; the fair belles up there didn't bother with togas but displayed themselves in peekaboo underwear or see-through wraps. Adelia learned how to replace difficult closures with ones easier to open quickly, so camisoles could be removed forthwith without damage.

Suzette Juliette created hair styles with feathers, ribbons, and sprigs of silk flowers for the prostitutes who loved to dress up and ride the streets in open carriages on their days off. But a hairdo also had to hold tight while a girl worked, without pins driving straight into her head as she writhed in simulated ecstasy. A style must withstand a man's rough hands as he crushed her head to his privates. Suzette Juliette learned to pull chignons over hair rats, thick pads that the prostitutes made of their own hair as it shed. A rat was buried then pinned in place so regardless of the activity, the hair remained full and bouncy.

"Of course, I doubt it's the *hair* that men want bouncy," Suzette Juliette whispered to Adelia, causing her to snicker. Most activities in those mysterious upstairs rooms were far beyond Adelia's imagination but not her curiosity. She wondered why the girls seldom talked about it hurting, the way her brother's rough fumblings had hurt her. She saw enough bruises on their bodies to know sometimes things went very wrong. The entire operation was illegal, of course, but nobody in Astoria enforced the laws since so many shared in the profits. That included the girls themselves.

"I get to keep a dollar fifty," said Sugar Candy as she held a cloth to her bleeding nose and lip while handing Adelia a chemise with a three-cornered tear. "It's worth it."

While fights could arise, they were unusual. Ambrosia catered to an upper class clientele unlike the bawdy houses closer to Uniontown. Adelia and Suzette Juliette sought customers in the bawds, too, but they always stayed together while they worked. Mrs. Borg and Harriet had each given them sharp lectures on this topic. The prostitutes in those hellholes were not merely fallen angels, they were badly soiled doves. All they could still offer was what any woman could offer a desperate man, and they were a nasty, tough, pathetic bunch. Many madams were Chinese, catering to sailors with diseases from around the world. In these quarters, Chinese were seen as dangerous, less than human even though they were twenty percent of Astoria's population.

The Dresser Girls promised themselves they would stop serving the bawds when they could afford to turn down business. "We will no longer come here when our purses are full," Suzette Juliette announced as they checked themselves for lice before walking back to the boardinghouse.

"When lots of uptown women come to us for clothes that require more than easy removal," Adelia answered.

"Or cast iron hair styles," Suzette Juliette added.

Ambrosia became Adelia's favorite workplace when someone was home to watch Ernest. It was clean, she could keep an eye on Harriet's swelling belly, and one morning when she was heading toward the side entrance that led to the saloon's kitchen, she saw someone she knew. It was the young man she had knocked over on the porch at the boardinghouse.

He was in front of Ambrosia's main entrance, shining enormous brass lanterns on either side of the door. The stained glass in each lantern portrayed a goatish looking fellow with pipes surrounded by girls whose skimpy clothing seemed comprised of well-placed flowers. Adelia decided she really must look at the mythology book she had noticed in Mrs. Borg's bookcase.

"We meet again in a doorway," she said. The man looked at her and his face lit in recognition.

Ah, those laughing eyes!

He was stocky, not quite handsome, but looked kind even with the angry scar that ran along his lower right jaw. The sleeves of his shirt were rolled back as he worked, and Adelia noticed corded veins in his muscles that stood out, not at all like her arms. She wondered about that, how the sight of a man's forearms could make her feel a little breathless. This fellow was bigger, older and meatier than Martin. None of that seemed a bad thing.

He bowed to her. "I am Aleksi Kotila, at your service."

"You are another Finn?"

"Only Chinese outnumber Finns in this town. Thousands of each of us brought here by labor contractors."

"I am Adelia Wright, niece of the chef here. You work for Mr. Borg as well?"

"Yes. Which is why I was at his home, to deliver receipts to his Missus."

"Ah. When you knocked me over."

"Yes. I am sure you had no fault in the matter whatsoever."

"What do you do for Mr. Borg?"

"I am a bouncer."

The word made her laugh. "You mean you jump up and down? Like a rabbit? He pays you for such?"

"You do not know this word, bouncer? It is not often an immigrant knows a word you locals do not. But then, I do not suppose you frequent the sort of place where the word is used. It means I bounce people out to the street if they misbehave inside."

"So...knocking people about is your business?"

He laughed. "Have it your way, Miss Wright. Your American author Horatio Alger is credited with the word. I just act out the part."

"You are a reader?"

"I am when I can get my hands on a book. It is the best way to improve my English." He looked a bit perplexed. "And what business do you have here this fine day?"

"Do you think I am one of the ladies employed here?" Adelia was feeling chirky. This flirting was fun.

"I certainly hope you are not, unless it is to aid with the cooking."

"I am a seamstress," she said, holding her sewing box slightly aloft so it would catch his attention. "I come to the kitchen to pick up and deliver my work. I know little else of places such as this."

"Would you like to see the saloon? I could let you in this way just this once since it is still closed for the morning." He opened the door. "You go straight through to the hall and turn left. It will take you to your destination."

She had never been in a saloon before, upscale or otherwise, so it was a wonder to her. The Ambrosia's walls were sleek dark wood with many arresting spots of bright color that attracted the eye. Alcoves with classical art, antique Grecian jewelry and weaponry, maybe real, maybe not. The floor and the enormous bar were slabs of marble, evoking Mediterranean riches of long ago. Statues of goddesses lolled in many nooks along the walls, holding aloft a variety of urns and amphorae. Adelia had no idea why these ladies held such things aloft, but it did mean their clothing had all but slipped away. The statues were nearly nude which must be fine with the city fathers who frequented the place. Maybe they deemed the carvings to be art. The seamstress in Adelia assumed it must be easier to hold those tiny wisps of fabric in place if you were made of marble instead of flesh.

Above the bar was a lengthy mural of lush foods with golden goblets and dinnerware. An orgy of women did unusual things with the fruit, and nymphs poured ladles of nectar onto the bodies of naked men. Ambrosia, indeed.

A side room featured billiard and gaming tables. The main room with the bar had tables for meals and a stage with filmy curtains. At one end of the room, three marble-looking divans rested high on columns of differing heights. "What are they for?" Adelia called over her shoulder.

"For the, ah, dancers," Aleksi answered from the doorway.

"Oh. The dancers. Of course." Adelia thought of Pretti Patti and her lute, then laughed all the way into the kitchen.

In the days that followed, Adelia managed to cross paths with Aleksi often enough that the two became friends. A relationship was not easy for them to arrange, what with a bouncer's schedule being so different from that of a dressmaker. But they managed a walk here, a lunch there. Aleksi found reason to be in the kitchen, and Adelia found reason to stay longer than alteration orders would truly merit.

In the early mornings, if she and Suzette Juliette had an appointment at one of the seedier bawds, Aleksi often took the time to accompany them. Mr. Borg had little to say in the matter; his chef would have threatened him with whatever kitchen knife was handy if he had said no. To repay Aleksi's kindness to the Dresser Girls, Adelia mended his shirts for no charge. Suzette Juliette cut his hair although she made it clear she was not now, and never would be, a barber.

Sundays the saloon was closed, the city fathers having decided it was too much of a good thing for the Lord's day. Those afternoons became a time Adelia and Aleksi shared with each other. She learned his story. Aleksi had crossed an ocean to escape starvation, then rounded the Horn and sailed north on another ocean. As with most Finns, he worked the Astoria port as a fisherman when he arrived. Unlike most, he came to the attention of a bar pilot one afternoon in a fight on the docks. When it was over, there was one man standing. Mr. Borg hired his bouncer on the spot.

His size got the job, and his brains kept it. Aleksi improved his English and did many extra chores around Ambrosia. He proved to be personable and honest as well as big, so he was trusted with handling money, taking the night's receipts from the bar to Mrs. Borg.

Adelia did not rush to kiss Aleksi as she had Martin. Aleksi was more than a love song with great lips. He actually interested Adelia. At nineteen, he was older than Martin, no longer a boy. He knew more, having been well-schooled in Finland. He told Adelia things she did not know. Their backgrounds had each been unkind, but together they found their spirits could chatter, tease, smile, enjoy. On top of everything else, Aleksi was a gentleman unless he was dealing with surly drinkers. Then he was terrifying.

Whether they would be more than friends was not yet clear to Adelia. But it was very clear to Aleksi. "A life among boozers, whores, and lowlife crimps who shanghai sailors is not the life for Aleksi," he told her one afternoon as they counted the masts in the harbor. "When I save enough, I will buy land where the air smells clean. Or maybe a boat. And I will take you with me."

She laughed at his joke. "Careful. If you do not follow through, they call it breach of promise here in America."

"It is the same in Finland."

"And why would I need a man to take care of me?"

"Girls are not safe without men."

"It has been my observation that girls are not safe *with* men."

* * *

It was nearly March. Adelia was in Suzette Juliette's room. Ernest, legs akimbo, sat on the bed with a chalkboard in his lap.

"Now draw a green D," said Adelia, helping him with the alphabet while she sat next to him, stitching.

Mrs. Borg had finally put herself in the Dresser Girls' hands for a make-over. She'd released her hair from its tight topknot, washed it in her bath that morning, and was now sitting on the only chair in the room.

Suzette Juliette brushed the raven tresses. "Why is your hair so dark, Mrs. Borg, when most of you Finns are so light?"

"The Great Hunger Years."

"What is that?" the hairdresser asked.

"Years of famine across Scandinavia decades ago.

Everybody left or died. Finns, Swedes, Russians, Jews. We emigrated to America and met people of many backgrounds."

"Look at my D, Addy. Look!"

"Perfect! Now an E in blue."

"Somewhere in all that mingling is the cause of my black hair. I am not so much a Finlander as Finlandish."

"I could make your hair red like mine, or maybe even blonde..."

"Color will stay the same."

"But if you want a new look..."

"Color will stay the same."

"No, an E has a line in the middle like this."

"Very well, Mrs. Borg. I saw something new in *Ladies' Home Journal* with hair short and rolled over the eyebrows. We could also have ringlets over your ears and..."

"Hair should never be too short for a bun. It is not practical."

Adelia had run into her own resistance to a make-over. She'd shown Mrs. Borg samples of materials lighter and more flattering than the heavy bombazines. "This fabric will move with you, heighten the, ah, assets of your fine figure."

"Horsefeathers! Materials like that won't last a year. Impractical."

Finally, they'd settled on a narrow lace binding that Adelia was working into the neckline and cuffs of one of the dark dresses.

"Mrs. Borg, horses do not have feathers, do they?"

"No, Ernest my sensible young lad, horsefeathers are something foolish like what Adelia was saying."

When hair and dress were finished, Mrs. Borg stood and stared at herself in a mirror. Her dark bun was still pulled straight back but maybe a little looser than the original topknot. Her dress was the same, with the tiniest row of lace to battle all that dullness.

The Dresser Girls felt defeat. But their client was thrilled. "Oh my dears! I...I love it! I will tell all my friends about such talented girls."

They heard a knock at the front door, and Mrs. Borg minced from the room with an actual smile on her face.

The girls looked at each other, and Adelia covered her mouth with her hands to keep from belting out a guffaw that Mrs. Borg would surely hear.

"Horsefeathers! Horsefeathers!" Ernest sang, apparently liking the sound as he scribbled with his chalk.

"Lesson learned," whispered the hairdresser to the dressmaker. "A make-over for some clients is just a make-do for us."

"Adelia. Please come." Mrs. Borg trilled from the floor below. She still must be happy or might not have added the 'please.'

As she bounded down the stairs, Adelia thought

about a little change for some being too much change for others. Suzette Juliette was right. The uptown clientele was nowhere near as venturesome as the prostitutes. To increase their trade with the neighborhood ladies, the Dresser Girls best remember to move slower into higher fashion. A bit at a time.

She was sure it would be Aleksi awaiting her. He often stopped to say hello when he made a delivery to Mrs. Borg. But it was Lucien P. Durand at the foot of the stairs. Adelia was so flabbergasted she forgot herself and ran to embrace him.

"My goodness!" he said when he unraveled himself from her arms. He held her back and took a long look. "How can a child grow into a woman in just, what, three months? Four? You are very beautiful, my dear Miss Wright."

She was so eager to release all she'd pent up that she blurted away with no sense of decorum. "Oh! I am so sorry to have left your camp in such a hurry. Hai must be furious, and Gerty..."

"Yes, well, you did steal Harriet away. They have survived although I'm told the pies are not quite such heaven. And it was the wise thing for you all to do, under the circumstances."

"You found Mrs. Munro? She has Ernest's lighthouse? Oh please, how is she? Are you here for good? Are you going back? Do you think Ernest could go with you to his mother? Could I..."

"Stop! You are like a kitten batting a ball of yarn! Come with me now. Do not bring the boy. I have a carriage out front."

"She is here? She is here?"

"Silence. Let us go." He held a finger in front of his lips.

Adelia squealed then ran back up the stairs to ask Suzette Juliette to keep an eye on Ernest while she was gone. "Show him the difference between an E and an F."

"I will, of course, but why? Where are you going? Who is that man?"

"I will tell you all when I return." Adelia, cloaked in mystery, now grabbed her cape, galloped back down the stairs, swept out the front door and into the waiting carriage like the heroine in a dime novel romance.

* * *

The Meriwether Hotel was small, elegant, and nearly as private as a home. Unlike Seaside House, the lobby here was modest since this was a hotel that valued discretion more than ostentation. Each accommodation, only eighteen in total, had its own sitting room. Lucien P. Durand maintained a suite of rooms at the Meriwether for when he was in town.

And he was in town now with his new wife, the former Florence Munro. He told Adelia on the carriage ride to the hotel, when she allowed him a word edgewise, that the two had married just before leaving San Francisco for Astoria.

That shut Adelia up until they arrived. She was completely flabbergasted. Mr. Durand and Mrs. Munro, married? How wonderful. Right? But did that mean she was no longer important to them? Was she to be no more than a reject once again? *What about me?*

When he threw open the door to his suite, she was standing there. The woman who'd been so missed.

"Mrs. Munro! I mean Mrs. Durand!"

"Adelia!"

Adelia was so nearly in shock she could hardly breathe. The two looked at each other, crossed the room, cried, hugged, cried some more. All thoughts of rejection were forgotten. Lucien P. Durand might as well have been a ghost for all either of them noticed him.

"Is my boy well? Will Ernest know me?"

"He has grown, and he misses you every day."

More tears. Minutes passed.

Mr. Durand finally broke through. "Now that the bodice of each dress is sodden with salt water, we have much to discuss and little time. Florrie should not stay in this town for long. We sailed in from San Francisco today and will head back in the morning, taking Ernest with us. My new son."

It hit Adelia life a physical blow. She was nearly in

shock to gain Mrs. Munro one day and lose both Mrs. Munro and Ernest the next.

But it was for the best, was it not? So she joining the other two in the talking and planning, all the while holding Mrs. Munro's - or she should say Mrs. Durand's - hand. The gentleman's eyes twinkled in what Adelia believed could only be the joy of creating joy.

Chapter Fifteen

February 1894

When plans were settled with the Durands, Adelia felt gutted like a salmon at a cannery. She was to be left on her own, by her own choice. She knew this time would come, when Ernest would be taken away. She had thought it through often enough. Still and all, how could doing the right thing feel so wrong?

Unsure whether she could trust her own feet to get her there, Adelia took the carriage back to the boardinghouse. She felt leaden as she climbed the stairs to go get Ernest.

Suzette Juliette was eager to be on her way to an appointment. "You must tell me all that is happening when I return."

Adelia was grateful her business partner rushed out the door. She told Ernest she had a big surprise as she packed up his few things. When he saw his valise, he panicked.

"Are we running away again, Addy? I like it here. Is that why you are sad? Should I be scared?"

"No, my love. We are going to see Miss Harriet first, then on to a wonderful surprise." She did her best to smile brightly for him. "I am not sad. I think I am catching a cold is all. Or thinking too much about a new dress to make."

"But where are we going?"

"It is a Pinkerton secret, and you will love it."

Adelia took Ernest to Ambrosia then released the carriage. The boy had never been to the brothel, of course, so curiosity soon replaced his anxiety. She deposited him in the storeroom off the kitchen. "Wait here for me. I will go get Miss Harriet."

She could not send Ernest away without Harriet's help in providing a cover story. Besides, the cook would never forgive her if she didn't have time to say good-bye to this little boy who had become a part of her own story.

Harriet listened as Adelia explained, a look of dread spreading across her face. "So they married? That was fast."

"Mrs. Munro is a woman who knows her own mind," Adelia assured her. "She loves life, and Lucien P. Durand is the type of man who is up for anything."

"They sound a fine fit. But Ernest. He will be happy?"

"He knows and trusts this man."

"And you? You will be happy?"

"It is the right thing to do. But oh, Harriet. Oh, Harriet."

When she got herself under control, she and Harriet went to the storeroom. Pretti Patti and Bad Madge had discovered Ernest. They were exclaiming about cuteness and handing out hugs and kisses.

"This is my nephew, you two, and you are scaring him. Now away with you." Everyone was a little afraid of Harriet so the prostitutes vanished.

"Those ladies did not have their dresses on, Addy," Ernest said, eyes round as an owlet.

"Let's keep that part of our Pinkerton secret to ourselves, shall we? Now say good-bye to Miss Harriet for a while. We are off on an adventure."

Harriet hugged him. He said good-bye. She hugged him harder. Then she sniffled. Suddenly her tears seemed to be unstoppable.

Adelia felt alarm. "Harriet, are you all right? Is it..."

"I am pregnant is all. Everything upsets me now." The word 'now' drew out into a howl.

"We will put together a story about Ernest's absence, Harriet, when you get home tonight. Now we must go." Adelia and Ernest slipped away through a kitchen crew who no doubt wondered what on earth she had done to their fierce boss. If it sweetened the cook up, they'd want to know Adelia's secret.

From Ambrosia, it was only three blocks up Ninth to the Meriwether Hotel. Adelia and Ernest walked hand in hand. She knew that when he saw his mother, she would lose his attention for good. And she needed him to remember her.

"You know how much I love you, don't you, Ernie?"

"Yes. Are you crying, Addy?"

"No. But Miss Harriet was funny, wasn't she? All that howling."

"Will you love her baby more than me?"

"You will always be my best boy."

They entered the hotel and climbed the stairs. Outside the Durand suite, Adelia sunk to her knees. She ran a comb through his hair and rubbed a trace of wagtail lip rouge from his cheek. She opened the child's valise, and pulled a toy from it, one that had been hers as long as she could remember. "I am giving you my lighthouse, Ernie. Keep it for me until the day we meet again. Until then, Tilly is yours."

"But why are you calling me Ernie...where are you" Panic flashed in his eyes.

The door opened. He turned and saw his mother. "Mama! Addy, it's Mama!"

The last thing Adelia saw before she left was the two halves melting into one whole again. Only Lucien P. Durand looked up in time to see her turn away, leaving her family behind.

Adelia rushed for the boardinghouse but her eyes were so full of tears and her head with such misery that she had no idea which way she was going. Just uphill, away from the hotel, away from the river, and the ocean that was for her to be the great divide.

A hand caught her from behind and spun her around. Mr. Durand drew her in, and she collapsed against his chest. All the hurts, the losses, the rejections in her young life poured down the front of his vest.

"Come back with me. Stay the evening with us. Let Florrie love you a little longer. She thought you'd both have more time. She is distraught."

"I cannot bear it. I have said my good-bye."

"At least see us off in the morning at the port."

"No. Mother and child are already gone from my sight. I will leave it that way." She pulled back, and they walked on, side by side, up the hill.

"You know she said you could come with us to San Francisco. I would like that."

"Mr. Durand. I cannot do that. We went through this already. It is time for Ernest to look to his mama instead of me."

"He had you both once."

"Things are different now. Who would I be? A nanny? A servant? I am not your daughter, not hers, not the same social class. I cannot teach him the things he needs to know to succeed in your world, because I never learned them myself. I would not fit."

"I know the role of the black sheep as I hold it myself. We could stick together."

"Thank you for your kindness, but Harriet will need me now. Her baby comes soon. I cannot leave the Captain and her when they have done so much for me."

"Maybe after the baby, maybe..."

"No promises, Mr. Durand, that you may not want to keep when the time comes. I will be okay. I have a place to live, a young man who cares about me, and a business to run...and damnation! They belong to you now. Not to me."

"I see that, I do. But they can belong to us both. We will all write and maybe next summer, it will be safe for us to come back to visit."

They had arrived at the boardinghouse.

Adelia said, "I have learned false hope is more hurtful than no hope. We will all be sad. Then we will all be fine. Our lives will go on."

Lucien P. Durand tipped his hat. "You are so young to be so old."

"I will be right back with the rest of the money Mrs. Munro, er, Mrs. Durand gave to me for Ernest's care."

"Adelia. How can someone so old be so silly? Keep the money, dear one. It is meant to be yours. I could not possibly give it back to Florrie without creating another tidal wave of tears, and I am quite damp enough already."

* * *

Until Adelia could get her story straight with Harriet, she could not stay in the boardinghouse. Suzette Juliette would be along with questions, and Mrs. Borg soon after that.

Her safest place to be, under the circumstances, was the Ambrosia storeroom. Harriet saw her come back and nodded slightly but kept away, busy with the evening meal. Adelia closed the door, turned the lamp low, and climbed onto the daybed that was there for the cook's comfort. She stayed still as death, but not that happy. Her tears had reached the bottom of their well and dried away, so even her shoulders didn't shake. She made not a move or a sound.

Adelia replayed her conversation with Lucian P. Durand, convincing herself she had made the right choice, that the wrong choice would have been going with the Durands. It was time to get on with her life. She knew pain would modify in time, but right this moment it overwhelmed her. She needed compassion, and Aleksi was there to offer it.

When he let himself into the room, she sat up and held out her arms to him. He swept her up in his strong embrace and settled her on his lap on the side of the bed, as though she were little more than a child. She whispered, "I am not asking you to find solutions. Just to hold on to me for a while."

That is exactly what Aleksi Kotila did until late afternoon became meal time. He left her then, to go to the door when the evening crowd arrived. Adelia, who had exhausted herself, slept until Harriet came for her at midnight, her own shift complete. Together with Captain Jokinen, who was in town for two nights, they walked home on the empty street to the boardinghouse up the hill.

Chapter Sixteen

Spring 1894

The next morning at breakfast, Harriet told Suzette Juliette and the Borgs that her brother had come to reclaim his son but not his daughter. Ernest was gone, but Adelia would stay. The tablemates seemed to accept this as the way of the world: a girl would not have the value to a farmer that a boy offered. They all would miss the little guy and were so sad for Adelia, of course, but she would adjust. Only Suzette Juliette, in tears herself, whispered to her friend, "Whatever I can do, however I can help."

The next day, Aleksi took her to an ice cream shop for her favorite strawberry sundae. She told him the true story as the ice cream melted into a sweet puddle. He, too, knew the heartache of lost family since he had been parted from his own; it was a misery they could share.

"Now you know I even committed murder for her and her boy. You should probably find a better sort of person to be around," she said after managing to eat the cherry if nothing else.

"Did you want to go with them, Adelia?" he asked, reaching for her hand when it trembled.

"Yes. No. I need to find my own way now." She squared her shoulders.

"Love lasts across miles, you know. It is a hard lesson to learn when you are only thirteen. But a true one. I miss my little brothers and sisters. And I might just die if you left me now."

"I will not leave. I have a new family here with the Captain and Harriet and Suzette Juliette. And you. Most of all, you, Aleksi." She gave him a watery smile. He ordered her another sundae. This time with a spoon for himself, as well.

As the days passed, Adelia adjusted, as everyone said she would. After a week, she was less sullen, even chatting again with the whores in the Ambrosia kitchen or the high born women who brought dresses to hem and bonnets for new ribbons to their Dresser Girl at the boardinghouse. If not exactly cheerful, Adelia managed polite.

In two weeks, she received a letter. Mrs. Durand must have mailed it the moment she arrived in San Francisco.

"...Ernest cried and cried for you, Adelia. Please write

to him soon so he knows you are well. Mr. Durand is excellent with him. My boy finally has a father who cares. And I have such a good husband. Did you know Lucien was the perfect mate when you sent him to me? He is yet another gift for which I am greatly obliged to you. You are in my heart and will always be. We will meet again soon, on an occasion that shall be happier for us all. Your loving Florence Durand."

Adelia wrote to Ernest right away, printing on the envelop flap, "For Pinkerton Eyes Only." In the days that followed, letters traveled between San Francisco and Astoria as fast as ships could sail.

Harriet and the imminent arrival of the baby became Adelia's immediate concern. The cook figured she was due in late April. Planning was fun. Together she and Adelia set up a nursery corner in the large room the Jokinens shared. They tried to come up with the perfect name for a baby boy or baby girl.

"Archibald?"

"Egbert?"

"Bruno?"

"Hortense?"

"Agnes?"

"Edwina?"

On Sundays, Aleksi built a cradle in the shed behind the boardinghouse, and Adelia sat with him, making baby clothes. The Captain entertained everyone at the dinner table describing Harriet's cravings. "She begs for sautéed reindeer! A true Finn is in that oven."

Business for the Dresser Girls was on the rise, but both of them were eager for things to move faster. Suzette Juliette one day lamented how long sewing took. "I can get more customers, but you are so limited by the time invested in creating a frock."

That comment ignited an idea which Adelia had nurtured for some time. She'd first seen the wondrous machine in magazines and catalogs. It was sleek and powerful and bursting with promise. It reflected who she knew herself to be, a creator of beautiful things. Mrs. Durand had seen the ability in her, in the hotel when she was still Mrs. Munro.

The Singer Vibrating Shuttle Sewing Machine Model 27 with Foot Treadle would vastly increase her output. Such a marvel, powered by her own legs! *The woman's faithful friend the world over,* claimed the advertisements.

Adelia knew she should save the last of the Munro money for a rainy day, along with the pittance she had left from the lard can in her father's home. She knew that. *But, oh! What a wonder, this Model 27.* Surely anything that increased her efficiency would lead to bigger profits. One couldn't get ahead without taking a risk. When she got proficient, she figured she could charge maybe nine dollars for a complete dress, plus smaller sums for alterations. She could take in so many more jobs than now. But still, at $125, Model 27 was a fortune.

Adelia had made hard decisions before. She did not shrink away now.

The machine, when it arrived in the Port of Astoria, was delivered to the boardinghouse on a horse-drawn dray. Adelia enlisted Aleksi to remove it from the sturdy wooden packing crate, then together he and Captain Jokinen muscled it up the stairs to her room. They had to first remove Ernest's settee so the mechanical wizard could fit against the one wall with a window.

This new roommate was about the size of a desk, in a handsome wood cabinet with decorative steel legs. When the cabinet was open, it revealed a glossy black steel machine with ornamental grapevine decorations. It looked poised to strike, ready for maneuvers. With its complement of accessories, it promised to hem, tuck, shirr, bind, quilt, ruffle, and button hole. Model 27 was built to last forever. Adelia just hoped she could live up to its potential someday soon.

The machine took over the empty time created by Ernest's departure. It filled lonely hours as Adelia spoke to it lovingly, learned its whys and wherefores, and conquered sewing techniques that were drudgery by hand. She experimented with scraps, marveling at the needle gliding up and down, lockstitching identical tiny bites. Her feet flew, heel to toe, on the treadle for sewing large pieces together, or they crept as a delicate material was puffed into a lavish sleeve. By early April, Adelia had made a suit for Suzette Juliette, a plainer but sophisticated frock for herself, a maternity dress that could cover Harriet's last pregnant month, and a tiny quilt that featured a lighthouse and sailboat at sea.

* * *

"I have a surprise for you," a balloon-shaped Harriet said one morning. "We are going to the Corner House today for lunch. You will take a break from your sewing machine, and I will take a break from the Ambrosia kitchen."

"Why will we do that?" Adelia asked. An outing like this was unprecedented. She knew polite society believed pregnant women should have the good sense to keep their scandalous selves in confinement. But working women could not merely hide themselves from sight. Nor was Harriet the type to buckle under to a constraint she found absurd.

"If I told you, it would not be a surprise, now would it?"

"I have not been to a restaurant since the Seaside House verandah." How the sun shined that day as she laughed with Mrs. Munro and Ernest out on the verandah. Not even a year ago. But a lifetime ago.

"This is nothing so fancy nor so dear. Still, it is a

chance to wear our new dresses."

The two strolled down the hill toward Commercial Street, both proud in Adelia's creations. Her own outfit was a sweep of dove gray with a deep ruby waist length capelet. The gown she'd made for Harriet was a plum print with a lavender band above the baby. The material spread around the chef's short frame, lush and regal.

They seated themselves at a table for four near the large panel windows overlooking the busy street. The lunch room was crowded with tables, hardly enough room for waiters. Luscious aromas of baked goods and roasts wafted through the crowd as servers carried trays high over their heads. Some customers raised eyebrows at Harriet, but most of the diners discussed their own business over laughter and clinking dishware. In the background a pianist played *You'll Miss Lots of Fun When You're Married,* a tune by the popular new composer, John Philip Sousa. The atmosphere was boisterous, a place where a newly prosperous working class could celebrate their success.

"Where is my promised surprise, Mrs. Jokinen?" Adelia asked.

"Look to the front door just now."

The first one in was the Ghostly Girl. Behind her came Ephraim.

There followed a series of hugs and greetings which involved name calling.

"Felicity!"

"Harriet!"

"Ephraim!"

"Adelia!"

The couple sat across from the cook and the dressmaker. Adelia knew her own face must beam like the other three, although she could no longer see how this boy had been the recipient of her first crush. What was she been thinking?

The gossip began to fly.

"...baby will arrive in late April..."

"...we married last month and Ephraim has found work in a Portland hotel..."

"...Albin and Katja send their love..."

"...became a full-fledged chef at a gentleman's club..."

"...you are no longer our little miss! You have grown so lovely. I might be far more jealous today..."

"...Harriet wrote to us so we knew where to find you..."

"...you made these marvelous dresses? Such talent you have!"

"...taking a steamboat to Portland this afternoon..."

The conversation ebbed and flowed as they ordered then ate their chicken fricassee and calf's liver with onions. Each had one of the new five-cent bottles of Coca-Cola. They agreed the food was ample but not very good.

"Katja says that is the entire point of American cooking. Get enough in your gut and you won't care if it is good," Felicity said.

"Oh! And you must know that we carried out your plan, Adelia," Ephraim said.

"Plan?"

"We knew you had to leave, and that we shouldn't ask why. Harriet was very firm about that before she headed for the logging camp. But you left a job undone." Ephraim may have tried for a face that looked severe, but his good humor shone through.

Nonetheless, Adelia sighed. "I left many things undone, and I apologize. I never meant for more work to fall on you."

"Oh, but this chore we loved. We executed your plan for the housemaids who cut up your dress." The Ghostly Girl actually developed a rosy glow. Adelia vowed she would never think the unkind appellation again.

"We gathered a pail of garbage scraps," said Ephraim. "Allowed it to stew a day or two. Albin added some fish skins."

"Then during the maids' work shift, I spread those scraps over their beds and put their quilts on top." Felicity began giggling and couldn't continue the tale.

"You were not there for them to find you, but they blamed you anyway. Oh, such a fuss! None of us knew anything about it, of course. But for several days we raised our noses and sniffed when either maid walked by. My goodness, what is that aroma?" Ephraim mimicked, holding his nose.

Their laughter drowned out even the mediocre pianist working his way through a Stephen Foster medley on the upright Baldwin.

Nothing can lift spirits like an afternoon of gossip, and Adelia was very thankful to Harriet for arranging it. She could not wait to tell Aleksi that she would soon have friends in Portland if they should ever want to visit a town even bigger than Astoria, although she couldn't imagine what else they could ever need.

"Well, they have riverboats that are brothels there. To escape land taxes," Aleksi said. "Maybe you could make mermaid costumes for the *Sirens of the Sea.*"

* * *

Adelia's attraction to Aleksi deepened. They played together, shared their stories and their flaws, teased and comforted. As spring bloomed, doling out the occasional sunny day, the two took many walks hand in hand to the east where the Columbia was free of odors, or to the west toward Youngs Bay. They each had a fondness for music so they joined audiences in the park to listen to brass bands play the new marches. Military instruments from Civil War bands were in ample supply so even the common man could afford to learn to play. When the couple had the admission fee, they visited a music hall, sighing at love songs or laughing at the lyrics of vaudeville.

Why won't the men propose, Mama?
Why won't the men propose?
Each seems just coming to the point,
and then, away he goes!
I've hopes that some distinguished beau
a glance upon me throws;
But though he'll dance and smile and flirt,
alas he won't propose!
And what is to be done, Mama?
Oh, what is to be done?
I have no time to lose, Mama,
for I am thirty-one!
At balls I am too often left
where spinsters sit in rows;
Why won't the men propose, Mama?
Why won't the men propose?

For the first time in Adelia's life she had free time and enough funds to enjoy it. She was not plagued with worries now that Ernest was home safe, not looking over her shoulder, happy with her work since Model 27 had changed her life.

"Will you marry me, Adelia?" Aleksi asked, not for the first time.

"Maybe, unless a better offer comes along." She grinned a chirky grin. She was only thirteen, and marriage was a very new idea to her.

"And who might a better offer be?"

"Oh...Walt Whitman pens a better verse, or Gentleman Jim throws a mightier punch, or Beau Brummell was a far more fashionable fellow, or..."

"Enough. None of them can kiss like this."

And he was right. His kisses had none of the tentative quality of Martin's. They were not sweet. They were deep and long, explosives ready to ignite. Adelia quite liked them and gave extensive thought to what might come next.

"Will you marry me, Adelia?" Aleksi asked in another park on another walk.

"Maybe when I am old enough."

"And when might that be?"

"Oh, years and years from now." Adelia was, in fact, pretty sure it was just two until the age of consent. "But we can practice now." This time the kiss was from her to him. She pulled him behind a row of flowering rhodies and pushed her lithe body close to his.

"Will you marry me, Adelia?" he asked when another week passed.

"How could I marry a man who works among prostitutes?"

"You show them how to dress, my dear seamstress. You are the one to expose this. And this." He placed his hand on one breast and then the next.

In the kitchen storeroom one Sunday, an afternoon the saloon was closed, Aleksi slowly undressed Adelia. "You could use easier buttons and hooks on your own clothes," he muttered as he worked. But the time it took was time she needed to assure her brain that her body knew what it was about.

Was this the man to soothe her curiosity and that annoying itch? He was a man she trusted, one who had taken his time and waited for her. Maybe he could erase the memories of her brother and the chicken coop floor. Or at least obscure them. He was worth the try. By the time he lowered himself onto her, she was more than ready, curling her legs over his broad strong back.

"Is this how the prostitutes do it?" she asked on another occasion.

"I do not know how the prostitutes do it."

"Or like this?"

"Dear God."

Adelia realized that the memory of her brother's aggression was loosening its grip on her. Sex could be fun instead of vile, beautiful instead of a battle. In time, Aleksi offered her an engagement ring to prove that marriage was indeed his goal. The delicate rose gold band held the tiniest of diamonds sparkling between two pearly white moonstones.

"Will you marry me, Adelia?"

"Yes."

* * *

Harriet's baby arrived in the Ambrosia kitchen a week earlier than anticipated. She was delivered by a midwife who was attended by three prostitutes while a fourth raced up the hill to get Adelia. The birthing of a *wanted* baby, one to actually keep, was cause for great joy in the brothel. Baby Girl Jokinen had many, many aunts. Mr. Borg even managed a bit of champagne for all his ladies.

"Her name, Harriet? What is her name?" Adelia asked, holding the wisp of humanity.

"She is Milla Adelia Jokinen. For Elias' mother and for you."

Named for me! I matter that much! Adelia beamed with pride and instant love.

By the time the Captain returned from the river, his wife and baby girl where resting comfortably in the boardinghouse, with Adelia attending in awe. She was astounded with the ease that Harriet breast fed, burped, and swaddled the baby, as though mothering skills were born along with Milla.

"Terrible Tilly has news of Marvelous Milla!" Adelia wrote to Florence Durand. *"A baby girl blessed my friends Harriet and Elias this day."*

Adelia knew she would never stop sewing clothes

for this little girl, her namesake and her newest joy. When Harriet returned to work, Adelia tucked the cradle close to Model 27 so she could look over the sewing machine and smile at the fashionable baby all through the day.

* * *

Joy is ephemeral. Maybe it had always been that way for Harriet. When Adelia thought about the accident after the fact, she believed it to be true.

Harriet , Suzette Juliette, and Adelia were strolling down Ninth. The afternoon was sublime, a May dazzler that brought color back into the Astoria storefronts after so many gray days. The sun felt marvelous on the ladies' cheeks and ungloved hands. They laughed at a ribald joke Pretti Pattie had told to Harriet.

Adelia was pushing Milla in the new wicker baby carriage. She and the baby were making gurgly, cooing sounds at each other.

"It is the height of safety and convenience," Harriet claimed. "The wheels can move independently. It's the most maneuverable carriage ever."

"That well may be, but I particularly love the frilly parasol over the basket. Adorable! Such decorative swirls on the wheels as well. Height of fashion, Harriet. Height of fashion. Very ahead of its time." Suzette Juliette approved of all things modern.

Adelia was aware of their chatter, but she was mostly in a world with the baby. Milla Adelia smiled up at her, or maybe it was gas. Adelia leaned down to make a miniscule adjustment to the lighthouse quilt. Later she thought if she had not been so absorbed, she might have saved them all from inconceivable pain.

The shriek of an terrified animal shot fear through Adelia's nerves. She lifted her eyes from the baby, and the world turned to slow motion. The happy sun became a blinding spotlight that imprinted the horror on her brain forever.

A beautiful bay horse reared high in the air as the surrey it pulled spun on loose stone. The traces lifted with the animal, tipping its carriage to one side. As it tilted, the carriage pulled the horse up and over. It fell, lurching into a heavily loaded dray and knocking the old mare hauling it onto her knees. The dray went over next, spilling its load of canned goods.

All three women froze beside the road, but Harriet was closest to the curb. The cans and pallets rained down on top of her. As the corner of one slashed open her head, she tumbled. She screamed for Adelia as she collapsed under the hooves of the struggling carriage horse.

The animal flailed in terror, trying to free itself. In the process it kicked Harriet repeatedly, landing terrible blows to her body and head. The women and horses all screamed, the sounds of petrified animals and humans indecipherable from each other.

Both drivers tried to separate their beasts and get to the woman beneath the wreckage. People ran to help, but Adelia was first. She grabbed Suzette Juliette by the arm and ordered, "Stay with Milla."

Then she heard a gunshot, and the carriage horse went still.

Broken bones, flashed through her mind. *Poor thing, poor thing.*

She plunged around the carcass into the fray. "Harriet! I am here," she called, stumbling through the cans of salmon that rolled everywhere. She fell, stood again, and was momentarily halted as two big men urged the old mare to her feet and led her away.

At last, Adelia could see Harriet amid the debris, a bit of flotsam so tiny and broken. So still. It was immediately clear that her stand-in mother had been trampled to death. In the street, surrounded by the odor of horse manure and fresh blood, by men yelling orders, by the sound of a baby crying, Adelia dropped to cradle Harriet's broken upper body.

She wished whoever had taken pity on the horse would now do the same for her.

Chapter Seventeen

Spring through fall 1894

A funeral was attended by everyone who worked at Ambrosia or lived in the boardinghouse. Everyone except Adelia. She stayed in her room with Milla Adelia Jokinen in order to cling to the grinning, finger-sucking, squirming, living memory of Harriet. She had no desire to see the battered body lowered into the ground. She knew how to care for the baby now, even feed it; she had given her a bottle often enough when Harriet wasn't there.

Harriet wasn't there. Would never be there. A wound had opened within Adelia, and she feared it would never close again. Of all the losses she'd battled, this was by far the greatest adversary, the one that could obliterate what joy she managed to find. She stared at the baby's pink cheeks and gummy smile, looking for the face of Milla's mother.

Adelia had been told that you can't control what you will remember in the future, but she thought of the little things now, trying to impress them in her mind so she could tell Milla one day. Harriet's favorite recipe, song, joke. The curl that never stayed tucked behind an ear. How Harriet often used the fingernails of one hand to push back the cuticles of the other. How she squinted at the newspaper type, always blaming the printer and not her own eyes.

Adelia wondered if Harriet knew she was pregnant when she gave that talk on birth control, in the cookhouse at the logging camp. The memory of Gerty egging the cookee on brought a smile to Adelia's face. Why was Harriet's past such a secret? Had she been a spy or a bigamist or a thief in a former life? She was a woman who carried her past as part of her present, the one muddling up the other. Harriet's secrets died with Harriet.

When the Captain came back to the boardinghouse after the funeral, he found Adelia in her room, still holding Milla. He sat on the edge of her bed since she had the only chair. To Adelia, he looked as though his bones had compressed, forcing his wide shoulders to droop like an old man.

With a great intake of breath, he started to speak, but Adelia interrupted. She'd practiced what to say to him. "I will do whatever you need, Captain. You have so often done everything for me. I can marry you and raise this child on your boat if you wish. Or I can marry Aleksi, and we will get a home and raise Milla there. Or if you prefer, I can raise her here on my own. I will do anything to help you now."

He smiled his sadness at her. "Adelia, you are not much more than a child yourself. At the moment, you sound like one."

"But I can do it. I can make it work."

"You lose what you love in this life," he said, frustration tightening his voice. "You should know that by now. But you still think things end well."

"I learned about loss when my dog Shep died," Adelia said. "I have fought loss ever since. And things can end well. They can, Captain. I miss Harriet, not as much as you do, maybe, but I will raise this child to love her memory." Adelia felt a pang of guilt. She had hurt Harriet, who always knew that Adelia longed for Florence Munro. That was the truth of it. Love was not an all or nothing game. It came in different strengths.

"Adelia. You know this baby is not really mine. I have no way of finding her real father even if he would want her."

"Yes." She could not get out another word without her tears sloshing all over Milla. The Captain was not going to accept her. It was agony to admit, but she knew he was on the righteous side of this tug of war.

"With Harriet, we would have been a jolly family. But now, I must admit that raising a child on my own is not right for me or Milla. And certainly not right for you."

"But I cared for Ernest and..."

"I will not saddle you with another child in trouble, Adelia. I have contracted with Mr. and Mrs. Borg to raise Milla."

"What? But they are *old*!"

"Not yet fifty. And age is not a crime. It means they are experienced. Their own four sons have grown just fine. Mrs. Borg took a shine to Ernest. He reminded her how much she enjoyed having a little one around. Milla will be happy here. And safe."

"But I..."

"You will see Milla each day as long as you live here. Mrs. Borg has told me how she will relish your help. Like a favorite aunt. But not a mother." He sighed heavily, straightened his spine and stood. "Do you understand, dear girl?"

She clutched the baby. Finally, she nodded. He took Milla from her arms and down the stairs to the couple who awaited her.

* * *

The spring and summer months passed into a stellar autumn, and the boardinghouse changed along with the seasons. The young couple who existed on virtually nothing but their own love moved out. Mrs.

Borg had no idea where they were drifting to, but the other residents all feared for the lovebirds' grasp on reality.

The Dresser Girls took over the rent on the large room to use as their work room, after the Captain vacated it to move back to his boat. They also kept their own small living quarters. Mrs. Borg put up with a parade of Dresser Girl clients, probably because she had fewer boarders to worry about. And both Adelia and Suzette Juliette were willing babysitters for Milla. It was an arrangement that suited everyone.

The town was bursting with growth, approaching a five-digit population. Adelia and Aleksi joined the celebrations that commemorated the completion of the south jetty which would help harness The Graveyard of the Pacific. The same year, they celebrated the completion of the railroad connecting Astoria to Portland and beyond.

Adelia turned fourteen in June. Lucien P. Durand appeared in July and again in September, on his business trips through Astoria, between San Francisco and the logging camp. He brought Adelia a set of ruby glass mugs as well as an ornate silver spoon, souvenirs from the 1894 San Francisco Mid Winter World's Fair. She gave him a pouch she made for Ernest from the softest deerskin. "So he can hide all his treasures," she said.

On the fall trip, Mr. Durand had exciting news. "I

have purchased the Seaside vacation house from Emma Watson. You remember the one, right? Hydrangea House, where I am told you and Ernest hid at one time. Mrs. Watson and her family no longer come to the beach. The house is a Christmas present for Ernest and Florrie. We can all meet at the beach for a fine time next summer. We'll be careful but by then, nobody will question Mrs. Durand even if they do remember a story of a missing woman named Munro."

Adelia hoped the remainder of 1894 would pass away in calm, leaving her time to adjust to a world without Harriet. Aching grief began its slow journey into sweet memories. Her business was growing, she saw Milla as often as she wished, Aleksi and she talked about marrying next spring at Hydrangea House. She was still too young in Oregon's eyes, but surely nobody would be there to stop it. However, she had been fooled by the cold dose of reality too often to trust it anymore.

* * *

George Wright was an assistant keeper on Tillamook Rock Lighthouse far too long. The first head keeper had only managed four months of 'the sad sea' before he called it quits, and George had been at it for years. The endless gloom, recurrent storms, unrelenting fog sirens, and tiny quarters left him jumpy, on the verge of panic most of the time. His crewmates took to calling him Chumpy, referring to his deranged state. But they only did this behind his back after the time he delivered a nose-ender blow straight to its target.

He had stopped going to his cabin in the woods since he no longer had a family there. He began to drink heavily, returning from shore leaves always pissed, often beaten, and smelling of Swilltown whores. Drying out on the light, he was foul in mind and language. He passed notes so he didn't have to speak with the other keepers. They did the same with him. When George actually issued death threats against others, he was deemed unstable enough to be ordered off the rock for good at the new year.

The new year wasn't quite soon enough. A hurricane in December descended on Terrible Tilly. The whole station, including the light tower, was repeatedly submerged with the keepers terrified within. Furious waves tore rocks free, projectiles of up to a ton, and hurled them at the iron roof and the light. Glass panes in the lantern room, shielded by strong wire, shattered nonetheless. The fog sirens clogged with seaweed. Water flooded the living quarters. The lens and revolving apparatus surrendered and for a time, ships at sea lost their source of warnings.

It was too much for George. His head was deeply cut by flying glass, and he nearly drowned trying unsuccessfully to shutter a window 136 feet above the normal sea level. After the worst of it passed, he stood outside, screaming into the night. The first tender that could make it to the rock days later dropped off supplies and picked up George for his final ride to the mainland.

He shacked up in a two-story hovel for fishermen in the Uniontown section of Astoria. George was disgusted by hundreds of immigrants pressing too close after his solitude at sea. Too many cheap saloons were mere doors away, so he drank in equal parts of nickel beer, rotgut and bitterness.

There was only one thing George Wright knew for sure. He wanted what was coming to him. He placed an ad in *The Daily Morning Astorian.*

Anyone knowing the whereabouts of Adelia or Wiley Wright contact...

Due to the excellent frocks she made, Adelia's name was known among the soiled doves, even the cheap ones down at the docks. One of them provided the information that George sought. It was a far easier way of making a buck than any other option the woman had.

* * *

Mrs. Borg sailed into the Dresser Girls workroom. Her face was so pale she appeared to have powdered with flour. "Adelia! Your father is at the door. I will not allow him in. He is repugnant."

Suzette Juliette looked up from the combs she was cleaning with carbolic acid. Adelia, cutting fabric on a board she placed atop a bed, blanched.. She considered hiding under the board. Maybe he would go away. How could he be here? *Repugnant?*

"Come now," Mrs. Borg snapped.

Adelia stood and marched resolutely forward, a prisoner heading for the gallows.

At the door, she peeked out the glass to the front steps, the ones she'd knocked Aleksi down. A wretch huddled there at the base. She would not have recognized him as anything but a dirty, unshaven bummer going door to door for work or hand outs. Even at his worse he had been a meticulous man, well kept in appearance. Could this be George Wright?

She opened the door and stepped out on the porch. He turned to her. They stared long and hard at each other until it became a fearsome game of who would speak first. Finally, Adelia said, "You have found me."

"And aren't you just the jammiest bit of jam in your frills, with your airs. Things work out well for a sneak thief, I see."

"What do you want?"

"The money you filched to begin. And the respect due a father."

"You may have the one, sir. But not the other."

He moved up the steps toward her. She smelled the alley, the booze. She saw madness in his eyes.

He reached out to touch her, but the door opened. Mrs. Borg stepped out with a stiff-bristled sorghum broom. Suzette Juliette followed wielding a steaming bucket of scalding water.

George backed down a step. He roared, "I am your father!"

Adelia faltered, feeling lightheaded. Whether she wanted to claim him or not, he was her father. He had earned little affection from her, but she had at one time mourned for his.

"Women do nothing but break a man down. You are your whore mother's child. Your brother Wiley would not treat me this way. Where is my son?"

"I have no knowledge of his whereabouts."

"Deserted him, too, did you?"

So her father did not know what happened, why Adelia had to leave. If Wiley had never confessed to attacking her, then maybe her father was owed an explanation for her departure, if nothing more. Adelia gritted her teeth, counting to ten as she thought. "There is a shed around back. Come there tomorrow at this time, but only if you are sober. If you can manage that, we will talk." She turned her back on him and faced her two soldiers. "Ladies?" The three entered the house single file and locked the door.

"And what was that about?" asked Mrs. Borg, leaning the broom against the doorframe.

"Yes. What was that about?" asked Suzette Juliette,

setting down the bucket.

They went into the sitting room where Milla slept in her cradle. These two woman, an odd duet to be sure, had both stood firm beside Adelia, albeit with a broom and a pail of water. Adelia could not help but chuckle as she looked at the weaponry. The two soldiers smiled as well. All three dropped into comfortable seats, warmed by the morning sun streaming through the windows.

"I guess I owe an explanation to such a brave regiment, willing to sweep and wash my enemy away." Adelia meant it. What humor lingered in the room was soon expelled, as she spoke softly to let the baby sleep. "My father is an assistant keeper on the Tillamook Rock Lighthouse. Or, considering his current condition, maybe the proper verb tense is 'was.'"

"An admirable job," Mrs. Borg said. "But one of great seclusion."

"I've heard it said that Tilly is the most treacherous light in the nation," Suzette Juliette added.

"The newspaper fears men trapped out there in a storm may become deranged. I suppose it is an occupation only appropriate for a lonely kind of man, one happy on his own." Mrs. Borg ended with a sigh of "Dear, oh dear."

"Aloneness may well have been the problem. My mother left my father just after I was born. I do not know why, but his moods or his drinking would be likely candidates. I see now that he blamed me for her loss, that I could never earn his affection if for no other reason than I remind him of her."

The two-woman audience cooed sad sounds.

Suzette Juliette was first of them to speak. "He lost a chance to have family through no fault of yours, Adelia." She turned away. The baby had begun to wiggle so Suzette Juliette gave the cradle a slight nudge with her toe to make it rock.

"He left my brother Wiley, too, who then had no man to civilize him for months at a time. When I was twelve, Wiley...assaulted me."

"You mean he raped you?" Mrs. Borg spoke the ugly word, one so dreadful it was virtually never uttered.

"He tried. My own brother." Adelia shivered. "That is when I ran away, and I have made my way ever since. Friends have more consequence to me than family."

Suzette Juliette turned back from the cradle. Moisture pooled in her eyes. "I was raped one night between our privy and the house. This was when I still lived at home. I was grabbed, muzzled with a rag, pulled into a filthy ditch. Afterwards, I told nobody but my mother. She said if I had not wanted it to happen I could have kept my thighs in the way. She blamed me and is ashamed her daughter is not a virgin."

"Many believe a woman must be complicit. My dear, your mother is delusional, or she knowingly perpetrates myth to cover an event that may have happened to her." Mrs. Borg's wrinkles pinched crow's feet around her eyes.

"You mean she could be what they call damaged goods herself?"

"Yes. And she cannot speak of it without being shunned by society or cast out by her husband."

Suzette Juliette shrugged her shoulders. "I don't know if that excuses her conduct toward me or only makes it worse."

"Women may be protected in the cities to the east," Mrs. Borg said. "I have never been there. Wealth and good name may wrap around them, keeping them constantly chaperoned. But out here? Where men outnumber us by dozens, even hundreds, to one? We cannot always be tucked away in safe quarters. I believe most women have been assaulted, often more than once." Her voice was husky with outrage.

"Oh, Mrs. Borg, has it happened to you?" Adelia could not think of this big, stolid woman being so overpowered.

Mrs. Borg picked up Milla who had begun to fuss. Holding the baby to her own cheek, she looked her sorrow at Adelia. "My advice? You keep this to yourself. Do not tell your father what your brother tried. It is a fact they both may use against you. That is the lot of women, I am sorry to say."

* * *

Adelia was not exactly afraid of her father, but she was not a naive child anymore. She knew booze and solitude could well have robbed him of every social nicety. She asked Aleksi to join her for her father's visit the next morning, telling herself it was because he was her intended. But it was also because a bouncer had his uses elsewhere than a saloon.

They were in the shed when George Wright arrived. He was filthy but did not stink of liquor. He had apparently made an effort at sobriety based on how sick he looked. In his fragile carriage, Adelia could see the shadow of the father she remembered. "This is my fiancé, Aleksi Kotila," she said.

George Wright turned his red rimmed eyes toward the young man. "A Finn, huh? Work on the docks?"

"No, sir. I am charged with maintaining security at the saloon called Ambrosia."

George raised an eyebrow and sneered. "Well, are you not the biggest toad in the puddle. A saloon too dear for us common folk. And it's the doggeries for most of you Finns."

Adelia put a restraining hand on Aleksi's forearm. "What do you want from me, father?"

"Like I said. My money."

She handed him a small pouch. "Inside is what I owe."

He counted the treasury notes and coins. "A simple return? Not enough, daughter. I will need more to feel well paid for your desertion."

"You deserve far less. I would not owe this much if you had raised me as a father should."

George squinted from Adelia to Aleksi. His mouth lifted into a sly smile. "Are you two already dancing the blanket hornpipe? Are you having your way with my daughter?"

Aleksi's fist caught his jaw and powered him across the shed into the wall. "You will mind your tongue, sir. I intend to marry this lady."

"Lady? Marry her? Ha, she is just a child. What are you, girl? Thirteen? Fourteen? You are certainly below the marrying age unless you have my permission. And that will take money. Hit me again, it will take more."

"You mean, sir, you are selling your daughter? You are no better man than is your son."

"What do you know of my son?"

Adelia snapped. "Enough. Both of you. Tell me, what is the price to be free of you?"

"Find me a decent place to live. Feed me. Care for me until I am back on my feet with respectable employment. Then I will permit you to wed. You have three days to work out a plan. After that you can both go to blazes."

* * *

Nobody wanted George Wright to have a room in the boardinghouse. Not the Borgs, not Aleksi, not Suzette Juliette. Adelia didn't either, and besides her money was tied up in Model 27. There wasn't enough left to rent another room for her father. But she needed to do something if she wished to marry anytime soon.

She thought about the stockroom in the Ambrosia kitchen, now that Harriet was gone. Maybe the Dresser Girls could do all their business out of their workroom in the boardinghouse.

"No, Adelia," said Suzette Juliette. "We still need that room to reach out to the doves down near the docks."

"No, Adelia," said Mr. Borg. "Don't want him near my girls."

"No, Adelia," said Aleksi. "I might just kill him."

Finally, her noggin landed on the shed out back, where Aleksi had built Milla's cradle and where, together, they had met with her father. Why not? They could clear it out. He'd be even closer to the privy than the boarders were, and there was fresh water from the pump. All in all, it would be cleaner and safer than where he was now. If he scrubbed himself up enough, maybe he could even come inside the house for meals now and then.

Negotiations with Mrs. Borg were delicate. On the one hand, the landlady had a sharp eye for a good deal and prided herself with driving a hard bargain. Adelia had overheard the iceman and the milkman discuss how tough she was. But Adelia knew Mrs. Borg trusted her and would value her help around the house, if only to free more of her time for Milla. In the end, Adelia agreed to prepare the breakfasts for all the boarders, and to clean the sitting room and stairwells once a week. She would also pay an extra fifty cents a day for food for her father.

Suzette Juliette helped with the shed. The two Dresser Girls removed everything from inside and stacked it in the yard. Much of the clutter was bits and pieces of furniture from the house, too worn for the boarding rooms. The girls thought some of it usable in the shed.

They washed cobwebs from the ceiling and walls, scoured the shelves built into one wall, swept the dirt floor down to the hard pack. Mr. Borg, a bar pilot with many friends at the docks, provided them with a sheet of tarred canvas too far gone to keep provisions dry on the ships, but perfect to cut down moisture on the shed's floor. Next they brought the clutter back in, working sacks, boxes and tools tight together on the shelves. Bigger equipment was stacked along the back wall. "Better insulated this way," Adelia said, taking a break to stretch her back.

They found a rag rug that they spread over the tarred pall, a wooden crate with label art of salmon leaping from cans to use as a nightstand, an iron frame for a single bed. Suzette Juliette was dispatched to the general store for a lantern, a ceramic hot water bottle, and a soapstone. Adelia could heat the bottle and stone on the kitchen stove and deliver them to her father's shed at night as foot and bed warmers. She filled a tick with fresh clean straw for a mattress then stitched heavy curtains to surround the single bed in order to trap in body heat. Meanwhile, Aleksi mended a broken chest they found in the clutter. It made an acceptable place to keep George Wright's clothes dry and free from insects - clothes that Adelia would wash when she did her own.

In three days, her father appeared again. Adelia was glad to see he wore new britches and shirt. He must have used some of the money she'd given him to fix himself up. Maybe he could make it back from the brink of desolation. Maybe.

She showed him how they'd fixed the shed, thinking it cleaner and safer than any housing for men on the waterfront. She told him of her willingness to provide food and laundry. In return, he would be expected to keep himself and his quarters clean, to maintain reasonable quiet in this family neighborhood, and to accept that drunken behavior would not be tolerated. "It is at least as comfortable as the cabin where I was born," she said in hopes of sealing a deal. "And a man of your experience with the sea can surely find work on the Astoria waterfront."

George looked around. He sniffed at the smell of carbolic and lye. He tested the bed. For the first time, she saw him smile. "Better plan a wedding date, girlie. Afore that Finn gets you in the family way."

"So you will agree to our marriage?"

"Thunderation, daughter! I do not want responsibility for you the rest of my life."

Chapter Eighteen

Winter 1895

An uneasy detente existed between Adelia and her father, George. They didn't yell and rarely snarled. She found their arrangement like that of a farmer and a large domestic animal. As long as she fed and cared for him, he settled down, minded his matters, came to heel. When he drank and caroused down in Swilltown, he kept it to himself, returning quietly in the night to his own shed to recover.

By late winter, George found work on the new jetty that narrowed the mouth of the Columbia by a mile. Having more purpose, he drank less and perhaps felt better about himself. He was allowed to come into the boardinghouse for meals and the companionship of the other boarders. Mr. Borg and he formed something of a friendship based on tales of the sea. But Aleksi and George Wright kept their distance from each other; on nights when the Finn was invited to dinner, George preferred Adelia serve his meals in his own quarters.

Astoria, Oregon, March 4, 1895

My dearest Adelia,

It is with extreme pleasure I inform you that Ernest and I intend to spend the entirety of June, July and August at Hydrangea House in Seaside, Oregon. I am sure you must remember it.

Our darling Ernest is growing at the rate of a colt. He is all long arms and legs, learning to control his new height. Nobody would recognize him now, and with the name of Mrs. Durand, I too feel safe from discovery. Our mishap is many months behind us now.

Ernest does not talk about his father, even when I ask. He changes the subject, telling me how he intends to be a Pinkerton man or showing me how to carve a stick (something he learned from someone he calls witless). I cannot determine as of yet how losing his father has affected him. If he is grieving, he keeps it to himself, at least for now. He appears to be captivated with Lucien.

I do think Ernest is unusually open to people he does not know. He has had such luck with you, your Captain Jokinen, Harriet. For Ernest, unfamiliar persons have offered an abundance of security and well-being. He has outgrown shyness of them. Far from it, he seems delighted to meet an outsider. The time may come when he must be taught judicious suspicion.

A thing I know for certain is how much he loves and misses you, Adelia. As do I.

Mr. Durand will join us at Hydrangea House

when his business allows for his absence. Otherwise, he shall spend time at his lumber camps or with his new involvement in railroads. Subsequently, I have a great deal of free time in store and would love to invite you to spend it with Ernest and myself. As you may remember, Hydrangea House has several extra rooms so by all means, bring your companions if you choose.

Your loving friend,
Florence Durand
Mrs. Lucien P. Durand, San Francisco, California

The letter thrilled Adelia even with the mention of their 'mishap' which brought the whole experience back to mind. Mrs. Durand still believed she had murdered her husband; Adelia never had the occasion to tell her the truth. It was not something she would put in a letter or mention when another soul was around.

And besides. After all this time, was confession the right thing to do, anyway? Would Mrs. Durand prefer to be told the truth or not? Would she want to know she was not her husband's executioner, but that she had cast a child in that role by her own failure to complete the act?

And what would it mean to Adelia? She did not feel unduly burdened by it. Maybe she should feel guilt, but she didn't. Joseph Munro might be a loss to someone, but not to anyone she knew. Besides, the further in the past the less real the event became.

Would a confession do any more than plow up old ground?

Her thoughts went back and forth as her feet treadled away on Model 27. If the law ever did accuse Mrs. Durand, Adelia would most certainly come forward. Until then, it was best to slap her yap shut.

She showed Aleksi the letter, and since it delighted her, he was pleased as well. Adelia wrote to Mrs. Durand immediately, asking her permission to marry at Hydrangea House in June. The permission was soon granted. *"Such fun! And Ernest must surely be your ring bearer,"* wrote Mrs. Munro.

In early June, Adelia would be just fourteen. "In the nick of time," she teased Suzette Juliette who celebrated her sixteenth birthday a short while before. "I do not want to be an old maid such as you." Adelia was working on two dresses for her trousseau as well as keeping up with her clients.

"Ah, but I am fine wine," Suzette Juliette teased back. "Not a tart like you."

"Did you call me a tart?"

"Would you prefer vinegary upstart?"

"Will you stand with me as my bridesmaid? Even though you are so much older than I? If you will, I shall make your dress."

"The honor as your bridesmaid belongs to me."

Together they ordered silk taffeta moiré from the dry goods store for Suzette Juliette's dress. "It sounds so French," the hairdresser oohed in delight.

Adelia decided Harriet would be with her, too. Carefully, she deconstructed the wedding dress she had made for her friend and turned the soft rose wool into a nip-waisted jacket with puffed sleeves. Adelia chose an ivory silk with a wild rose pattern to create a high necked dress to wear beneath the jacket. She could feel Harriet's approval for her practicality. After the wedding, she would cut off the gown's short train, and it would be suitable as her Best for years to come.

"And please, Suzette Juliette, do my hair as you did Harriet's with roses twined into the back."

Aleksi's suit was worsted wool with cuffs and lapels trimmed in silk, but Adelia would remove those adornments so he could use it in the future. He asked Captain Jokinen to be his groomsman, probably more to please Adelia than himself. Aleksi didn't care who was there, other than his bride and himself.

Suzette Juliette, the Borgs with Milla, Captain Jokinen and the wedding couple planned to go as a group to Seaside, a short ride on the new Astoria & Columbia River Railroad. They would meet the Durands and other guests at Hydrangea House.

The only one in question was George Wright. Adelia had no idea what shape he would be in. "Have you a suit for my wedding, father?" she finally asked. "You plan to come, do you not?"

"I plan even better than that, daughter. I will have

a surprise for you when we gather at the train."

And a surprise it was when the lovely June day finally arrived for them to travel. They planned to stay the night at Hydrangea House, and the wedding would take place the next morning. The jovial group gathered in time to board the train, with valises, hat boxes, and a large picnic basket.

Milla, at fourteen months, was a wiggly handful in Suzette Juliette's embrace when the hairdresser's sense of a nearby attraction went on alert. She whispered to Adelia, "Who is that handsome fellow coming down the platform with your father?"

Adelia looked. She gasped. It was Wiley.

Her brother. Her enemy.

"Look whom I have found!" Her father boomed, slapping his son on the back. Wiley's attention was fully on his little sister.

Adelia panicked. What should she do? Her father didn't know what her brother had done, but she needed him at the wedding to approve her age for marriage. Would he come if she told Wiley to leave? Or if Aleksi attacked him?

She felt lightheaded when Wiley grabbed her tight and crushed her to his chest saying loudly, "Ah, little sister. Pretty as a picture as always." Into her ear he then whispered, "Does that sapskull know what a whore you are? That you tried to seduce your own brother?" His boozy breath was as fetid as his words.

Aleksi stepped forward and grabbed Wiley's shoulder, pulling him backwards, away from Adelia. "We four gents have a, ah, wager to settle while the rest of you board the train," Aleksi announced to the rest of the wedding party. To Adelia he added, "Excuse us for a moment. We will not be long." To the Captain, he added, "Elias, escort Adelia's father if you will."

As Adelia was summarily ordered to board with the Borgs, Suzette Juliette, and Milla, the four men walked a few paces down the platform. Two appeared to support the other two with arms tight around them. The Finns were not particularly tall men, but they were particularly muscular. George and Wiley Wright offered little resistance. From the train window, the rest of the wedding party peered at them as they stopped, faced off in a square, began gesticulating. Adelia's nose pressed to the window of the train car.

When the men boarded the train, just as it began to squeal and puff away, there were only three of them. Wiley had apparently decided against attending the wedding. George looked pale and took a seat away from the rest of them. When Aleksi took the seat next to his intended, she asked what had happened. She put a hand on his chest but was embarrassed to see her fingers shaking, so she removed it.

"In Finland we would say there is no cow on the ice. That means there is no need to worry." He put an arm over her shoulders.

"But why would he come here?"

"Your brother was surprised to find you have told me about him. He thought the shame was yours, not his. He has reason to think otherwise now."

"What did you tell him?"

"That the next time I see him near you, I will kill him. Elias said he would be my second."

"And what of my father?"

"Your father has just discovered what a disgusting mongrel he raised. He will approve our wedding, and then I am done with him. Whether you choose to carry on a relationship with that man is up to you."

Adelia remained quiet. Aleksi was a caring man, a protector. Any woman would be lucky to have him at her side. But he had no experience with a conniving ne'er-do-well like her brother. Aleksi thought the issue was dealt with, but Adelia was not so sure. She feared Wiley would keep trying to get what he wanted, now that he knew where she was.

A dark cloud had appeared on her sunny day. It was not until they stepped off the train in Seaside that her euphoria returned. A little boy, all knees and elbows, flew down the platform and grabbed her as she knelt down to him.

"You are back," Ernest said. "I thought you had left. Like my father. I thought I might never see you again, Addy."

"My dearest boy. All through our lives, we will

have adventures with other people in other places. But we will always come back to each other. Always."

* * *

That evening the men played cards and told tall tales while the women prepared Hydrangea House for a ceremony the next morning. Mrs. Borg frosted the wedding cake that Mrs. Durand had baked.

"It is outstanding," gasped Adelia, surprised by Mrs. Borg's artistry.

"Harriet is here guiding my hand," Mrs. Borg explained. "I could not do these sugar roses all on my own."

Mrs. Durand distributed vases of hydrangeas to all the guest bedrooms, while Adelia and Suzette Juliette decorated the sitting room with pink roses and peonies. This tiny room was special to Adelia since it was the 'floral cave' where she and Ernest had hidden away the first time they stayed in this house. She chose it for her ceremony.

The wedding took place the next morning so guests could catch the late train back to Astoria. By nine a.m., they assembled in the flower cave. From the old Seaside Guest Hotel, the scullery team reunited. Katja and Albin came accompanied by Albin's accordion. Ephraim and Felicity arrived from Portland.

The men pushed furniture back so there was room in the flower cave to stand, although quarters were cramped. Bride and bridesmaid waited in the kitchen, where they could hear but not be seen by the guests as they assembled. Adelia gave Ernest his instructions about carrying the ring on the cushion once he heard the music begin.

Ernest did as told, almost. When Lucien P. Durand hand-cranked the phonograph to play a cylinder of *Here Comes the Bride,* the boy gleefully galloped into the room yelling, "Here's the ring! Here I come!" The guests burst into laughter as he clutched the little silk cushion in one fist and waved the ring in another. Ernest wedged himself between Aleksi and the Captain in front of a smiling rental pastor.

Adelia and Suzette Juliette came in together, right behind the child although neither of them ran. The jolly crowd gasped at the beauty of the two Dresser Girls. This was not a ceremony for those of solemn demeanor. Adelia even heard a whistle although none of the men later admitted to such an infraction of the rules. Little Milla wailed out her own music before Mrs. Borg shushed her with a bottle of apple juice.

Only one face was sour. George Wright stayed long enough to give his approval to the rental pastor, then he left the house. Adelia presumed he awaited the next train back to Astoria. He did not stay long enough to hear the pronouncement of man and wife.

After the ceremony and a beautiful luncheon in the garden, Adelia and Aleksi turned to their gifts. The Borgs had already given them Aleksi's time off with pay, so the newlyweds could stay at the cottage with the Durands for a week. And Suzette Juliette had privately presented Adelia with lovely naughties to wear beneath her wedding dress.

Since Adelia had worked at the hotel as a pot scrubber, the scullery crew gave the couple a brand new cauldron, pot, and loaf pan. "You already know how to care for them," Kajka pronounced sternly. "Now learn how to use them. And do not you let me catch you doing them harm."

The Durands provided a handsome purse of cash, as well as a metal shovel designed for clam digging. "I trust it will work better than the stick you had when first we met," Florence Durand said.

"What luxury!" Adelia laughed. "I will teach my husband how to use it on the beach tomorrow."

Ernest's gift was wrapped in a drawing he'd done of Adelia, his mother, and himself on the beach. The sun and Terrible Tilly both had broad smiles in the background. Inside the wrap was Adelia's old souvenir lighthouse. Ernest said he didn't need it now that they would be so close to each other so often. It could shine its light on Adelia once again.

Captain Jokinen had brewed a large batch of *sahti* on his boat, straining the mash through juniper boughs for a distinctly sour, herbal flavor. "Aleksi hasn't had real beer since he left Finland. Now everyone must share this treasure from the time of the Vikings."

After sharing a wee bit too much *sahti,* Albin stopped all conversation with a lively beat on his squeeze box. Then Katja, much to everyone's surprise, performed a Finnish *polska* around her one-legged Swede. Next, she started a Finnish line dance with the whole party skipping to the beat. The Finns loved it, and the non-Finns were soon laughing aloud at the terrible racket as the chain covered the ground, twisted through arched arms, careened across the yard and through the cottage. Mrs. Durand's red curls flew free, Mrs. Borg loosened the top button of her dress, Aleksi removed his wool jacket for the greater freedom of his linen shirt.

Oliver, a young cousin of Lucien P. Durand, was at the party, as well. He was paying the Durands an unexpected visit from England. Adelia did not fail to notice that as the Finnish dances progressed, Oliver drew closer down the line toward Suzette Juliette whose charms bounced and twitched in good fun. When Aleksi finally claimed exhaustion, Adelia picked Ernest up and swung him to and fro.

After the raucous dances, Lucien said it was not a proper wedding without a waltz, so Albin managed to pick one out for the newly married couple. Then he played it again, and the other couples joined in whether they knew how to glide or not. All this dancing face to face, in each other's arms, was a bit wicked. Adelia and Aleksi approved.

When the dancing ended, and Ernest had been put to bed in the room where little Milla already napped, the singing began. Mrs. Durand sat at the Steinway upright and played a tune she knew to the words on a song sheet.

Have you ever noticed when you're going by the sea,
The things that people do with impunity?
If they did the same things when they're up in town,
Moral Mrs. Grundy on her face would wear a frown.
Father, mother, all the family
Trundle down to have their paddle by the sea.
Mother takes her stockings off upon the sandy shore,
And shows a lot of linen that she's never shown before!

When it's wet in town she lifts her skirt and shows
A little bit of ankle and some nice silk hose.
If fellows look at her silk stockings she'll say,
" How rude!" and frown
You can do a lot of things at the seaside
that you can't do in town.

The whooperups next warbled their way through Stephen Foster's *If You've Only Got a Moustache* which promised that facial hair was the way to cut a fine dash with the ladies, and *He Was Such a Nice Young Man* who stole the family spoons while the ladies' heads were turned.

None of the men could be persuaded to sing a bawdy song they'd heard in Ambrosia so Adelia, Suzette Juliette, and Mrs. Borg, all of whom overheard the wagtails plenty of times, let loose with a version of *Sweet Betsy from Pike* that reddened every cheek in the room. After that, Mrs. Durand refused to play anymore, and the party soon broke up. At dusk, guests left for their homes or the evening train to Astoria.

* * *

That night, Adelia and Aleksi were exhausted but still buzzing with excitement and half drunk as they entered the room assigned to them. He was eager and drew her near, but she pulled away. She opened a dresser drawer and took out a small booklet.

"Sit upon the side of the bed, my love. We have had carnal knowledge before, but on this our wedding night, Pretti Patti thought I might need advice. She gave me this little book."

"Oh no. Advice from an Ambrosia wagtail." Aleksi feigned a long groan. "I will wear no toga."

Adelia laughed at his comment."It is not a fashion guide. It is instruction on personal relations within marriage."

"Are they not the same as outside of marriage?"

She set the manual down on the dresser and began undoing the buttons on her dress. "Oh no. For instance it says in there I should be resigned right now, that sex will be revolting but must be endured for the rest of my life."

As the dress pulled away, her silken chemise began to show. It was filmy and lacy and in key places, daringly see-through. "You on the other hand, will now turn into a slathering beast intent on the grossest of behavior."

"That may be true," said Aleksi. He began to remove his own clothing.

"Early on in our marriage, I must devise all manner of ways to reduce sexual contact. Lest you think I like it which would be most improper." She shimmied out of the dress altogether, displaying garters, hose, and wispy fabric.

"I like that you like it." He removed his clothes at double time.

The last of her wisps dropped to the ground. Her beautiful lithe body was visible in the lamplight. "And the lights should always be off to keep you from seeing me nude. Or me from resting my eyes upon you."

"Then I should probably not have removed that last bit. Or maybe I should turn up another lamp."

Completely happy, completely naked, they made love. Again. And again. It was sweet and rough and answered all the questions they could think of for the moment. They lay drenched and spent.

"That is a very good manual, my lovely girl," Aleksi whispered.

"Except the part that says we should do this no more than twice a month."

"That is a chapter best ignored."

* * *

Adelia and Aleksi enjoyed what was no doubt the first lazy week of their lives. They went to bed early and stayed in bed late. Lucien and Florence knew why, and let them be. Not so Ernest who knocked once then barreled in. He landed on the bed, bouncing and yelling, "Get up! Get up! The day begins! It is sunny."

And so it stayed for the week. They spent so much time on the beach that Adelia turned the color of coffee with cream, thriving in the sea air.

"It smells not at all of canneries and sewage," Aleksi observed. "Just the good fresh brine."

"We must evacuate that smelly city more often," Adelia agreed.

They hiked to the top of Tillamook Head and stared at coastal waves surging across Tillamook Rock, the spray reaching high up the lighthouse tower.

"Your father spent months at a time out there? Takes a hard man to do that."

"Or did the one create the other? I think Terrible Tilly does not care much for humanity. It saves some, but breaks others in the process."

Aleksi was no philosopher, but he tried. "Like some bonfires are lit not for warmth but to lure the unsuspecting."

"Something like that. It reveals how fragile we are, how dangerous the things around us. I fear that safety is just an illusion."

"Now you have me, Adelia. I will keep you safe."

The friends enjoyed each other for seven days. When the tide was low, Ernest and Adelia taught Aleksi, Lucien, and Lucien's English cousin, Oliver, how to dig for razor clams. They built a fire and feasted on the beach. One afternoon, the townsfolk gathered to play baseball, but Lucien, Oliver, and Aleksi didn't take part. The two Englishmen, even though fans of cricket, and the Finn found this American game incomprehensibly slow and boring. But they all enjoyed a sport introduced just that year called Mintonette. They put up a net in the hard-packed sand, and two teams volleyed a ball back and forth. Mrs. Durand whipped them all, clearly the champion at serving the ball and smacking it back across the net. Adelia spent one entire day with Ernest on the beach building castles and sharing secrets, while Lucien and Oliver taught Aleksi how to play golf at the course owned by Seaside Guest Hotel.

Adelia was tickled by Oliver, finding delight in his interest in Suzette Juliette.

"Is she French nobility perhaps?" he asked.

"Perhaps...perhaps not," Adelia teased. "A woman of some mystery."

"Is she married? Promised?"

"She does have friends. But the man to win her has not yet appeared."

"Would I be able to call on her when I am in Astoria?"

"I did not know you intended to be in Astoria."

At dinner on their last evening with the Durands, Oliver finally explained his presence at the summer home. "I was entrapped, you see. It is not uncommon in English families of wealth."

"Entrapped by what?" Adelia asked, still innocent.

"Entrapped by whom?" Mrs. Durand asked, far more worldly.

"I was at a summer house party. The manor house was hot from all the lanterns and the dancing. I went out to have a smoke and take the cool evening air."

"I see where this story is going." Aleksi raised his brows.

"I circled a pond in the garden, only to find the second eldest daughter of the family circling in the other direction. She had apparently tripped, developed a limp. Of course, I gave her my arm."

"And of course, she was a lovely young woman,"

Lucien offered. "This is fiction as old as time."

"Yes, I admit. The girl is a proper bit of frock. But not to my liking as a lifelong mate."

"Ha!" laughed Lucien. "My young cousin plays the field, betting on every horse in the race..."

"Exactly. And why not until I find my favorite?"

"Please, gentlemen. Oliver, go on with your story. I cannot wait for the details," Mrs. Durand said.

"When we returned to the house where her father was glowering at us, she leaned harder on my arm and announced we were betrothed."

"Could you not say it wasn't so?" Adelia asked, taken aback.

"Not in England, not if you wish to remain a gentleman. I could not call her false without being the worst of cads, nor could I marry her. I had no choice but to leave."

"So many scoundrels in our family!" Lucien said amidst laughter. "Fortunately, the Durands are now out of young men until Ernest is old enough to break hearts. Oliver joined me here and will manage my logging interests while I build my railroad concerns."

"I think it is possible, Oliver, you should stay away from Suzette Juliette." Adelia tried to appear serious.

"But she is the exact type of girl that interests me."

"Maybe. However, if she were to entrap you, you would never break free."

"Ah! Who can resist such a challenge?"

In the morning at the train, Adelia and Florence both cried. Ernest snorted. "Girls cry too much. You will be back soon, Addy, I know that now."

Florence gave Adelia a key to Hydrangea House. "You are welcome to use the cottage whenever you choose, when we are here this summer, or after we return to San Francisco for the winter. It is comforting to know it will be looked after when we are gone."

"Such a wonderful opportunity. We will cherish it, won't we Aleksi?"

But the next time she came to stay at the cottage for more than daytrips, he would not be with her.

Chapter Nineteen

Summer 1895

Adelia saw no reason to move out of the boardinghouse, especially since Mrs. Borg made such an effort to keep her as a tenant. Instead, Aleksi moved in. They took the room vacated by the dreamy young twosome who had floated on their way.

"A room for big dreams," Mrs. Borg said. "The kind you two should dream."

George Wright moved to quarters elsewhere now that his care was no longer a contract with his daughter. He was somewhere in the city, but Adelia made no effort to stay in touch. She might have on her own, but her husband refused to have anything more to do with the man. Adelia's father became a subject best not discussed.

Meanwhile, the Dresser Girls prospered. Little Milla grew chubby and opinionated, at home in the workroom as long as she had a wooden spool to gnaw or a hair brush to pound like a drumstick. The ladies of the upper town who came for hair or alteration appointments doted on this child whose gummy smile was irresistible.

"She's great for business," Adelia observed.

"Just wait until you have one of your own," Suzette Juliette responded. Only Suzette Juliette knew that Adelia was practicing some of the less dangerous birth control methods taught to her by Harriet.

"We want to wait at least a full year," Adelia told her friend. "When we can afford a home; when we know we can support a child."

"When, when, when," Suzette Juliette muttered with open disapproval. "Is it not the whole point of marriage for a woman? Now that you have wed, a baby cannot happen too soon."

"It can if you do not know whether you want one at all."

"Pshaw. All women want babies. Haven't heard such bunkum in all my born days."

Adelia wasn't moved by Suzette Juliette's rant. "Don't get all wrathy. You lecture like a schoolmarm." Adelia's own childhood wasn't the kind she would wish on another youngster, nor was Aleksi's, for that matter. Maybe it was true they were both overly cautious. But still. Adelia visited Mrs. Durand and Ernest in Seaside in July and again in August on daytrips. Aleksi was working so he could not go, but Adelia took along her sewing equipment, all except Model 27, of course. There was always needlework she could do by hand while chatting with friends. Suzette Juliette went with her on these short visits, pretending a lack of interest in Lucien's cousin, Oliver.

Mrs. Durand and Ernest came to Astoria as well. The round trip on the train could easily be done in a day, with plenty of time for a lunch with Adelia at the Corner House and a stroll down the burgeoning Commercial Street to examine new goods in new stores.

Adelia wished Harriet could take part in her happy new life, even see Milla's first steps. Mrs. Borg seemed to hear what she was thinking as Adelia walked the baby across the sitting room.

"I am sure Harriet is watching," said Mrs. Borg. "She watched me frost your cake, she watches me raise her baby. She knows I raised four boys but worries about a girl. As do I."

"I miss the Captain around here, too," Adelia said. He rarely visited the boardinghouse anymore. Elias and Harriet had been Adelia's family for such a brief time, but that's what she'd learned about life's inconsistencies. Change was inevitable and usually came from unexpected quarters.

* * *

It was a dreary afternoon, not yet raining but threatening to bluster. "Come on, Adelia," Suzette Juliette urged. They needed to make a trip to a bawd down in the worst end of Swilltown. "Let us go before the sky breaks loose."

"Aleksi? Can you accompany us now?" Adelia asked once she had packed up her valise with freshly mended clothes.

"I must finish this last one." Aleksi was installing carpet rods on the new runner that went up the stairs to the rooms of delights. "I will be right with you."

"Okay, we will start out slowly."

True to their word, Adelia and Suzette Juliette ambled, enjoying a bit of window shopping, especially at the new pastry shop's raisin sponge and molasses cakes, orange chiffon, angel and devil's food. They simply had to go in so each could purchase a pink-frosted shortbread to nibble as they continued their walk along the wooden road. Noise and congestion of drays and carriages, hawkers, sailors, Chinese workers and raucous drunks increased as they neared the worst end of town. If it hadn't been so noisy, one of them might have heard him approach.

"Greetings, girls. You are each sweet treat enough."

The detestable voice was just behind them. Adelia spun around, the last of her biscuit dropping to the sodden walkway beneath her feet. A river rat rushed to scuttle away with the crumb.

Wiley grabbed his sister by the upper arm hard enough to bruise it. She saw the bone-handled bowie knife he held under his coat and knew danger was very real, very close.

He pushed her toward a battered door. "Go through there. Both of you." He held the knife where Suzette Juliette could see it, too. In the crowd of people and vehicles hustling by in all directions, nobody else noticed.

"We shall do no such thing. To hell across lots with you," Suzette Juliette snapped. She was not wise to this man the way Adelia was. She did not know how Wiley hated to be sassed.

The knife caught Suzette Juliette across the front of her corset. Its stays helped block the swipe from deep penetration but blood from her midriff soon dampened her frock.

"I will not ask another time. And I will use my iron mistress far deeper on whichever sauce box utters the first sound."

The door was actually a tall wooden gate that opened into a tight alleyway. The girls entered and huddled against the coarse-hewn wall of an old warehouse. Adelia felt nothing so much as fear for her friend. She supported Suzette Juliette who was now sobbing in equal parts pain, fury, and terror.

"I will sample your fruit when I find you alone, little sister. But since you have obliged me this time by providing your friend, I believe I will pluck her first." Wiley picked twine from his pocket and pushed it at Suzette Juliette. "Tie her hands."

"I will not..." Suzette Juliette began but Adelia interrupted.

"Yes. You will. Here." Adelia held her hands crossed at the wrists in front of her friend, and Suzette Juliette looped the twine around them.

"Tighter," Wiley commanded.

The coarse fibers cut Adelia's skin as Suzette Juliette drew the twine fast. Her brother pushed her down into a pile of old broken barrels that splintered as she fell on them. Her wrists were immobile. She would need to act quickly before her hands lost all feeling.

"Watch. Don't move. You might learn a thing or two," he mocked.

Wiley took his time. He first twisted buttons from the bodice of Suzette Juliette's dress then with the point of the knife, cut through her camisole. "My, my. What heaven have we here?" She cried as he squeezed a breast hard, enjoying her pain.

Behind his back, Adelia chose a loose stave from one of the ancient barrels and tried to grasp it tightly. Her tethered wrists were numbing her hands.

"On your knees, whore." Wiley pushed Suzette Juliette down. "Unbutton my fly."

His attention was fully on her friend. Adelia

gathered herself together and lunged, swinging the slat across the back of Wiley's head. He bellowed, wobbled, but stayed on his feet. Adelia made ready to strike again, but her weakening hands dropped the impromptu weapon as her brother rounded on her.

Wiley smashed her hard in the jaw with his right fist, then sunk a left hook to the area of her liver. Adelia folded to the ground, limp. Immobile.

She fought to stay conscious, to stop what was happening although she was powerless. Suzette Juliette screamed for help. As Wiley turned back to her, the gate broke open, and Aleksi burst through. The big Finn grabbed Wiley by the neck and slammed his head into the warehouse wall with a spine-jarring thrust.

He roared in fury, ready to strike again, but Suzette Juliette yelled at him. "No, Aleksi! Adelia needs a doctor. Now, Aleksi. Now."

Her voice reached some center of reason still intact within Aleksi's animal fury. He paused to consider. Wiley appeared out cold. Aleksi removed his coat and tossed it to Suzette Juliette, then picked Adelia off the ground. She clung to him, in shock, nearly without breath. Adelia saw her brother begin to move, but she was helpless to tell her husband or friend.

Suzette Juliette donned the coat to cover her nakedness, picked up Adelia's valise, and ran to the street. She stopped a cab by waving the valise in front of the horse, scaring it to a halt. With her own blood soaking the coat, Suzette Juliette clambered into the cab and supported Adelia as Aleksi handed her in.

"Take her to Ambrosia," he said. "I will run for the sawbones and get him there. Tell no one who did this. The bastard is mine if he is not yet dead."

Suzette Juliette nodded. "Better you kill him than the law forgive him."

Aleksi yelled "Ambrosia! Go!" to the driver. He turned back to the alley, but it was empty. Wiley had escaped out the other end. Aleksi had no time to follow now. He sprinted away to get Doc Alford, the man who took care of the wagtails whenever they needed more care than a saloon could give.

Outside Ambrosia, Suzette Juliette shrieked for Mr. Borg, who came running. He and the cab driver carried Adelia inside and placed her on the daybed in the kitchen storeroom. She was aware enough to whimper and moan, but nothing more. Aleksi arrived with the doctor. Doc Alford washed his hands and arms, a health precaution that medical men had just begun to practice.

As the doctor prepared to examine his patient, Aleksi knelt down to her. Adelia's eyes were closed, but she smiled at his nearness. She knew who he was and where she was. "Our first place," she said, weakly patting the bed. "Our first time."

"I love you," was all he could manage.

It was enough. She did not raise an arm or her

eyelids, but she struggled to say, "All will be well."

The doctor shooed Aleksi out. After that, Adelia lost consciousness. It was up to others to tell her what happened next so she could reconstruct the story.

Pretti Patti was dispatched to get Mrs. Borg, who arrived to tend Suzette Juliette's wound. The long scratch below her breasts had bled in anger, flushing itself out. With the doctor's guidance, Mrs. Borg applied a solution of alcohol and iodine then wrapped the wound in a clean piece of muslin kitchen towel.

Tense minutes of waiting crawled. The one time that Adelia cried out in pain, Aleksi cried out as well. "Why has this happened? What shit bags the men in her family be."

When Doc Alford was finally through with his ministrations to Adelia, he opened the doorway to the kitchen to find Aleksi pacing just outside, surrounded by prostitutes in togas who were whispering comforting words the young husband did not hear at all.

Doc Alford waved them out of the way like a flock of robins, then told Aleksi, "Your wife's youth and fitness have saved her life, but she cannot be moved for some time, as much as several weeks."

Her jaw had been dislocated, but the sawbones popped it back into place, causing that loudest cry of pain. He temporarily bandaged her around the chin and head to hold the jawbone in place. If swelling didn't knock it back out, and if Adelia refrained from speech or yawns, she would recover.

"However, once weakened, her jaw could easily dislocate again if hit. I suggest you try keeping her away from her family," the doc advised. With a glance toward Suzette Juliette, he added, "Keep *her* away from them, too."

Adelia's liver was bruised and would manifest as back pain when she awoke, although the broken ribs would bother her more. Doc Alford believed she would recover in time, especially with the help of laudanum in a mixture with opium.

Aleksi sighed. It was a relief, but he didn't relax. Now he could loosen the reins on his rage. Through clenched teeth, he growled to Suzette Juliette that he was going to find his wife's brother. Nothing she could say would have stopped him. She showed no desire to do so.

For the next week, Mrs. Borg, the wagtails, and Suzette Juliette took turns nursing Adelia. She was drugged much of the time and hazy the rest of it.

In those early days, nobody told her that Aleksi had never returned. Or that her father had disappeared, too.

It was Mr. Borg, with his contacts in the shipping trade and his associates in other watering holes and brothels, who finally ferreted out what had most likely happened. George had been drinking in a swill mill when his son staggered in. The younger Wright had a bleeding head wound, so he drew attention from other patrons, but he told them to bugger off. He sat and drank with his father.

In time, a furious Finn entered, big as an enraged bull. In the tale told to Mr. Borg by the barkeep, this monster grabbed the younger man, slammed his face on the table, then lugged him to the alley by the collar and seat of his pants. The older man followed, begging the Finn for mercy. But the brute beat that young man to death.

While this was going on, the bartender sent a boy for the crimps. They paid him for tips like this, criminals on the loose or men too drunk to defend themselves. They slithered into the alley as fast as river rats and knocked both the Finn and George Wright senseless. Then they pulled up a trap door in the alley, a door that opened to the filthy water lapping around the stilts below. They dumped Wiley's body into the stench of the river, to be eaten by whatever favored rotten meat.

George Wright and Aleksi Kotila were lowered through the same hole, unconscious, into a rowboat ready to haul them to a sailing ship.

"You mean both have been shanghaied?" Mr. Borg asked, not terribly surprised. The dreadful act was common enough in the port of Astoria.

"They be crew on one ship or two separate ones steaming to Asia or around the Horn by now," answered the barman. With a shrug he added, "I imagine the codger has already been booted overboard if he proved too old to pull his weight. But that young brute? A captain will have paid top dollar for him. You won't likely see him again. Not in this lifetime."

* * *

Adelia's body mended. When she could stand the jolts of the short journey, she was carried by horse-drawn cab to the boardinghouse. As she healed, she began to eat solid foods, breathe deeper, sit in a chair, even use Model 27 again. Everyone assured her that Aleksi would find his way home if anyone ever could.

She knew that. She knew he would try. But the odds were impossible. Nobody knew anyone who had succeeded. She wanted to trust in a tiny flicker of hope that he would soon appear, grab her up, hold her tight. She did not want to think it was dotty to cling to such idle wishes. She fought nightmares of him on a ship half a world away.

Her mind wandered back to the dog Shep that had died when she was a child. She'd discovered then that life was a sneaky adversary, and nothing in her experience altered that view.

Adelia was changed forever. She was no longer so quick to smile or laugh. There was no family for her, never would be. She stopped looking for more, deciding the people she now knew were all she would need. She didn't want to expand her circle of loved ones, not ever again.

What she did want was to go back to the ocean, the beach, the place she had first felt anything like the comfort of home. "I'm returning to Seaside," she told Suzette Juliette. "Mrs. Durand has given permission for me to move to Hydrangea House."

Tears slid down Suzette Juliette's face, and Adelia ached for this girl who had been raped by one man, now assaulted by another.

"This city is a dreadful place," the hairdresser said. "But I cannot bear to lose you."

"You would never have suffered such harm if I had not led my brother to you." Adelia burned with guilt.

"You and your brother are not one and the same," Suzette Juliette snapped. "His death is a loss to no one. You are a loss to everyone."

"Then come with me. The Dresser Girls can work from Seaside as well as from here. We will start again. The women there have more means, the tourists are wealthy and fashion forward. We will do well."

Suzette Juliette nodded. She helped her invalid friend board the train that would take her to Seaside and the caring arms of Mrs. Durand. At the station, her words to Adelia were, "As soon as I can ship our belongings and say our good-byes, I will be with you. We will both live a better life in Seaside."

Chapter Twenty

Spring 1906

A decade passed. For years, Adelia went through a quiet hell. No amount of questioning of crimps or port authorities, no amount of help from Mr. Borg, the wagtails, or Captain Jokenin, brought her any answers about Aleksi's whereabouts. Law enforcement did nothing to help.

What she found was that shanghaing was as common as dirt. Men were abducted from shore and forced to labor on merchant ships that headed for Shanghai often enough to give the practice its name. They had no choice in what ports they'd go to or for how long. They didn't make enough for passage to get back. Only by luck would one ever return to the port where he was taken.

Dead or alive, Aleksi was gone from Adelia's life. For five years she tried to stay hopeful. After that, she gave in to reality and tried to remove him from her mind. But the misery was always there, annoying as a tickle in the back of her throat.

She was twenty-five. In the decade since Aleksi disappeared, she turned Hydrangea House into a classy boardinghouse, running it with the brisk efficiency of her mentor, Mrs. Borg. The Dresser Girls had rooms at the front of the house for commerce. One was a discreet beauty salon and the other an upscale dressmaker's shop.

The Durands were always close. Their private quarters in Hydrangea House stayed private, ready and waiting for them to venture up from San Francisco. The trip became easier each year by either ship or train.

Ernest was sixteen, but he was still a little boy to Adelia. Only he could tease her that he was older than she when she had married. He alone could evoke her silly side now and then, get her to run on the beach like a girl, or play volleyball against that terror of the net, Florence Durand. Adelia was aware that he fancied himself her protector these days, not the other way around.

Adelia didn't open her heart to new people, but she clung to the ones from her past. The business hardened her nearly as much as her personal life had. Dealing with suppliers and clients of her dressmaking business, as well as tenants in the boardinghouse, sharpened her. She was always on the look-out for the next thing to get out of line, even though her life appeared stable. And she was right to be watchful. Two things happened in 1906 that rocked her life again.

* * *

"Ernest, could you call Zeus into the house?" Adelia had already hissed at the little cat, assuring it that she would feed it to the next dog who passed by. It ignored her, knowing this human was all bluff.

Ernest named the white cat after the one owned by Emma Watson all those years ago. This was his third Zeus, in fact, although this one was a little female. She was waiting for the nuthatches to appear from the birdhouse for the chance to nab a tasty treat. Adelia, who was trying to get the rose bushes pruned, would rather miss that particular drama. She was on her knees working at the base of the hydrangea that towered over the roses. Her back, never strong after the beating by her brother all those years ago, would not allow her to do this chore much longer.

"Come on, Zeus, get out of the garden," Ernest yelled out of the house. Then he stepped onto the front porch. The sixteen-year-old had coppery hair, now rich and lustrous like his mother's. He was gangly but finally growing into his enormous feet and long arms. Adelia was proud that he had the confidence it took to look someone straight in the eyes. She liked to think she was in part responsible for that.

Ernest wasn't looking at Adelia now. He was looking over her head. In a voice more friendly than wary, he called, "Can we help you, sir?"

Adelia followed his sightline up and over her shoulder. A man stood outside the garden fence, staring at her. "Who...?" She stopped. She set down her clippers, got off her knees, and brushed off her skirt. "Aleksi?" she whispered. Then louder, in a cry tamped down for so long, "Aleksi!"

She ran for the gate then out to the walkway in front of the cottage. He was in tatters, he was gaunt, and his sun-wrinkled face spoke of an older man. But his smile was unmistakable. Aleksi was home.

The Finn dropped a valise and knapsack, then opened his arms to her. "My wife. My life." She sank into him, fitting the way she did ten long years ago.

Zeus, disgusted by such a display of human emotion, skulked back into the house. Ernest gave the couple a moment then loped forward, offering the Finn his hand and a wide smile.

"This cannot be little Ernest," Aleksi said, looking up into the boy's eager face. "How tall you have grown."

"Too many women around here to look after, so I had to grow. Can't tell you how glad I am that you are back." Ernest picked up the valise and knapsack then carried them into the house.

Adelia had awaited this day, dreamed of it, finally accepted that it would never come. And now, she felt nothing so much as shy. She blushed like a new bride, feeling unequal to the situation, absolutely tongue-tied.

She'd been a child when he was abducted. Now she was a woman, one whose face and body had suffered with the passing years. Would Aleksi love the one as much as the other? Would she love this man as much as the boy?

Aleksi seemed to have no such doubts. "You are more beautiful than even in my best fantasies," he whispered to her before they turned to follow Ernest.

She found her tongue. "Where have you been? How did you find us? You are so thin. Are you well?"

"A cool drink and a biscuit would be nice," he answered with a laugh. "I could use a place to sit, my love."

"Of course, of course. My manners!" As they walked into the house, his arm around her waist, she could feel how he limped and leaned on her. There was a huskiness new to his voice.

She took him to the flower cave where Aleksi and she had married, and where Ernest and she had hidden years before when Mrs. Munro was on the run. It was less ornate these days, with creamy drapes and upholstery that Adelia had made. Now hydrangeas were an accent, not overwhelming blotches of color.

Adelia went to the kitchen to arrange a tray of lemonade and macaroons, taking a moment to remove her gardening apron, attend to her hair, and catch her breath. When she came back to the cave, Aleksi was asleep. His gaunt frame overwhelmed the loveseat, but he appeared at peace, legs sprawled over one bolstered end where his feet just missed the lamp table. Adelia set down her tray and touched his forehead, feeling the alarming heat. Was this exhaustion or something more wicked? She lifted his head and twisted her small frame underneath it, until she held it in her lap. She looked down at him, studying this apparition from the past. The stubble of his beard was not blonde but gray. His lips were thinner and cheeks not so round. He slept with a frown now. A cut appeared below his eye and an angry red sore like a rope burn festered around his neck.

Was he the same? Was she?

Adelia had lived through the early years of his absence by saying her husband would return. With dogged determination, she refused to state otherwise. She made up stories of the things they would do, based on the things they had *said* they would do. She would become the first famous American dress designer. He would buy land and build structures until he had a farmstead bigger than all of Finland. They would have three children, two girls and a boy, each with a super talent, be it musical or mathematical. These dreams carried her through her lonely reality. She was not hallucinating; she knew they were not level-headed sensibility. But she chose to believe them anyway. She had to in order to survive.

After those years, when Adelia left her teens behind, she admitted it was time to grow up, to put away all things childish. She lived quietly like a widow, accepting the day to day sobriety of making it through life as a singleton. There would be no fame and fortune, but there would be safe harbor for herself and the few souls she allowed to matter.

Nobody else could get close to her anymore, not really. She was reserved, pleasant, an attentive landlady. People liked her well enough. But she was not available as a confidante or friend to anyone who wasn't already inside the castle walls. Adelia could exist that way, surrounded by those people who knew what she had lost and who did not ask impossible feats from her.

And now. Here was the dream of her youth come to call. Aleksi was back. But he was not that boy. She was not convinced she could allow this unknown person back into her inner circle.

"Adelia, do you and Aleksi want..." Ernest galumphed into the flower cave, saw the situation, shut down his question, and crept away as quietly as a sixteen-year-old could creep.

Suzette Juliette entered, stared, kissed Aleksi's cheek and then Adelia's. "Do you want a doctor?" she whispered, tears running down her cheeks.

Adelia whispered back, "We should allow him sleep first, I think. When he awakes."

Other boarders were not yet home, and Mrs. Durand was still in San Francisco. Ernest had come ahead for an early start on the summer since his school lessons had ended. Adelia had a request of Suzanne Juliette. "Please advise the boarders that I will not be preparing an evening meal."

"Yes. It is a fine time for them to try one of the new restaurants in town."

Still Aleksi slept, and still Adelia held him.

* * *

At dark, Aleksi stirred. Adelia called to Oliver and Ernest to help him up the stairs to the necessary room. After that, they walked him to Adelia's bedroom. She threw back the covers so they could lie him down. Aleksi was not quite delirious but having trouble with events and time.

"Ernest, will you go for the doctor now?" Adelia asked. "I have seen one's shingle just two streets down."

The boy was half way down the stairs, bounding like a greyhound, before she could so much as thank him.

"Is it exhaustion?" Suzette Juliette asked as she helped Adelia strip Aleksi down.

"Yes. And likely more. He is very weak." Together, they washed him. His body was painfully thin and riddled with wounds and scars. Adelia's tears fell silently as she worked, and Suzette Juliette kept quiet, no small feat for the boisterous woman. By the time the doctor arrived, the patient of the Dresser Girls was clean and ready for examination.

A strange little man bustled into the room announcing, "I am Dr. Black. Ha ha."

Adelia looked up to thank him for coming and choked back her surprise. He was rotund in the chest but his lack of height and toothpick legs combined to give him the look of a bantam rooster. He even strutted.

And he certainly was sure of his dominance over the two hens. "Leave us, ladies, so we men may have a chat, ha ha," Dr. Black ordered. He herded the Dresser Girls out of the room with a demeaning "Shoo! Shoo!"

Adelia awaited medical advice in the kitchen while Suzette Juliette heated a pot of broth in hopes Aleksi would be up to sustenance.

"Possibly we should dunk Dr. Black in your pot to give it more chicken flavor," Adelia muttered. It was beneath her. She didn't care.

"Why does the man ha, ha so? Is it because he

thinks he is amusing?" Suzette Juliette asked.

Ernest came into the room with a theory. "Maybe he's a jackass with a lisp. Ha ha instead of heehaw."

Soon, Dr. Black strutted in and seated himself across the table from Adelia. He was so short that from her point of view, only his head appeared above the table top.

"Tea, please," he ordered Suzette Juliette, not noticing she wasn't a servant of the house or of his.

"Now then, Mrs. Kotila." He reached up and across the table to pat Adelia's hand. She wanted to snap at him to quit the condescension. But she wanted his information even more.

"Mr. Kotila is certainly exhausted and dehydrated. Be sure he drinks as much as you can force down him. Water, ale, tea, whatever he will take." He patted her hand again, and she removed it from the tabletop to the safety of her lap. He then tented his fingers. "I fear your husband has had a hellish journey to get home to you, Mrs. Kotila. You have a rather difficult job on your hands to bring him back, I fear."

In the next moments, he told her what she needed to know. She decided she should not judge the bantam so harshly. A crowing man may get away with being a blowhard, if he is a knowledgeable blowhard.

For care of Aleksi's numerous wounds, she should first treat all wrappings and gauze with carbolic acid. Everything must be extremely clean. Next she should apply a solution of iodine and potassium to the wounds before wrapping.

"It will sting but it is an antiseptic, the best we found for use in the Civil War. Nothing better since. Have him eat fish, too. Iodine may be good on the inside as well as the out. Who can be sure." Dr. Black frowned for a moment, then asked if he could speak with her alone.

"Just going!" Suzette Juliette said. "Come along, Ernest. We must beat those carpets and stoke those fires and butcher that hog and..." It trailed off as they moved down the hall.

"Saucy one that, ha ha. Now then." The doctor checked over his shoulder to be sure they were alone. "As your husband is a sailor, I took the opportunity to check all wounds for signs of venereal disease. Syphilis. You understand?"

Adelia was not sure she did. Was he implying all men behaved like beasts when away from their womenfolk? Or just sailors? Nonetheless, she nodded.

"I found no such rashes or warts. Excellent news for you, my dear."

There was something more. Aleksi had been lucid enough to tell the doctor he suffered attacks of malaria. "There is no cure, now that he has been bitten by mosquitoes on some god-forsaken continent. The parasites live on in him. Shivers, headaches, seizures, sweats. They will plague him from time to time, in varying degrees of potency. I am sorry to tell you, my dear, that between the disease and the medicines for it, many men become sterile."

"We have no plans for children, Dr. Black," Adelia said. "This is no cause for worry." After being ripped apart from Aleksi for ten long years, she could not imagine wanting to care for anyone but him, now that he was home.

"Well, then. That is good, then. Now, between bouts of malaria, keep him away from mosquito-infested areas and keep him cool. By luck, Oregon may be one of the very best places for him, ha ha."

He handed her a scribbled note. "I do not often tout herbal remedies as most are ineffectual, but you might look for sweet wormwood tea. The Chinese use it, have forever. Send someone to purchase it in their part of Astoria. Don't go yourself, of course. God knows where you would be shanghaied. Ha, ha. If you can get him to drink it, it may stave off virulent attacks. And, if you believe in Indian ways, stock up on willow bark, meadowsweet, Oregon grape, whatever suits you. In teas, gargles, poultices. It won't kill him, and it might help you feel better to be so involved in his nursing."

As he stood to go, he had one more warning. "Stay away from all the bottled herbal tonics available everywhere. So many are dangerous. They *could* kill him, ha ha." He applied a tall hat to his head and stopped at the door long enough to tell her he would come back in a day or two.

By the time he left, Adelia actually felt grateful to the irritating, pontificating, womanizing little poop.

* * *

In the morning, Katja joyfully prepared a giant breakfast for Aleksi. "He is home," she beamed at Albin, when he entered the kitchen with an armload of firewood.

"Who is home?"

"Aleksi, you Swede oaf. Aleksi is home. Our Adelia is bride again." Katja and Albin had finally grown too old for the heavy load of a big hotel. They worked now at Hydrangea House, overseeing the cooking, cleaning, and handyman chores. Without the strict rules of the Seaside Guest House, they at long last had married and lived under this roof, trading their labor for room and board. They were family.

Adelia took the laden tray upstairs. When she entered the room she was momentarily alone. She turned and saw Aleksi coming back from the necessary room. He had managed to dress himself.

"You must be careful, Aleksi. You are sick with far more than exhaustion."

"No, my darling wife. I am well now. I am strong as iron again, now that my wish has been granted. My only wish was to find you and devote the last days of my life to you." Even with all this spoken bravado, he opted to sit back down on the bed.

"Those last days can start tomorrow. For today, have breakfast. Katja will kill you herself if you do not get meat on your bones. Then rest. Today is for talk."

"Katja the dancer?"

When Aleksi laughed at the memory of the line dance led by the rotund Finn, Adelia noticed molars missing from his upper left jaw. Her husband had been through endless abuse, physical and mental. "Yes. She lives here with me now."

"And the man who played the jolly music when we wed?"

"Yes. Albin is here, as well. Hydrangea House is a safe place for many whom you have already met. And for you."

He ate. Adelia sat with him and altered a shirt of Oliver's, swiftly shortening the arms for Aleksi. They talked, although it would be a long time before he told all the details of his harrowing tale. She feared some were too hard to ever tell. Or to ever hear.

Aleksi talked about his abduction, about coming conscious aboard a freighter on his way to Asia. At first, he was whipped and beaten repeatedly to break the rage in him, and chained so he would not leap overboard. In time, he became a good sailor because he discovered that exhaustive work was the only way to dull his misery. For a decade, he sailed from port to port around the world, with no choice of where to go. At long last, Astoria was once again a destination. Aleksi jumped ship outside Swilltown and after a talk with Mr. Borg, came to Seaside.

Adelia told him about her slow recovery from the beating by her brother, how her jaw still ached during the long winter rains. And her back was not as dependable as it once was.

No, Aleksi did not know what became of her father. He was not on the same ship with Aleksi. In fact, he did not even know the man had been taken. Nor did he care, although he did not wish this fate on anyone.

He confessed he meant to kill Adelia's brother that day behind the waterfront tavern in Astoria, and Adelia assured him he did. She added that in her eyes, killing Wiley was justified. She reminded him of how she had killed Mr. Munro. She had been pushed to the worst, as had Aleksi. "You do anything to protect the people you love."

"You are the most lovable of murderers," he said to her.

"Your murderous nature is balm to me," she answered with a smile.

Adelia explained she, along with Suzette Juliette, abandoned Astoria for Seaside. The Dresser Girls continued their duties here, although a genuine salon was now separate from a genuine sewing room. Adelia operated Hydrangea House as a boardinghouse for the people who mattered to her.

Aleksi expelled a breath, one that caught ragged in his throat. "May I be one of those people who matter? Live with you here close to the sea, but never again sail upon it?"

She realized just how beautiful his broken smile and scarred face were to her. Yes, she loved this man that the boy had become.

They talked until Katja must have become worried it was time for lunch. The couple, fully dressed, were locked in each other's arms on the bed when the old Finn tiptoed in with a tray for two. Adelia stirred just enough to be aware.

"Sleep and love. That is the sustenance you both need," Katja whispered. "Food can wait. I am so happy with the turn life has taken."

* * *

In the next weeks, Aleksi rallied. He was eager to return to healthy employment, unhappy to be a burden on his wife.

"You are not a burden."

"A man who does not work is a burden."

"What you are is stubborn."

"You would be one to recognize stubborn when you see it."

One mild March day, sitting side by side in lounge chairs on the beach, Aleksi said to his wife, "I could farm."

Adelia stretched in the sun like a great cat. She looked over and smiled at her husband, pleased he was looking ahead. She knew from his cries in the night that his years at sea haunted his dreams. "The area here is marshy. It is not good farmland."

"Hmmm. Okay. I could teach Finn at the school."

She laughed. "You could teach it to me, my love, but I doubt the local children have a great need of it."

"I could open a saloon," he said. "I know the business."

"I do not think Seaside is ready for wagtails in large number. Nor am I. And you are not yet in shape to be a bouncer."

"Not a saloon that needs roles such as those. A nice place for men to gather for a proper game of cards and conversation."

"Aleksi, I believe such a proper place would fail due to boredom."

This time, he laughed. "I suppose you are right. Maybe the Captain and I could brew *sahti* together, selling it in modern bottles."

"Modern or not, to American taste buds, *sahti* tastes like sour piss."

"Such language, wife! Actually it tastes like sour piss to Finns, as well. Maybe I should just be a clam digger and sell my wares door to door."

"I do not think you should put Mr. and Mrs. Adams out of business. They were good to me when I needed their help."

"How about traveling salesman with elixirs and powders and rattle snake oil?"

"Harvesting the oil is far too dangerous, and you are never to do anything dangerous again."

"I was a builder before I left Finland. I can make places."

They held hands and watched the ocean rise and fall. It was beautiful. They were back together, having fun, and both hopeful for a future, as long as neither allowed black memories to settle like a heavy fog.

"I have been thinking, Aleksi. I would like to move the salon and the dressmaker shop out of the house, to have more room in Hydrangea House. A new place for the businesses to expand. Maybe both side by side on one of the main streets. Would you happen to know anyone who could build such a place as that?"

"My dear wife. An entire village of stores in Finland owes its existence to me."

But on April 18, all plans were put on hold. Before the Golden Gate telegraph offices collapsed, word got out to the world that an earthquake had struck San Francisco, and what little was left standing was burning to the ground. Any word of Florence Durand was cut off. Dread descended on Hydrangea House.

The wait for news was excruciating.

Lucien P. Durand appeared in Seaside the following day. Both he and his horse were exhausted and soaked through with rain. He had been at the lumber camp when the Captain arrived with word of the disaster and had ridden all night to reach Ernest. He ached to save his wife, but first he needed to be sure the boy did not take off to look for his mother. If either of them tried, he knew they would fail. His railroad contacts told him the army was turning away everyone approaching the city.

Thousands of San Franciscans were dying, crushed in the ruins or burning in the flames. Hundreds of thousands were homeless, gathering in camps or clogging the roads and rails as refugees. There was nothing to do but wait for news. Mrs. Durand would contact them when she could. If she could.

Chapter Twenty-One

April 1906

Mr. Durand, Ernest, and the rest of the residents at Hydrangea House worried themselves to the verge of illness. Nobody left the premises, wanting to be there when a telegram arrived, for better or worse. They wandered room to room, picking up magazines and setting them down, watering overwatered houseplants, straightening straight book shelves.

Zeus grew tired of so many humans accusing her of being underfoot, when it was so clearly their own fault that they would not get out of the way. She positioned herself atop the new upright ice-making machine in the kitchen and swiped at anyone who came too close.

Only Adelia stayed relatively calm. She had such a long, complex, terrifying, exhilarating relationship with the resourceful Florence Munro Durand. If anyone was capable of a quick-witted escape, it was this ingenious woman. Adelia wholeheartedly believed in her. She only wished she could comfort Ernest the way she could when he was a child.

Time crawled. When at last a telegram reached them, it was only one day before the lady herself descended from the train at the Seaside station. Husband and son met her with great thanksgiving. She had no luggage to carry, so Lucien offered to carry her. She managed a smile at his solicitude and pointed out that she had survived complete with usable legs.

Mrs. Durand was alive but fatigued and had a terrible story to tell. She shared it with everyone at dinner that night, after she had time to bathe and rest. Once she started, no one interrupted, anymore than they would stop a sermon in progress. Even the clatter of silver and the clink of crystal eventually felt too interruptive. Eating and drinking came to a halt as everyone listened to Mrs. Durand speak.

"Mrs. Brodie, the lady I met when I first arrived in San Francisco, has been my friend all these years. When Mr. Durand is up here in Oregon, we often get together to play euchre or see a moving picture at the Bijou. This time, we had tickets for *Carmen* performed at the Mission Opera, starring the great Italian tenor, Enrico Caruso. Oh! You know how I love opera. I was wild with excitement.

"Mrs. Brodie and I dressed to the nines, saw the

great man deliver an outstanding performance, had a late dinner, then stayed downtown together at the Palace Hotel. It was a perfect evening for two middle-aged ladies having a night on the town.

"In the early hours of the morning, the hotel began to shake. It rocked and swayed. As I drowsed, I thought I must be aboard ship, sailing from San Francisco to Oregon or the other way around. But Mrs. Brodie shook me awake. We went to the window, raised the sash. A nightmare was on the other side of the glass.

"We clung together and gaped at the sight. Buildings were collapsing all around us. Never have I seen such a thing. Down one went...then another...and another. Boom, boom, boom! I do not think the shaking lasted a full minute, but the hotel walls began cracking and plaster fell from above, covering the beds and the floor. A great hunk of masonry hit our window from the outside, shattering the glass. We had to get out.

"I am pleased to report that neither of us lost our head, but we were terribly frightened. We dressed in a minimum of time and garments, grabbed up our evening handbags from the night before, took each other by the hand, and threw open the door to rush from the room. But the hall was packed with other guests in various stages of dress. We were soon squashed together as we pushed down the grand staircase, like cattle through a chute. Five floors we descended, clinging to each other, trying not to trip on our skirts or be shoved off a step. At the base of the stairs, the mass of us pressed out to the street.

"The mayhem was worse outside, but there was no getting back in. Stores, banks, offices all around us were tumbling and disintegrating. Dust was so thick we could not clearly see. The street was a river of ruination. People screamed as they were hit by bricks or leapt from windows or merely succumbed to terror. Bodies lay everywhere, limbs missing or broken to impossible angles. The noise of the shattering city was indescribable.

"In the confusion and dust clouds, I lost contact with Mrs. Brodie. I felt her hand slip away from mine and never saw her again through the manic crowds. I still have no idea what became of her. I can only hope she found her own way out of hell.

"I was spun this way and that, bruised by crazed humanity, until I collided with a tall portly man who was holding to a trembling lamppost outside the hotel. When I looked up at his face, I saw it was Enrico Caruso himself. I hadn't known the Metropolitan Opera company was also staying at the Palace.

"I yelled above the din what a fabulous show it had been. I did not do this because it was a good time for a chat, but to appeal to his vanity and seek his protection. At least he did not push me away. He seemed dazed, actually, muttering about his belongings. In time, his valet came out of the hotel, carrying an abundance of luggage. The two men began to walk uphill, winding through panicked pedestrians, around rubble, past terrified horses trapped in the traces of overturned wagons. I wanted to help the poor beasts, but I stuck like a burr to the great Caruso.

"I suggested we find a building still standing in which to shelter. Signore Caruso said we would be safer out-of-doors. Maybe an Italian knows more of earthquakes than a less worldly woman like me. I held my tongue. And he had said 'we.'

"We made it onto Union Square. Caruso and I sank to the ground to rest in the open area, while the valet fended off looters who eyed the luggage. We watched together when the Palace Hotel sunk to the ground. After that, it was not long until we saw heavy smoke and flame increasing all around. So we rose and began to walk uphill, shuffled this way and that by soldiers, some helping and others stealing what they found in shattered storefronts.

"Such disaster we saw! Wounded souls by the dozens. Bodies ripped open. Oh, the misery. And the smell. At one time, my skirt hem caught fire, but the valet helped me rub it out when I knelt in the dirt. The unnamed, unknown little man was such a hero to me.

"By nightfall, exhausted and filthy, we found a hard bit of ground in a park on one of the city's seven hills. There we stopped for the night to pass over us.

We could see across the bay, over Alcatraz Island to Oakland. In between that land of safety and us, the golden city burned through the night. The roar of fire and shrieks all around kept us from speaking. We did not sleep, had nothing to eat or drink. But the great tenor, his loyal valet, and a lady with no credentials whatsoever, huddled together and cried.

"The next day, the valet was able to stop a man with a rickety cart and horse. The driver wanted an appalling amount of money, more than Caruso had when he evacuated the hotel. I said, "Signore Caruso, you have the name to get us out of this city. But I have the cash." I opened my evening bag, a glittery bit of glamour from the opera, now ridiculous in the light of day. I handed the required bills to the driver.

"We rode in the cart atop the luggage that Caruso's valet had shepherded all this time. It was a long slow trip downhill through ruination toward the San Francisco Bay. Dangerous, too, with the number of desperados out for anything they could get.

"We passed piles of rubble, each of us wearing scarves over our noses and mouths to fend off smoke and dust and the aroma. Firemen battled flames while soldiers released people trapped under beams and cement. Once soldiers halted us, but one of them recognized Caruso and let us pass.

"It was late afternoon when we arrived at the waterfront ferry building, where Enrico Caruso's fame and my fortune saved our souls. We were escorted to an already packed ferry. People were pushed out of the way to make room for the three of us. The little boat left dock immediately, taking us to Oakland. Once there, we hired a carriage to the train station. Signore Caruso was given immediate passage on a train headed east. I boarded, too, and soon was on my way. The squeal and steam of the engine was a comforting balm compared to the noise and smoke we had just lived through.

"With the help of a kindly conductor, I transferred to the north when I finally reached a station outside the disaster area. I must have been in shock, because I do not know where I was, only that I was on my way to you. As soon as I could, I sent Lucien the telegram, and I purchased a dress and comb from another woman on the train, a lady who had not just traveled through the lowest levels of hell. At last, I arrived here to be with my family and friends.

"I do not intend to leave ever again. I am at Hydrangea House for good."

* * *

Adelia was delighted with Florence Durand's decision to live out life in Hydrangea House. The great loves of her life, her collected family, had come home to roost. Aleksi, the Durands, even Suzette Juliette.

What a superior selection to the family first doled out to her, back when Terrible Tilly was the only light in her life.

In the next two years, Hydrangea House was transformed once again. As far as Adelia knew, it had begun life as a vacation home for the rich. When the Durands purchased it, they allowed Adelia to transform it into a boarding house. And now, it was blossoming as something new.

The Durand family moved in and, even though Lucien was often gone, they simply needed more room. This was not a family used to making do.

"You have managed this house for many years," Aleksi said in bed one night. "Will they ask us to move, do you think?" Aleksi had promised to devote his life to making Adelia happy, and he was as alert as a barometer at spotting bad weather ahead.

"Of course not, my darling. And she would never complain. But, Aleksi, she *does* own Hydrangea House. Let's do our best to make it comfortable for her family."

So Adelia and Aleksi went back to work the next morning on their plans for a separate building to house the Dresser Girls' businesses. This would vacate the front rooms of Hydrangea House to rehab anyway the Durands wished.

"At least one more necessary room, Aleksi..."

"Can we expand the flower cave, Aleksi? I'd like to have a library there..."

"I need a den, man, big enough for railroad business at one end and logging at the other..."

It wasn't just the Durands with requests. As reconstruction was underway, Suzette Juliette and Oliver let it be known that, at long last, they wished to marry.

"So you won't die a spinster!" Adelia teased. "I was sorely worried."

"Could you install a door in the connecting wall between our rooms, Aleksi?" Suzette Juliette asked. "We will sleep together in one room and use the other as our private parlor."

Adelia asked tenants not "in the family" to leave. Her final count was the three Durands, Oliver, Suzette Juliette, Albin and Katja. Adelia also kept a room for Milla who suffered teenage rages under the no-nonsense guidance of Mrs. Borg.

Milla became a frequent visitor. She was four years younger than Ernest so she gave him a little sister to tease. He gave her an older brother to admire.

Or maybe that's wrong, Adelia thought. She recalled her first crush on Ephraim all those years ago. Would Ernest and Milla stay friends or would they become more? Adelia could not tell. Whatever might be, the girl's nearness gave her a chance to tell Milla all about Harriet. This was not a conversation Adelia would have had in front of Mrs. Borg, who loved the girl but had no understanding of her. "Raising girls is not like raising boys," she had once said to Adelia. "I believe I am too old to change, and she is too young to care."

When everyone had their say about their quarters in the house, Aleksi nodded. He commandeered the table in the flower cave where he fussed with sketches and figures. He hired an architect. The two used arcane Finnish phrases as they developed plans. Sometimes, passing the entrance to the cave, Adelia thought those phrases were loud and heated enough that she was glad the language remained a mystery to her.

But Katja huffed and chuckled. "Not since the old country have I heard words of such rudimentary meaning. It reminds me of home."

Finally, on another night in the bedroom, Aleksi pronounced, "Including the expanded dining room and renewed kitchen and two new necessary rooms, this house will nearly double in size. The Durand pocketbook best expand as well. We may have to rename this house Hydrangea Mansion. "

For a year, life for everyone was a chaos of noise, dust and displacement as the building crew hustled to follow Boss Aleksi's orders. He was unstoppable, and Adelia delighted in the results. He managed to complete Hydrangea House in time to host the wedding of Oliver and Suzette Juliette.

And the stores weren't far behind. Aleksi was a whirlwind there, too, overseeing a separate crew for the structure that housed the Dresser Girls Hair Salon and the Dresser Girls Frock Shop, side by side. In his spare time, he kept Model 27 in fine repair, even creating a second machine with parts he gleaned from here and there.

The big Finn came to the attention of the Seaside city fathers. They must have felt an injection of new blood was in order, and this stout fellow, Aleksi Kotila, seemed just the ticket. Even his wife was a woman of substance, a whiz at business, and who would think such a thing possible of a lady? Aleksi was asked to join the city commissioners. He was highly complimented and mightily amused. "From Swilltown to Seaside, I am counted a success! What a country this America is."

Adelia hired another seamstress after Milla proved impossible to teach the finer points of needlework. Her dress shop featured custom-made clothes, of course, but also a small collection of readymade wear. Adelia never really liked repeating the same dress in different sizes. She had to agree with Milla that it was pretty damn boring.

"Why recreate when you can create?" the girl had said to her.

With the first two stores complete, the Kotilas created a third in the row. It was Aleksi's brain child. "Something for me to do when all the building is complete, lest I put myself out of work," he said to Adelia.

Seaside Variety was created to delight tourists with products that were made locally. Aleksi first stocked his store with crafts and foods from the people who had helped his wife through the years. "These are the good folks who brought you to me," he told Adelia.

On its shelves, Seaside Variety carried Tillamook Rock Lighthouses hand carved by Mr. Witless. Specialty cheeses, branded The Old Settler, were brought up the Elk Creek Road by a farmer whose barn once provided haven to a twelve-year-old on the run from her brother. Bess Adams Fancy Canned Clams sold enough year round to see the Adams couple into retirement. Indian blankets by the Ida Rose Ladies were in more demand than they could supply; their little group soon expanded to another Chinook and two Clatsop weavers. The Ghostly Girl provided a line of skin care that included Harriet's Magnolia Balm, Florence's Sweet Violets Hand Cream, and Seaside Girl perfume. Aleksi even tried his hand at brewing Captain Jokinen's Finnish *Sahti,* but nobody ever made a repeat purchase.

Adelia knew what Aleksi was doing with Seaside Variety, of course. He was attempting to force aside bad memories by overwhelming her with good. That was fine with her. As he helped her mend, he was healing himself.

* * *

Adelia's journey had come to an end. If it was affection she sought all those years ago, she had surely found it. She was surrounded by so much collected family, she was rarely alone anymore.

"I may have left home without affection, but at least I took father's money and brother's boots with me," Adelia said one evening when walking the beach with Aleksi. With a chuckle, she added, "I was never above a little revenge."

"It is one of your outstanding traits, my dear."

"Yes. Along with my easy-going nature."

The ball of the sun, just dipping itself into the ocean, caused the sand to sparkle with refracted light. The couple stood for a moment, watching Terrible Tilly blink away a mile out to sea, isolated and alone.

They had lost ten years together, she and Aleksi. They were wrenched apart like that beached whale all those years ago. Each of them had been beaten until their bodies were no longer strong. Either might cry out in the night or suffer a dark spell. But the core of who they were remained resilient. Love survives almost anything.

Adelia knew life for her collected family would go on its messy, agonizing, boisterous way for as long as she lived. Speculation about sorrows and joys to come was a waste of time. Whatever was ahead, they would manage it.

The Dresser Girls businesses were humming

along, and Hydrangea House bustled with life. Adelia had all she needed to feel content. Even more than that, she was happy.

Chapter Twenty-Two

Spring 1957

Adelia Wright Kotila died in the winter of this year. I think she was seventy-eight, but in truth, neither of us counted the years toward the end. Where's the sense in that? Adelia went quietly in her room at Hydrangea House under the care of my wife, Milla. I feel as though I lost my best friend. I feel that way because I did.

My mother, Florence, willed the old place to Adelia years ago. I lived here through my late teens until I left for school in Seattle. My step-father, Lucien, died in a logging accident while I was away. It was right that my mother and I be together to grieve the passing of that fine man. So I moved back to Hydrangea House to live with her and the Kotilas.

In those years, Suzette Juliette and Oliver lived here, too. They raised their baby boy, Lucien, in

Hydrangea House, but they moved to England when World War I began over there. It was Oliver's real home. Apparently, he had been forgiven for whatever reason he left in the first place. It was a great sadness for us all when Adelia received a letter from Suzette Juliette telling us Oliver had died in that miserable war.

My mother lived long enough to see me become a Pinkerton man. It's just as well she was gone before I enlisted when America joined that 'war to end all wars.' I hope she knows I married Milla, that we raised a daughter who is now a chef like her grandmother Harriet, and that I continue to house a long line of cats named Zeus. I hope she and Adelia are laughing together again.

I was shipped home from Plymouth, England in 1919. I'd been gassed in the war in France, then sent to an English hospital before the long trip home. Milla was at the front, too, one of the ten thousand American nurses. When she came home, she took over my care, but in truth, I never completely recovered. Weak lungs are a result of mustard gas. I couldn't go back to the Pinkertons. Now I'm an administrator at the library here in Seaside.

Adelia lived out her years in the house with us. She never quit creating on old Model 27. Right up to the end, she made sure the women in this family and in this town dressed in spectacular style. She sure loved that machine.

Aleksi passed two years before her, from a final bout with malaria. She grieved, of course, but she also felt grateful for all the years she had with him after the wretched shanghai incident.

I guess I am the only one she allowed to call her Addy. To everyone else, she was Adelia. Maybe she felt her name was her first real possession. That and an old dog and this little toy lighthouse. I've kept it all these years. The paint has pretty much worn off. But you can still read the legend *May Your Light Always Shine.*

By and large I think it has. For Adelia. And for me. Certainly she was the light of my childhood. Without her, my mother and I may never have...well, that would be a different story.

Adelia willed Hydrangea House to me. Someday Milla and I are sure to will it to our daughter, and maybe she will do the same to our granddaughter, Florrie, if the old place is still standing.

Today, I put Adelia's urn on the front seat between my granddaughter and me. Florrie's dog sprawls across the back, panting in the excitement of a car ride. I drive down Highway 101, the segment that was once the Elk Creek Road. I turn off at Ecola State Park then go on to the top of Tillamook Head. There, Little Florrie and I hike to the best vantage point of Tillamook Rock Lighthouse. I'm slow as my lungs weaken fast now.

She wants to carry the urn so I let her, taking the dog leash myself.

Florrie is fascinated that Adelia is inside this plain metal container. But not *all* of Adelia is in there. Not the part that laughed and played games and told the best stories. Death is a difficult concept for my granddaughter. She has never so much as seen an animal die. She is a child both loved and sheltered, one never in fear of finding the next meal.

It's a rare mild day with the wind just right, and I've been waiting for it to come along.

"Why today, Grampa?"

"Because today the wind blows briskly out to sea."

"So Adelia will go with it?"

"That's the plan. Out toward the lighthouse. You see it there."

Adelia told me years ago exactly what she wanted me to do with her ashes. "Toss me at Terrible Tilly," she'd said. "We are bound to each other."

I take back the urn, open it, cut through the plastic inside with my pocketknife, and let the ashes fly, dispersing them as far as I can. Florrie watches, and her face clouds as she toys with tears. But then she is over it. She is a sunny child by nature. As soon as the cremains are all gone from sight, she leaves me to go admire the buttercups in early bloom.

I take my time to say good-bye to both my friend and to the lighthouse, since the Coast Guard intends to shut it down later this year. I guess Adelia and Terrible Tilly are taking their final bow together. I am aware of the quirk of fate, me standing here on the edge of a fragile cliff, mourning the woman who kept me safe all those years ago.

I pat the head of Florrie's old rescue dog. "Come on, Shep. It's time to go home."

THE END

AUTHOR'S NOTE

In the 1870s, sailing ships by the thousands were ripping open their hulls on jagged boulders hidden off Tillamook Head on the Oregon coast. Shipwrecked sailors climbed onto outcroppings, only to be pounded to death by waves pitching fist-sized rocks. Others swam for shore, but found no ledge on the pitiless face of the Head. This strip of coast near the entrance to the Columbia River earned itself the nickname Graveyard of the Pacific.

Something had to be done. Ships approached daily from the Orient, the Horn, Alaska and California. Commerce could not stand so much loss of cargo and crew. But a lighthouse on the Head, high above the sea, would too often be shrouded in fog, its warning flash invisible to ships below.

The nearly impossible got underway. Tillamook Rock Lighthouse was to be built in the sea, over a mile out from the headland on a great mound of basalt. It would be far more visible from there. But this sea stack was never meant to support life, other than resting seabirds and sea lions. The rock did not want men on its back. Coastal tribes never went near, knowing it was cursed by their gods.

The first mason to survey the rock in 1879 slipped from it and fell into the sea. His body was never found. The project was considered madness by locals from Elk Creek in the south all the way up the Oregon coast to Astoria at the mouth of the Columbia River. Local settlers refused to build it. The government brought workers from far away, and stashed them in a keeper's quarters at a light in Washington territory. These men were kept isolated from those who might tell them what they were up against.

Construction began on as calm a day as possible. The first mission was to get four of the unsuspecting workers aboard the rock. A supply ship approached it, refusing to get too close. It launched a dory with a crew to row the workers alongside the rock. The boat bucked and lurched, a bit of flotsam with no place to land. The men hurled themselves from the dory to the basalt sea monster, literal leaps of faith.

There was no shelter. They clung to the sea stack like limpets, soaked by salt spray, buffeted by high winds, threatened by half-ton sea lions. Other workers arrived. In time, they excavated a shallow niche on the northeast side where they built a shanty, bolted it to the rock and covered it with canvas. This flimsy construct was now their home.

They chiseled ring bolts into the basalt so ropes could be strung from a ship to the rock. Then they built a system of derricks and pulleys to winch supplies across in a sling. Newcomers were hauled over dangling in a breeches buoy, a contraption with canvas pants attached to a life ring. With the ship pitching and rolling at one end of the line, the hapless souls were often dredged through the freezing sea.

It took over a year to blast off the top thirty feet of the rock for a flat enough surface to build Tillamook Rock Lighthouse. Storms and the sea destroyed many starts before it was complete. The lighthouse got built, possibly because workers had no way off the rock unless a cutter happened by on a very smooth day. The light was eventually dubbed Terrible Tilly for its overall attitude toward men.

One bleak night, just before the light was to go live in the winter of 1881, the construction crew awakened to a voice in the dark issuing the order to come about.

"Hard aport!" a commander seemed to cry.

The workers saw running lights, then all went dark. Even the shriek of a January gale could not mask the creaking and flapping of rigging and sails. By morning light, they saw the remains of the *Lupatia*, a British barkentine en route from Japan to the Columbia. Soon thereafter, a rescue party at the beach south of the Head found twelve bodies of the sixteen man crew strewn along the shore.

Only one member of the crew survived. A Shetland Shepherd, the mascot, swam over a mile to reach that beach. She was there with her dead man crew when rescuers arrived, howling her fear and misery into the wind.

Tillamook Rock Light was extinguished the final time in September of 1957. Its beam had flashed at five second intervals, visible eighteen miles to sea, for seventy-seven years. But modern marvels like radar and wireless communication made it obsolete. It was replaced by a buoy even further out to sea.

Terrible Tilly remained cantankerous to the end. She was the most expensive U.S. light to operate and was widely considered the most treacherous. Tilly caused some keepers to threaten duels, refuse to speak to each other, leave under fear of derangement. One was removed from the light after putting ground glass in another keeper's food. Nonetheless, it must be remembered that the Tillamook Rock Lighthouse saved thousands more lives than she inconvenienced.

The lighthouse still stands, most easily viewed from Cannon Beach, Oregon. Five investors from Las Vegas purchased it soon after its closure for $5,600. A variety of owners through the years hatched a variety of plans, the more notorious to turn it into the Eternity at Sea Columbarium. The ashes of a few souls are actually out there, soaking in their urns, storm after storm.

The vandalized shell of Tillamook Rock Lighthouse is part of the National Register of Historic Places and the Oregon Islands National Wildlife

Refuge. Humans have long since abandoned it. But the seabirds and sea lions who owned it for hundreds of years have gladly taken it back.

ACKNOWLEDGMENTS

The inspiration for this book is Tillamook Rock Lighthouse, the ruins still visible from pull-offs along Highway 101 on the Oregon Coast, in the area of Cannon Beach. If I hadn't been fascinated with that distant specter, I would never have begun the research that has led *Fog Coast Runa*way in varied directions, many of which came as a surprise to me.

There are fine histories of the lighthouse featured in *Fog Coast Runaway*. One of them was written by a keeper on the light, James A. Gibbs; *Tillamook Light: A True Narrative of Oregon's Tillamook Rock Lighthouse* is about existence on the rock more than half a century later than my story takes place. Nonetheless, its portrayal of day-to-day lifestyle is still highly applicable.

The time line is accurate, from the early days of the light in the 1890s through the San Francisco disaster of 1906. Enrico Caruso was in the earthquake and fire...I have altered his story only to include the presence of Mrs. Munro at his side.

The lyrics of folk, music hall, and bawdy songs are real and unchanged although they vary greatly from source to source. Their original writers are mostly lost to time but, as always with music, their presence adds great life to my story. I doff my verbal hat to those storytellers of long ago.

The quote from the journals of Lewis and Clark, spoken by Ida Rose, is what William Clark penned about Tillamook Head after he traversed it over eight decades before Ida's time. The climb was ever a monster, but worth it for its fabulous view.

Now about the slang, from 'case of the morbs' to 'butter upon bacon' to 'all-fired ratbag.' You can find it all if you search the web, logger stories, sailor speak, brothel terms, or read the literature published before 1890. While it has been a particularly entertaining part of writing this historical novel, it is definitely not politically correct. I apologize for the accuracy of terms that are now slurs to immigrants and natives in specific, and to women in general.

Liisa Penner, Archivist at the Clatsop County Historical Society in Astoria, introduced me to the history of Finns as well as Chinese on the docks and at sea. The Society's Heritage Museum is also a stronghold of many tales of sin and sex from the old-time brothels of the waterfront. Elaine Trucke, Executive Director of the Cannon Beach Historical Center and Museum, is a gold mine on the fascinating Tillamook Rock Lighthouse; and if you want to know what flowers bloomed in 1890s Seaside, the Seaside Historical Society Museum is a must visit. I believe the people who work at these societies, preserving the days of our long-agos, are among the nation's heroes.

The same can be said of the librarians who dig with the enthusiasm of pit bulls. Old records in the North Tillamook Library Manzanita Branch and the Seaside Public Library gave up their secrets to me.

For sharing in the research and many trips up and down the Oregon coast, I thank my sister, Donna Whichello. She is the silent partner in all my books, researching, editing, cheerleading.

My critique group of Jon Eekhoff, Heidi Hansen, Kimberly Minard, Melee McGuire, Jill Sikes put up with me week after week. This is no small feat since I tend to the moody. I must also thank Renee Rosen for her guidance and concern.

For this gorgeous cover, I am beholden to Veselin Milacic; for the equally attractive interior, my thanks to format developer Heidi Hansen.

Finally, I wish to thank my beta readers: Jan Shamberg, Donna Brubeck, Ursula Stomsvik, Jayne Nichols, and Linda Sharps.

I hasten to point out that any errors in text or in context within *Fog Coast Runaway* that may come to light are my own, the fault of nobody else.

ABOUT THE AUTHOR

Linda B. Myers won her first creative contest in the sixth grade. After a Chicago marketing career, she traded in snow boots for rain boots and moved to the Pacific Northwest with her Maltese, Dotty. You can visit with Linda at facebook.com/lindabmyers.author or email her at myerslindab@gmail.com.

CHECK OUT LINDA'S OTHER NOVELS

Fun House Chronicles
Bear in Mind
Hard to Bear
Bear at Sea
Bear Claus: A Novella
The Slightly Altered History of Cascadia
Secrets of the Big Island
Creation of Madness

Please leave a review of *Fog Coast Runaway*
or Linda's other books on www.amazon.com.

Made in the USA
Middletown, DE
29 June 2021

43196994R00205